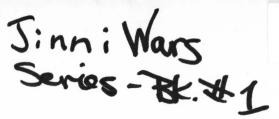

Jinni Wars
Series - Bk. #1

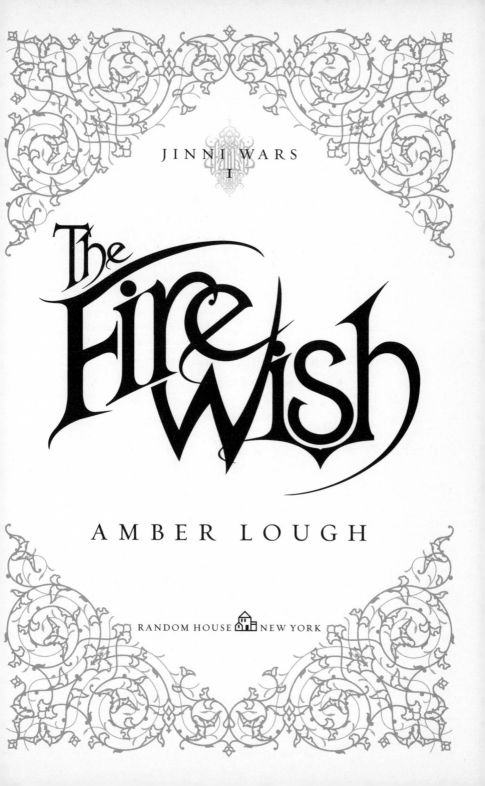

JINNI WARS
I

The Fire Wish

AMBER LOUGH

RANDOM HOUSE 🏛 NEW YORK

Text copyright © 2014 by Amber Lough.
Jacket art: title lettering, smoke, background texture, and spine ornament copyright
© 2014 by blacksheep-uk.com; lamp image copyright © Cre8tive Studios/Alamy;
archway image copyright © Maurizio Blasetti/Trevillion Images;
back cover ornament copyright © Azat1976/Shutterstock.
Interior title page and chapter opening ornaments copyright © Azat1976/Shutterstock.

Visit us on the Web! randomhouse.com/teens

Educators and librarians, for a variety of teaching tools, visit us at
RHTeachersLibrarians.com

Library of Congress Cataloging-in-Publication Data
Lough, Amber.
The fire wish / Amber Lough.—First edition.
p. cm.
Summary: "When a princess captures a jinn and makes a wish,
she is transported to the fiery world of the jinn, while the jinn must take
her place in the royal court of Baghdad."—Provided by publisher.
ISBN 978-0-385-36976-3 (trade)—ISBN 978-0-385-36977-0 (lib. bdg.)—
ISBN 978-0-385-36978-7 (ebook)
[1. Genies—Fiction. 2. Princesses—Fiction. 3. Wishes—Fiction.
4. Courts and courtiers—Fiction. 5. Baghdad (Iraq)—Fiction. 6. Iraq—Fiction.]
I. Title.
PZ7.L9237Fir 2014 [Fic]—dc23 2013010943

Printed in the United States of America
10 9 8 7 6 5 4 3 2 1
First Edition

For

Elizabeth and Henry

✦   ✦   ✦

Oh Beloved,
take me.
Liberate my soul.
Fill me with your love and
release me from the two worlds.
If I set my heart on anything but you
let fire burn me from inside.

—RUMI (1207–1273)

✦ I ✦

NAJWA

THE EARTH AND all her layers sped past while I traveled to the surface. I was smoke and flame, swirling through granite, through shale and sand. It took only a moment, and then I emerged, myself again. I stepped onto the dirt and shielded my eyes from the blinding star in the sky. I was in a human's garden, just as I'd wished.

"Shahtabi," I whispered. It wasn't a long-lasting wish, but it kept me from being seen by humans. It kept me safe, and it was the first wish I'd learned in school.

The sun beat down on a garden filled with flowers and their spiny pale green stems. It cast shadows—real, sun-made shadows—on the dirt. The garden was soft, without a trace of crystal. Instead, it had roses. Delicate, fragrant blossoms opened on the ends of the stems, yellow and pink in their centers.

A bird landed beside me on a branch and turned its head to look at me. It had shimmering feathers that it fluffed out before turning its head another way and taking off. Just like that, it was flying through the air, straighter than a bat. I had seen a live bird, and I had seen it fly!

But I was here for a flower, so I squeezed my hand around a stem. I was about to break it free when I heard music.

I dropped the stem, leaving the flower to bounce on its bush, and looked in the direction of the music. An arched door stood open. Someone, a human, was in there playing one of their stringed instruments. An *oud*.

The notes fluttered upward, and then dove into a melody I recognized. I couldn't name it, or remember when I had heard it, but it felt familiar. It was like breathing in a scent that made you sad, but not remembering why.

I should have gotten the flower and headed straight back, but I didn't. I tiptoed to the doorway. It was darker inside, and after my eyes adjusted, I saw a young man about my age bending over an oud and plucking at the strings. His sun-darkened fingers danced over them.

I *knew* this song. It swirled around in my memory, elusive and haunting. Why did it sound familiar?

The young man finished playing and put down the oud; then he pulled off his turban, tossed it onto the floor, and ran his fingers through his hair. It stood up, messy and thick.

I pressed my back into the doorway and took in the room. Shelves lined the walls, filled with bound books. Charts with numbers and maps of the stars covered the walls above the shelves, while scales brimming with broken rocks stood scattered on the single table in the room's center. It was a kind of laboratory, but one in which human boys played music.

The music hung thickly in the air, like the scent of incense, as he stood up and went to the table, taking two long strides before picking up a stone ball off one of the scales. He stared at the ball, which was so large he had to hold it with both hands. Then he turned it over, where it caught the light in milky-white layers. It was selenite. We used it to house the flames of our streetlamps, but it was heavy. I had never seen anyone rolling it in his hands, pressing it close to his face.

"How is this going to work?" he asked the almost-empty room.

My face started to tingle. Soon my *shahtabi* wish would fade, and he'd see me standing in his doorway. I backed out of the young man's laboratory while he was still staring at the selenite ball. Then I turned and ran to one of the rosebushes.

I was in a pool of hot sunlight when the wish died out, with a thorn-riddled stem between two fingers. Quickly, I bent the stem till it snapped, gasping as the thorns pricked my skin, and held the rose tight against me.

"*Mashila,*" I whispered.

My body fell into a cloud of smoke and flame, and I dragged the rose with me, its bit of pink dusting the air like a blush.

✦ 2 ✦

ZAYELE

"I DARE YOU to cross it," Destawan said. He pointed at the remains of an old bridge. It spanned a river with water bubbling and white with cold.

I wouldn't have minded if the bridge had still been fully intact. But then it wouldn't have been a good dare.

When the first spring melt happened, the river flooded and took with it bits of the bridge. The thick, woven ropes managed to stay on their posts, but most of the wooden strips were worn away and rotted. No one bothered to fix it, because there was a nice stone bridge just a few hundred feet down the river.

Destawan smirked. He was visiting from another village while his father came to trade with mine. He had gotten four of the children to follow him around, and it made him cocky. Or maybe he'd always been cocky.

"Don't dare Zayele," my younger brother Yashar said. He stared at Destawan with his unseeing eyes. "She's a young woman now."

"Then why is she here with us?" Destawan said. "They said you were the fastest climber, so it's either that or Truth."

I'd only known Destawan for a day, but I could tell he wasn't going to give me an easy question to answer. He'd want me to admit to something humiliating. I'd rather fall in the river than give him that.

"I'll do it," I said.

"Zayele—" Yashar pleaded.

"Don't worry about me. It'll be easy." I moved away from the children. They had come to see what Destawan would dare me to do. Now they ran alongside me, saying stupid things like "Don't do it, Zayele," and "It's just a dare." I ignored them and fixed my hijab so the wind wouldn't blow it off my head. Then I took off my shoes and carried them in one of my hands.

"Zayele," Yashar whispered. "Help me." He reached out for me, and I turned to take his hand, guiding him down to the bridge. We stepped over the broken rocks and the clumps of green grass. Everything was clean and bright today, glowing beneath gray clouds.

Down by the bridge, the water roared, crashing into the biggest of the boulders that stood in the middle of the river. The boulders dared the water to take them down.

Destawan laughed and jumped up on a giant brown rock that flanked the river. We stood there in the shadow of the gorge, watching water flow by. The bridge was only a few feet above the river, so it wasn't the fall that would hurt. It was the rapids. Yashar gripped my hand and wouldn't let go.

"It's really not that bad," I told him. "The wood's almost

gone, but there's so much rope. I could walk it blindfolded."
Bad choice of words, I realized.

"Are there any rotted bits on the rope? Does it look secure?"
Yashar hadn't always been such a worrier, but since he'd gone
blind, things bothered him more than they used to. I patted
his shoulder.

"It's not that far, really. Just twenty or thirty feet." I pulled
my hand out of his and set down my shoes. Then I smiled at
Destawan. "If I fall in the river, be sure to tell my father it was
all your idea." His eyes narrowed, which only spurred me on.

Each of the ropes that had been the railing was tied to a
boulder on the riverbank. The ropes were made from woven
grass, as thick as my arm, and they were heavy and wet from
last night's rain.

I'd have to trust that whoever had woven the ropes had
done a good job.

I grabbed one of them with both hands and walked sideways. I didn't want to get spread out if the middle ties broke
apart. Step by step, I moved along the rope. My ankles clicked
together each time I finished two steps. Within a few feet, I
was out over the water.

My toes were turning blue in the cold, and beneath them
was the white water. It was impossibly fast. I could swim, but
not in that.

I had to keep moving. The wind was stronger here, coming
down the gorge, and my hands were getting stiff. After a while,
I looked up to see how much farther I had to go. I was midway
over the river.

"Zayele!" the children screamed. I couldn't tell if they were cheering for me or warning me, but I didn't want to look back. I didn't want to see their faces.

One more step. Then another. And another, with the water rushing, rushing past. Where did it all go?

I didn't want to think of how cold it was. I only thought of movement, of the other side. And then, finally, my left hand touched something hard and unmoving. It was the wooden post on the far side.

Behind me, everyone cheered. I was shaking a little, but I turned around anyway and lifted a fist into the air. Then I cupped my hands around my mouth and shouted, "Your turn, Destawan!"

He shook his head and everyone laughed. Then he pointed at the village, and we all turned to see six horses trotting into the village center. We rarely had visitors this time of year, because the mountains were still frozen and no one had any crops yet.

I ran down to the other bridge, where I could cross over and get a closer look. Our village pushed up against a cliff, a little above the riverbank, and the horses and riders lined the street along the river. One of the horsemen carried the black banner of the Vizier of Baghdad. The vizier hadn't been to our village since the night my uncle and his wife were murdered by jinn, and something in me turned cold.

+ 3 +

NAJWA

I WAS THE last one to return from the surface and found everyone standing on the wool rug in Faisal's artifact room. The other students were all holding flowers or leaves, just like I was. I was the only student training directly under Faisal full-time, but everyone had to take the transporting class, even if they weren't training for the Eyes of Iblis Corps. It looked as if they'd all passed and would move on to their other teachers. It would just be me now.

Atish made his way over, holding a red poppy blossom in front of his dark, intense eyes. I was used to his handsome face, but now it looked strange in contrast with the young man I'd just seen on the surface. Before we'd all left for our test, Atish had promised he'd find me something pretty up there and I had laughed it off, brushing aside the feeling I got whenever it seemed he was trying to shift from longtime friend to something more. I hadn't wanted him to think of me, especially while we were each on our first mission. Now the poppy he held was as red as the drops of blood on my fingertips, and I hesitated before taking it from him.

"For you," he said. I nodded in thanks and wiped the blood against the petals, where no one would notice.

"Najwa, where did you get that?" Faisal's deep voice rumbled across the room.

"The red flower or the pink one?" I asked. I held each one up, gingerly holding the rose. So pretty, but so sharp!

Faisal motioned for me to bring the flowers to him, and as I made my way past the other students, I saw Shirin. She was sniffing her flower, which looked like a thistle. Her nose touched the tip, and she pulled back and rubbed at the spot where it had poked her.

When I got to Faisal, he held out his hand and I gave him the two flowers. He returned the red poppy, ignoring it. Then he pulled the rose petals apart, studying the stamen. "Where did you get this?"

Faisal was never this sour-faced. He was my affectionate, and often eccentric, uncle, who didn't bother with flowers and such things most of the time.

"I got it from a rosebush."

With a frustrated sigh, he strode on his short legs to his bookcase, then thumbed the spines. It was such a curious thing to see him so stricken that the whole class fell silent. When he found the book he was looking for, he pulled it off the shelf and flipped through its pages.

Then he looked up at the class. "You passed. What are you still doing here?" This was strange behavior, even for Faisal, but they took leave without asking any questions.

I leaned in as close as I dared and saw he was looking through a journal, with drawings of arches and flowers, Arabic calligraphy, and a few building layouts. He stopped at an illustration that matched the ombré rose I'd brought back.

"Najwa," Faisal said. He cleared his throat and held the book out to me. "This flower comes from only one garden." He tilted his chin down and frowned.

Faisal's gaze hadn't left mine. It was like he was studying me, trying to find out if I matched something in one of his books. I shifted on my feet, feeling my face flush.

"Which garden?" I asked.

"Janna's garden," Faisal said. He snapped the book shut and sniffed the flower. "The former caliph's dead wife."

That meant I'd been to the palace in Baghdad. No one could wish herself into the palace. Strong jinni wards, put up after the start of the war, kept us from getting in. But I had been there. The flower proved it.

I had gotten past the wards. No one, not even the Corps, had done that!

"I was in the palace?" I couldn't hide the surprise in my voice.

"You penetrated the wards, Najwa." He sounded disappointed, which was strange. It wasn't as if we were forbidden to go there. It was just impossible to get in.

"Come with me," he said. Then he turned and left the artifact room, still holding the rose.

I followed him down the hall and into his small office. It was plush like human homes, with overlapped rugs covering the stone floor and oil lamps casting golden halos of light along the walls.

Faisal was a magus, which meant he had the sort of wish-power that came to only a few in a generation. He was also Master of the Eyes of Iblis Corps and in charge of training any magi and those entering the Corps. I wasn't a magus, but I was the only one in my year training for the Corps. Once, when I was lamenting the fact that I wasn't a magus, Faisal said it was his love of humans, and not his wishpower, that made him a good observer in the Corps. He knew the way human minds worked, and how their hearts beat. He understood their stories, their faith, and their superstitions. Most of all, he knew why they kept trying to get into our tunnels. They wanted safety, just like any jinni, but for humans, that meant wealth and power. They wanted our jewels, and they wanted our wishes.

Faisal sat down cross-legged on a rug and bid me to sit before him. I obeyed, folding up my skirt beneath my knees. The floor felt miles away. No matter how hard I pressed my finger into the rug, I couldn't feel the stone.

"My little Najwa," he said with a sigh. I winced. I wasn't that little anymore. "I knew that if anyone was going to get past the wards, it'd be you. It's one of the reasons I'm training you for the Corps. What wish did you make in order to get in?"

"I don't know," I began. I brushed at the rug again, over a pair of birds woven into a yellow tree. The trees above hadn't been so pale. They had glowed, more real than emeralds. "I didn't mean to go there. I'm sorry."

"I'm not upset with you. What words did you use?"

"I wished to go to the most beautiful garden." I couldn't look at him, so I dug at a green spot on the rug.

He chuckled. "Was that it?"

"I—I don't know. I wanted to make an impression, but I didn't put that into any words."

Faisal's face cracked into a smile. "You made an impression, all right. This flower is proof that the human citadel is not impenetrable. We can get in."

"I don't know if I could do it again."

He waved at the air. "I'll have someone else try the same wish. Maybe wanting to make an impression is the key," he said, winking.

I sighed. "So I passed?"

He nodded, and then leaned forward, drawing his eyebrows together. "What happened up there? I haven't been there since . . . since I was about your age."

I told him everything. When I was finished, he sent for a messenger by blowing into the flame of one of his lamps. I got up to leave, but he stopped me.

"Who do you think that young man was?"

I shrugged. "I don't know. A scientist?"

"Think about it for a minute. How old was he?"

"About my age."

"Yes. And he was playing an oud? In a laboratory?"

I didn't see where he was heading. "Well, it could have been a room where they stored rocks, I guess."

"Najwa, use your training. Put everything together. Who would play music wherever he liked? Who would feel comfortable doing that in a laboratory, of all places?"

I stared at the flame he had blown on, thinking. What did I know about the palace? Nothing more than what Faisal had told me. There was the House of Wisdom, where jinn had once studied alongside humans. It was full of books. There was the Grand Mosque, the harem full of women and children, and the rooms for the royal family and all the people who worked for them. There were stables for horses, and warehouses for food and other riches.

The royal family was large, but the only people older than ten were the caliph, his harem ladies, and his two sons. One of his sons was a warrior, and he had been seen in some other city recently. The other one hadn't been seen outside the walls in a while. He was reported to be in the House of Wisdom often, so maybe he was a scholar. And worked in laboratories.

"The prince? The younger one, I think."

Faisal nodded. "In the clothes you described, near Janna's rose garden, and in a laboratory. I think there can only be one person such as this."

"I can't believe I was in the palace." The young man's face reappeared in my memory, smiling a little while he played his oud. "And I saw a prince."

"Prince Kamal," Faisal said, smiling. "He was quite the inquisitive toddler when I last saw him."

There was a knock at the door, and the messenger came in. Faisal stood to greet him, so I took that moment to leave, my mind buzzing. I'd been to the palace. I'd seen the prince.

4

ZAYELE

THE VIZIER WAS here, and everyone was standing around like idiots. After Yashar caught up to me by the stone bridge, I told him who was in the village, described what the horses looked like, and told him how the black banner whipped in the spring wind. He wanted these details because he used them in his poems. He was only eleven, but he could weave words better than anyone else.

As we got closer, his hand tightened in mine. I was watching the horses stomping in the dirt. The men sat in their saddles like they'd been sewn into them. But not the vizier. He had to be the one dressed all in black, with a turban and jeweled daggers stuck into his belt. He didn't carry a shield or sword, like the others. More than all this, he was smiling, his face wrinkling above his cheekbones. His eyes were the color of cold river water.

He was talking to my father, who reached up and helped him off his horse. My father gave him a hug and kissed his cheeks. By then, Yashar and I had gotten close enough that we had to be wary of the horses' hooves.

"My cousin," the vizier said, "it is good to visit my home."

He was one of us, but he'd left when he was young to study at the House of Wisdom, in Baghdad. He had made everyone in our tribe proud, rising through his school to become vizier, which helped us when it was time to pay tribute to the caliph. I'd never seen him before, and though I had known he was a real person, seeing him step right out of the stories and into my village was jolting.

"Come, let me give you tea," my father said. The vizier nodded and followed him into his tent, leaving the horsemen to dismount and guide their horses to the field that spread atop the gorge.

"Why is the vizier here?" Yashar whispered.

"We'll find out soon," I said. Then I squeezed his hand and took him with me to the women's tent.

They weren't truly tents, but long ago, my tribe had moved from place to place, and so we called them that. They were partially made from stiff felt and stone, but on the inside, they were more tentlike than not. I swept the flap aside and brought Yashar in.

A single lamp lit the interior. It was midafternoon, so the babies were sleeping and some of the women were resting beside them. My mother was one of them.

I knelt beside her, and she propped herself up on her elbow.

"Yes?" she asked, sounding less annoyed than I'd expected.

"We have visitors." As soon as I said it, she sat up.

"Who?"

"The vizier," I said.

"Did your father greet him?"

I nodded.

"Any word of why he is here?"

"No."

She looked past me at the door, and saw Yashar. "What is he doing in here?" she asked.

"He can't stay out there right now. It's not like he can see you anyway."

She sighed and stood up, then went to Yashar. She wrapped her arms around his shoulders and pulled him into her. "Son," she whispered, "you've got to learn to stay in your tent. You're getting too old for this one now."

"But Zayele said—"

"This is a tent for women. Now go out there and help with their horses. I'm assuming he brought men with him?" We both nodded. "Then go. One of the other boys can help you, Yashar."

She led him out and spun back around, probably to get her hijab and jewelry on. Left alone, I followed Yashar and wandered toward the path that led to the horses. Almost every child in the village was assisting with the new horses, including Destawan.

I groaned. "Destawan is up there."

"Let's just stay here, then, by the well." Yashar led me to the circle of stones that marked the village's well. He knew his way around, even though he'd been blind for six months.

We sat down, facing the entrance to our father's tent. "Why

don't you go in there and listen to what they're saying?" I asked. Yashar shook his head. "But you're allowed in there. You could spy on them for me."

"Zayele, I don't spy. We don't spy. Besides, I'd probably bump into the vizier and get thrashed by his horsewhip."

"I'm sorry."

"Stop apologizing. I can't stand it."

It was my fault Yashar was blind. It made writing poems harder, and that was my fault too.

I sat down, leaning my back against the stones, and fiddled with my hair where it was tucked up in my scarf.

"I don't have a good feeling about the vizier being here," I said.

"Do you think it's the jinn?" Yashar asked. "Are they coming back here?"

"No. The men would have more soldiers with them, not just guards. He's here for something, though. It doesn't make sense otherwise."

Yashar got up to get some water just as our father stepped out of the tent. We both paused, waiting to find out what he would do.

Father motioned for me to go to him. When we got closer, he smiled at me, ignoring Yashar. He did that a lot now.

"Zayele."

"Yes, Father?"

His smile was forced. "The vizier would like a word with you."

"Why?"

Father patted my shoulder, as if that would comfort me.

"He is looking for a bride for the caliph's son. If we're fortunate, he will choose you. Now go and change your clothes. Let your mother know you're being presented. We will be waiting for you." Then he waved his arm at the women's tent, directing me, before he turned to Yashar. "Stay away until the vizier is gone." He turned and disappeared back into his tent.

A *bride*? Tears welled up in my eyes and I ran toward my tent, digging my nails into my hands and leaving Yashar alone. If they sent me away, he'd always be alone. I couldn't look at him right now. I couldn't think about that.

On my way there, the clouds split open and hard rain raced from the sky, flooding the path between the tents.

✦ 5 ✦

NAJWA

RELEASED FROM MY class with Faisal, I went out into the vastness of the Cavern. It was a crystal bubble inside the earth—a geode so large it fit all the tribes, the city, and the Lake of Fire. But it wasn't as vast as the sky, and compared to the surface, it felt tighter, like a bowl turned upside down. Did everyone feel this way after their first trip to the surface?

Gypsum shards jutted out from the walls, catching the lamplight and scattering it every which way. The shards were as sharp as bat teeth, and I'd had nightmares of them falling and crashing through my house.

The Lake of Fire swept along the side of the Cavern, lapping at the crystal spears on the edge. Unlike in the human stories, it wasn't a lake of molten rock. It was decorated in fire. Gases bubbled to the surface, where they caught fire, sending licks of flame dancing across the shallow waves. The flames were blue-hot, but harmless.

Wishlights lined the streets and the crescent wall that curved along the lake. No one remembered who had built the wall, which was wide enough to walk on. Children raced on it, ignoring their mothers' pleas to slow down. Brightly painted goats pulled carts beneath the wishlights, taking one tribe's produce to trade with another's. Everything glittered.

And at the far end of the lake wall, sprawled out like a napping dragon, lay Iblis's palace. It was carved out of blue marble and pumice, striping it in glimmer and suede. Minarets dotted the width of the palace like the peaks on a dragon's spine. They were where the guards stood, watching over us and keeping an eye on the handful of tunnels.

Between the school and the palace were the markets, hundreds of homes carved into the sloping Cavern walls, and the street of fountains. And in the center, connected to the Lake of Fire by a bridge-dotted canal, roared the waterfall. It spilled out from a crack in the wall, stirring the air and water. Ten feet wide and fifty feet tall, it poured into the lake before mixing with the gases of the earth.

I stepped over the cobblestones to the first of the fountains and sat on a bench. I had always believed the Cavern was the most beautiful place in the world. I'd been told that nothing sparkled like the Cavern. But it wasn't true. The sun in the sky sparkled like nothing else, and the flowers had been so alive. So delicate and fragrant. Even the air itself had been fresh and clear.

I hadn't been on the bench long before Atish and two of his friends, Cyril and Dabar, left the school and headed toward me. Atish smiled from afar. He was so sure of himself, especially now that he was going into the Shaitan. It was all he'd ever wanted. He claimed he just wanted to protect us all from humans, but he probably wanted some glory as well. Being in the Shaitan meant you were more than a soldier. It meant you were loyal without question and had the sort of wishpower that endured in battle.

The past few months I hadn't been able to think of Atish without mixed feelings. Any of the other girls would have given the jewels in their hair for his attention, but I could only think of him as Atish, the boy who'd played with me when my mother kicked me out during her card games with her friends. As we grew older and were selected for our trades, the whispers and rumors strengthened. It was common for a Shaitan soldier to wed someone in the Corps. They went together, the warriors and those who told them where to go and whom to fight. But whenever he held my hand, his was too hot, or too thick, or too familiar. I could only ever see the boy who'd played with me, even when that boy grew into a man, with bronzed skin and a strong, sure jaw.

Atish stopped in front of me and flexed the muscles in his chest so that I would have no choice but to see them. I looked up into his face and raised my eyebrows, noticing how he and his friends were still wearing their training clothes, which were nothing more than wide pants and leather vests.

"How was your special class?" I hadn't meant for it to sound condescending, but it came out that way. Fortunately, he didn't seem to notice, and his friends hovered behind him, watching me with curiosity.

"So are you going to tell me what happened with Faisal?" he asked.

"Nothing happened, really," I lied. "He was in a hurry." I

couldn't tell him about the palace. Or the prince. The moment I realized this, I felt a pang in my stomach.

Smiling, he sat beside me, took one of my hands in his, and rubbed at the tender skin between my thumb and forefinger. It was the spot where Faisal would tattoo his mark on me once I was done with training. "What did you see when you were up there?" he asked.

"Just a garden, really. And a room with lots of rocks in it. What did you see?"

"A hill covered with poppies. There weren't any humans nearby." He leaned closer and then paused, looking at his friends. They already bore the golden lion mark of the Shaitan, which Atish had yet to receive. "It's a good thing, since I can do fireballs now."

"*What?*" I asked. "When did that happen?"

"After the transport test. Rashid pulled me aside and asked if I'd like to try it, so I did." He swallowed and looked away.

Rashid was the Captain of the Shaitan. Why would he have thought to test Atish this soon? "It's like they're planning for you to be in a Dyad."

"They aren't," Atish said. "Besides, there aren't any magi for them to pair me up with. And I'm relieved. I mean, to be in a Dyad would be amazing, but there's only one person I'd want to be with, and she didn't turn out to be a magus."

My cheeks burned. When we were children, we would play at being a Dyad, the powerful partnership of a Shaitan and a magus. But when Faisal told me I wasn't a magus like him, the dream died. I hadn't thought it would keep Atish from wanting to be in a Dyad, though.

Shirin appeared then, carrying a shallow box with a mixture of colored bottles. They held powdered stones and resins, which she needed for her own classes.

"What's going on?" she asked, putting the box on the seat and settling down between it and me.

"Atish can do fireballs," I said. He hadn't been able to cast them a few days ago, which was the last time we'd been alone together. Those times were few and far between now that he'd gotten further along with the Shaitan. We used to spend all our time together. I had always been the first to know.

"Oh," she said. "I guess you're too good for us lowly still-in-school jinn, then."

Atish was grinning. "I'm getting the mark today. Now that I passed the test, I'm qualified. I'm *in*."

Now I understood why Cyril and Dabar were with him. They hadn't been interested in Atish before. But now that he'd passed their test, and Faisal's, he was done. He'd completed everything, and he'd done it early. It was exactly what I'd always expected.

"You're one of them now," I said, forcing a smile. I was happy for him—he'd realized his dreams—but something had shifted. He was one step away from Shirin and me now.

"Almost." He tipped his head toward the school, where he'd have to go back now. They'd mark him, and that'd be it. He'd be an adult. He'd be Shaitan. He'd move out of his home and into the barracks, living and breathing weaponry and strategy until he died in battle.

"I, uh, I guess I'll see you later?"

"Yes," he said. "I'll see you tomorrow."

The three boys turned and left, leaving Shirin and me alone at the fountain. We watched the water spill down a stone leaf, dripping into the basin. Then I realized she was grinning at me.

"That was weird. Cyril and Dabar just stood there, like they were afraid to speak in his presence or something." She paused to rearrange her bottles, knocking a few down and setting them right again. "So tell me, what was Faisal so upset about?"

"Nothing." I stirred the water, wondering if it was the same temperature as the water in the palace fountains.

"Najwa. I'm not stupid. The flower you brought back really disturbed Faisal."

I shook the water off my hand and leaned forward, resting my elbows on my knees.

"It was just a flower he really liked. I think he saw one once when he was up there. But there is something," I said, smiling.

"What?" She was practically glittering, like she knew what I was going to say.

"I saw a human. A young man our age."

She squealed. "Was this, um, human boy worth looking at?"

I laid my hand on top of hers. "Shirin, think about it. He was a *human*."

"Well, he wasn't a goat."

I chuckled. "No, not a goat. He was . . . he was wearing a long white robe, and he had a turban on, till he took it off."

"He took off his robe?" Her eyes glinted, mischievous.

"No. His turban. His hair was all curly, and fell over his forehead."

"Shards, Najwa. You liked the way he looked, didn't you?"

My face was very hot, and I smiled, looking away from her. "No. I was just observing. I'm trained for that, you know."

"Right," she said. "So what did he do?"

"He was playing an oud, but it was in some sort of laboratory, and—"

"He's a scientist. And he plays music. Anything else?"

"He was just . . . he was just there." I wanted to tell her. But I couldn't. If she found out that I had gotten through the jinni wards, she'd stand up and boast about it as loudly as she could, right there by the fountain. Faisal would never trust me with any Corps secrets again.

"Good thing you didn't describe him to Atish," she said, "or he'd find the boy and shoot a fireball at him."

"No, he wouldn't," I countered. I thought about the wards, and how they had suddenly come down without any warning. We had been fighting the humans for years, but we'd never gotten ahead. Now we had an advantage, and I was the one who had discovered it. I just couldn't tell anyone yet.

Shirin groaned. "Here comes Faisal now."

Faisal was heading across the cobblestones.

Sighing, I shrugged at Shirin. "Break is over, I guess."

"Human boys for you, broken bones for me. Sometimes I wonder if I chose the right path." Shirin was training to be a physician, which meant she had to do some things I'd never have the stomach for.

We headed toward Faisal, but I kept talking. "But you love it; don't deny it."

"I know. I do. But the hospital is all girls, and Razeena

likes it that way." Razeena was the head physician. She was dry and quiet—the opposite of Shirin.

When we got to Faisal, he nodded at me. "We have a problem, Najwa."

"Uh-oh," Shirin said. Faisal raised one eyebrow at her and she shut her mouth, then scuttled toward the school.

"Did I do something?" I asked.

Faisal shook his head. "Just come with me, please."

Then he turned and we went past the school, past the training field, and across the stone square. The moment my foot touched the first obsidian tile, I knew where he was taking me, and I quickly brushed at the wrinkles on my dress.

He was taking me into the Command of Iblis, where the Corps met. I'd never been inside, because no one but the Corps was allowed. I knew only rumors about it. Supposedly, you had to wear a mask inside to keep your identity hidden, and it was where the Lamp was stored, which we'd used before the war. It was just a statue now. Also, there was supposed to be a chamber dripping in real, ever-blooming wisteria, where the Corps rested between assignments. Soon I'd find out if any of this was true.

"It seems," Faisal said as we waited for a pair of guards to open the door, "that you're the only one who can get into the palace."

· 6 ·

ZAYELE

A RIVER OF mud slithered past the women's tent, and I had to leap over it to get inside. My mother and one of my aunts chased the children who kept darting in and out of the tent. When my mother saw me, her frustrated face softened.

Everything welled up inside me then, and I could feel the tears coming faster. I wiped the salt and rain off my cheeks, and she hugged me. "What happened?"

"The vizier is looking for a bride for the caliph's son. Me." I ran to my bed and threw myself into the tangle of blankets. I was not going to cry anymore. I was not.

I felt her hand on my back. "Zayele," my mother said. "How can you be certain?"

"Father told me," I said, pressing my face into the blankets. "He said to come back and get ready to be presented. That if I was lucky, I'd be chosen. As the bride."

She was silent, pressing her hand into my back. Then she

pushed my hair aside and leaned down close to my ear. "You've always known something like this would happen."

I glared at her. "Marriage, yes, but not now! And not to a prince. I'll have to go so far away."

"Come." She pulled me up till I was sitting. "Let's clean off the tears."

I allowed her to wipe my face while she called to my cousin Rahela. Rahela was a few years older than me, and she never spoke back to the adults. If she'd been told she was going to Baghdad to be handed over like a prize, she would have been grateful. She wouldn't have stuffed her face into a pillow.

She sat down beside me and took my hand. "What's wrong?" she asked.

"Your uncle told her she is being considered for one of the caliph's sons," my mother answered.

"As a bride?" Rahela squeaked. She was as surprised as I was.

"Zayele," Mother said, "they can come to get you at any moment. You need to get ready."

"Even in the rain?" My voice was bitter, but I didn't care. "Wouldn't they want their *bride* to stay dry?"

"Zayele! I know you're upset, but you have to appear calm in front of the vizier. You have to represent us with honor. If you're going to be a princess, you have to act like one."

Rahela nodded, and I glared at her. "She's right, you know," she said. "Some of us wish we had this chance." She ignored my moans of despair and took out one of our nicest dresses from the box by my bed. Then she shook it out and motioned for me to change. I slipped off my hijab and my dress and wiped some of the mud off my ankles. Then I put on the other dress. It was stiff, like I'd wrapped myself in tree bark.

The dress was pomegranate red, with yellow vines and flowers embroidered across the chest and around the wrists. Rahela and I had made it a month ago, sitting by the winter fire and poking ourselves with needles. We'd spent hours embroidering the tiny blossoms and laughing about the men who would see us in it. But this was all wrong. Rahela was supposed to wear it first.

"That's better," my mother said as she got up to run after my baby brother, Anji, and handed Rahela a brush. "Help her," she said. Rahela started brushing my hair.

"But—" I tried to pull away, but she held my shoulder tightly.

"Just let me get you ready."

When she was done with my hair, she took one of our favorite hijabs. Then she took out another box filled with kohl and brushes.

"Close your eyes," she said. She rested her hand on my cheek and then drew with the kohl around my eyelids. It was thick and heavy, and since I'd turned fifteen, I'd worn it three times. Today wasn't any better.

In a few minutes, the man in my father's tent would be looking at me, trying to see if I was fit for a prince.

"Why did he have to come all the way here?" I asked.

Rahela shrugged her bony shoulders. "I guess to check on the tribe. And maybe to bring something back."

"But why should we care about what he wants? He hasn't been here in years."

"It's an honor—"

"He *saved* us!" my mother said. She was like a hawk, watching and hearing everything. She had been at the front of the tent, but now she loomed over us. "After the jinni killed your uncle and aunt, the vizier fought the demon *by himself*. If he hadn't been there—"

"I know," I said, stopping her. But her eyes flashed and she shook her hair.

"You don't know. You were a baby. We owe him our lives. He kept the jinni from killing us all." Her hands were shaking now, and she wrung them.

There wasn't anything I could say. Yes, he had saved us. Yes, my aunt and uncle were murdered. But I didn't want to leave. I didn't want to be a wife. "I just wish it wasn't me."

"He's the reason you're alive."

"He is planning on giving you to one of the princes." Rahela wiped a stray mark at the edge of my eye. "That can only be good for you."

"Good? They live in a city. It's hot and no one goes outside. There won't be any mountains to climb. I probably won't even be allowed to go anywhere by myself."

My mother shook her head. She was sitting down now. "I've heard the princes are both young and handsome."

"They are?" I paused. That wasn't as terrible as I'd feared. "Well, I don't care."

Rahela pulled me with her off the bed. "I know you're nervous, but the vizier is here, waiting to see you. Once you get in there, be quiet and just answer any questions he might have." I looked up and she gave a lopsided grin. "Don't look at him like that. Calm eyes, Zayele. Calm. Now stand up and let us see you."

I sighed, but I did what she asked. Rahela, my mother, and some of the other women scanned me from forehead to hem. The dress hadn't gotten any more flexible, so I still felt like a tree, but I could see they were pleased. My mother cleared her throat as if she was going to say something, but then changed her mind and tied the matching hijab over my hair, knotting it at the nape of my neck. It cascaded down my back, over my hair, and halfway to the floor. I was covered except for my hands and face. Those I had to leave bare, for the vizier to see.

Someone whacked at the tent flap with a stick and we both jumped. "Ready?" a man asked.

"Yes, one moment," Rahela replied. She knew I wasn't going to say anything. I went to the opening. All I could see was the rain gushing from the sky and the man's leather boots.

"What was the use of changing if I'm going out in that?" I asked. Mother sighed in disappointment and picked up a camel-hair shawl. Then she handed one end to Rahela and they held it over me. Rahela nudged me with her foot.

We stepped out into the wet and inhaled the cold air. The shawl kept most of the water from hitting me in the face, but it poured down on my mother and Rahela, drenching them. The man said something gruffly about the mud and headed toward my father's tent. We followed and passed a line of crocuses, all squashed into the mud by the vizier's guards. The sky was gray and the shadows were gone, as if they didn't want to meet the great vizier either.

I looked past the tents to the mountains. The snow was

starting to drip. Soon grass and wildflowers would be racing across the valley, and the camels would get as fat as pregnant goats. But if the vizier took me away, I'd never see any of that again.

We reached the tent and the man parted the flap.

"You women can go back," he said. Mother nodded, and she and Rahela each kissed me on the cheek.

"Allah be with you," my mother whispered. Her skin was pink with cold, and she squeezed my shoulder too tight, her fingers a stony clamp. Then she released me, gently, into the tent and left with Rahela.

Someone had lit a lamp inside. The flame danced on the walls and across the faces of the most senior men of the village. All of them were quiet, watchful.

My father was sitting on a cushion in his most formal robe. I knew every inch of it—I had woven the cloth, with Rahela's help, selecting the greens and browns that he preferred. Beside him, in a robe of black and gold, sat the Vizier of Baghdad. His long fingers tapped at his knee.

"This is my daughter, Zayele," Father said. He paused and glanced at the vizier, who nodded at me with narrowed eyes.

"Zayele, you are as beautiful as these men have claimed." The vizier's words were polite, but something heavy tinged his voice. "In fact, you look like your mother." I blinked. He continued, "Are you obedient? Faithful? These are some of the questions I must ask as I choose a gift for Prince Kamal."

The vizier started tapping at his knee again, but he stared straight at me. I didn't dare move, but I found my voice.

"Thank you for saving us. Before," I said. It was a pitiful

thing to say, but it was what came out of my mouth. "I believe I am faithful. And I'm obedient." Of course I was obedient. Anyone who knew my father would know that if I wasn't, I would be banished.

"I am sorry I could not save everyone, and I am sorry that a war began that day." He stopped tapping his fingers and turned to my uncle, twisting his head like an owl. "She is exactly what Baghdad needs. Someone fresh, but also a reminder to the people of what they are fighting for. She was here when the jinni first attacked, and she was saved."

My father pulled at his beard and smiled. "Hashim, I'm glad you've come for her. I think you're right. She will remind the caliph of the resourcefulness of the al-Rahman line. With her, you will have a hundred of our soldiers. Each one of them is willing to rid the world of the jinni plague."

"I'm certain the caliph will appreciate this year's tax tribute more than usual, Sergewaz," the vizier said, grinning. His teeth were surprisingly bright, and if he hadn't been so old and creepy, he would have been handsome. "Zayele, you're going to be this young prince's first wife. It's more than any other tribal woman can hope for."

It was like being hit in the stomach. The vizier and my father had made their trade. I was going to marry the prince, and my tribe's warriors would have the honor of taking part in the war. My father waved his hand, shooing me out of the tent. "Go let your mother know you will be leaving with the vizier tomorrow. Your cousin Rahela will go with you, so you will not travel alone. We have other issues to discuss now."

I could feel my face burning in anger, and I almost opened

my mouth to say what was on my mind, but then Father picked up his cup of tea. He was done with me. I turned on my heels and fled the tent. Outside, I picked my dress up to my shins and ran, splashing mud every which way. I went past my own tent, around the herd and to the cliffs.

I climbed them, not caring how they ripped at my hands or how slippery they had gotten in the rain. The dress snagged on the rocks, and the embroidered flowers were soon frayed and crushed like the crocuses we'd passed earlier. And all I could think of was that I was glad the dress was ruined. I was glad I couldn't wear it in front of the prince.

I climbed higher, wanting to escape, to turn into someone else. I wanted to feel the rain and wind blow through my clothes. At last, I made it to where I expected to find Yashar. He had started a small fire beneath an outcropping and sat crouched behind it. Smoke billowed around the edge and disappeared in the rain while the wood popped and steamed.

"Zayele?" he asked. He lifted his head and turned his ear to me. I ducked under the outcropping and sank down beside him.

"It's me," I said, and patted his hand. For a long time, we sat while the steam escaped from the fire, twirling in the air. The wood turned black and chunks of it fell down into the searing coals, where they died. Then Yashar rested his head on my shoulder.

"Are you going to leave with the vizier?" he asked. I grunted. "I won't know what to do when you're gone," he croaked.

"I don't want to go."

His head lifted off my shoulder. "What do you mean? Isn't it what girls want? To marry a prince?" He looked at me, furrowing his brows, and I shuddered. His irises were milky white with scars. They were like pearls, and unnatural. He could see light and darkness, nothing more than that, while I could see his blinded eyes every time I looked at him.

"I don't know. It's just that I belong here, not in Baghdad. Not in a city. Not to some prince." My heart twisted in my chest. Without me, how would Yashar make it? What if he fell down in the gorge and couldn't find his way out? What if Father cut him off? Ever since he'd gone blind, our father had thought he was deadweight. But I *knew* he wasn't. "Maybe I can find a way out of it and stay here."

"No," he said. He poked at the fire with a blackened stick. "You have to go. If you stayed, they'd make you marry someone from the al-Himza tribe. Maybe Destawan."

"Eww."

He chuckled, and I pretended he was really laughing and not breaking apart like I was. "You'd have to milk his stringy camels."

I shoved him and he smiled, a real one this time. "Baghdad is a long ways away," I said. "But anything could happen on the journey. Maybe I'll figure out how to come back home."

"Then you'd just be stuck here with us," he said. A spark popped and hit the stone between the fire and our knees, leaving a scorch mark.

"While I'm gone, don't let anyone hurt you."

"Don't worry. I may be blind, but I'm not missing a brain."

The water was pooling on the ledge and reaching toward my toes. Would it rain like this in Baghdad? After a while, the wind shifted and the outcropping couldn't hold back the rain anymore. We leaned against the stone while the fire sizzled and steamed until nothing was left but mud and char.

✦ 7 ✦

NAJWA

BEHIND THE DOORS stood an obsidian desk, and behind the desk sat a woman. I expected that we'd walk past her, but Faisal paused. She seemed to recognize him, but when she saw me, her smile thinned.

"Who's this, then?" she asked Faisal. She wore her hair twisted up in a gold-and-topaz clip, leaving a few strands hanging down. These she had dipped in bronze and filed at the points. She held one in her hand, twining her fingers around it while she looked me over.

"This is Najwa. She is expected," Faisal said.

"That's fine, but I need to check her in."

I glanced at Faisal, hoping he'd say something to get us past her quickly, but he nudged me toward her. "Najwa," he said with an annoyed sigh, "she needs a finger."

"Why?"

She said, "Just give me your hand, and you'll see what he means." She sounded like she enjoyed what she was going to do to me.

If this was what the members of the Eyes of Iblis Corps did the first time they came here, then so be it. I held out my hand and she took it in one of hers. Then she took one of her pointed strands of hair and pierced the tip of my finger. I bit my lip and watched her collect the drop of blood onto a small circle of copper and then cover it with a sliver of clear glass. Then she let go of my hand.

I brought my finger to my lips while she punched a hole in the copper circle, made a mark on the back, and hung it on a board behind her. I had noticed the board when we came in, shimmery with dozens of copper circles, but I'd thought it was just decoration. Now I looked closer and saw that each of the circles had a dark stain on the surface, pressed beneath a thin circle of glass.

"What is that for?" I asked.

"It's to keep track of everyone who can enter the Command of Iblis," the woman said.

"But why the blood?"

Faisal wrapped an arm around my shoulders. "Just in case."

That was the end of it. I could tell they would say no more, and I rubbed the sore spot on my finger, hoping that soon I would find an answer.

We left the entrance and entered the main hall. It was a circular room with walls of red and gold divided equally by four arched doorways, and in the center stood a lamp on a pedestal. It was the twin to one in the palace. Together, they had been the passage between the worlds, allowing jinn to transport without wishes and letting humans serve as ambassadors in the Cavern. The Lamp was made of pure gold and shone as though someone polished it every day. It stood, all alone, beneath a domed indigo ceiling. A sparkling, purposeful pattern spread across the ceiling.

"That's our chart of the stars," Faisal said. I had almost forgotten he was with me.

"Those are stars?" I whispered.

"No," he said, chuckling, "those are diamonds. We had them set in the same pattern as the stars in the sky."

"That's what the night sky looks like?" I said.

"Yes. And someday, you'll see it for yourself." Then he pulled me away to the doorway straight ahead, and we went around the Lamp and into a corridor. We passed two closed doors, both dark, and then stopped at one that was painted in the same red and gold as the main hall.

Faisal turned to face me, placing his hands on my shoulders, as if he was preparing to steady me. "Najwa, this is the Room of Iblis," he said, and I felt my jaw go slack.

I swallowed, and then said, "Why are we here?"

"I told you that you're the only one who can get into the palace. That proves you have special abilities, so we are going to bring you into the Corps."

Heat spread across my cheeks. "Today?"

He smiled, let go of my shoulders, and put his hand on the door. "Prepare yourself," he said, but he didn't give me any time. Suddenly, the door was open and I could see at least ten other jinn inside, all looking straight at me.

They were officers in the Corps. A woman stood by a map laid out on a table, and I recognized her as the one who always reported to Faisal. I had seen her in the hallways of the school, but she had never acknowledged me. The other jinn in the room were younger than Faisal, but more experienced than me. They had been to the surface countless times, some in the middle of a battle. They'd never taken notice of me, but I'd always known who they were. Whether it was something in their eyes or just the way they observed the world, I could always tell when someone was in the Corps.

Behind them all was the Eye of Iblis. It wasn't an actual eye, of course, but one whole wall of tiled quartz. Faisal had told me it was the way the jinn could see what was going on in the world. But without actually seeing the Eye of Iblis, I hadn't understood him. Some of the tiles flashed with images from other places, and some were bare and white, waiting patiently to show the room something. The Eye of Iblis was ten feet tall, twenty feet wide, and so bright that it silhouetted the jinn before it.

Faisal motioned toward the room. "Are you going in?" I felt faint, but I went in anyway and stood aside. Faisal went to the woman by the map. She nodded at him and turned back to give me a strained smile.

"Good, she's here," she said. Then, to me: "Are you ready?"

Faisal cleared his throat. "I haven't had time to explain what we want her to do, Delia. Najwa, each of us here has tried to enter the palace using your wish, but the closest we can get is the wall outside." He paused, waiting for me to say something.

"I—I'm sure someone else can get in," I said. My voice was quieter than I'd meant it to be.

One of the other jinn snorted. "We tried. Do you know

how exhausting it is to transport yourself over and over? We're done." I could see now that he was leaning back against another table, using it to prop himself up. The transport *had* been tiring. I couldn't imagine doing it repeatedly.

Delia shook her head. "You have to go back, Najwa. We needed someone in there a year ago. *Ten* years ago. We need to bring you into the Corps as a full member."

The same thing had happened to Atish. He'd finished his tests early, and the Shaitan had taken him. Somehow, getting into the palace had lifted me into the Corps, and they were going to give me a real assignment. I started to shake, nervous and excited at once.

"Najwa?" Faisal said. "Do you understand what Delia told you?"

"I understand," I said. Delia smiled, and this time it was genuine. The other jinn stepped back as she made her way to the center of the Eye of Iblis and pressed both hands against it. The images blinked and were gone, leaving it just a wall of blank crystal. Then she pulled on the center tile, and it slid out like a drawer. She reached in and pulled out a stick of sapphire the length of my forearm but as narrow as my thumb. One end was sharpened, and when I saw it, I knew what it was for. The mark of the Corps was sapphire blue, and this was what made it. She brought it to Faisal, who asked me to hold out my hand.

While the other jinn surrounded us, he held the sapphire point above the webbing between my thumb and forefinger.

"Najwa, we welcome you into the Eyes of Iblis Corps," he said. Then he wished, *"Iblishi."*

A blue light came out of the rod. It was a thousand and one heated pricks, all in one tiny spot. I gasped but held my body still, afraid that if I cried out, they would see how much it hurt. I watched as the light moved, drawing the mark, and then it was done.

That was all it took. Years of studying with Faisal, years of learning about humans and how to watch them, and all it took was a few seconds to join the Corps. I held up my hand. The rounded eye of an owl, the size of my smallest fingernail, stared back at me.

"Welcome, Najwa," Delia said. "In a few moments, the sapphire dust will reach your heart and become part of you." Then she winked. "You will be able to show us what you see whenever you press on it."

This was something Faisal had never told me. Everyone got a mark to designate their profession, but that was all it was. The Shaitan's lion mark was just a bit of gold powder set inside their skin. The physician's mark that Shirin would receive, an emerald snake wrapped around her wrist, was only that. Wasn't it? Or were all the marks a secret way for the members of each profession to communicate?

"How do you see what I see?" I asked Faisal.

"It goes to the Eye," he said.

"Can I practice?"

"Certainly," he said, nodding at my hand. "But it might be sore there."

Everyone was silent while I gazed at the mark between my thumb and forefinger. The skin was sensitive, but it was not broken. There weren't any punctures. How had the mark gone through my skin without damaging it?

I looked up at the wall, and then at Faisal. Gently, I pressed, and a giant graying beard spread across the Eye of Iblis. I jumped back, letting go of my hand, and everyone laughed. The image of Faisal's face flickered on the wall.

"Couldn't you have looked at someone prettier?" one of the jinn joked.

I turned to Faisal. "That is amazing! No wonder you know so much about the humans."

"Yes," he said. "I'm sorry we can't have a proper celebration, but we have to brief you and send you on your way."

Delia nodded and went to place the marking stick back into the Eye. When the drawer slid shut, she tapped the quartz and made a whispered wish. A brown line spread across the surface, branching out in both straight and curved lines. Within seconds, a map filled the entire expanse of the Eye. The map was of a large compound.

"Is that the palace?" I asked. I wanted to go closer, but I didn't move, afraid I'd break some rule I hadn't heard of yet.

"Yes," Delia said. "Can you find where you went this morning?"

The palace was a series of rectangular rooms of all sizes, and I couldn't tell which rooms had roofs and which did not. There were no indicators of bedrooms or gardens.

"She was in this garden," Faisal said, walking forward and pressing his finger against a large rectangle. Beside it was the laboratory I'd seen Prince Kamal in.

"Yes, I think that's where I was."

"You are not sure?" This came from another jinni, the one who'd said he was exhausted. I tried not to stare at the pointiness of his nose.

"I was there."

"And you can get back inside?" he asked.

Faisal put up a hand and stilled the jinni. "She is going to try."

I nodded. I was afraid to answer the other man, afraid I'd not be able to get to the palace this time. What if it was all an accident, and they'd given me the mark before I deserved it?

"For now, anything you can learn will help," Faisal said. "It's been fifteen years since anyone has been there. Just return to that laboratory and watch for a little while. There is no need to walk around yet. We only want to get another glimpse. If you see nothing, come back. If you see the prince, or someone else, watch what they are doing. You have been trained for this. You will do fine."

"Yes, but I haven't finished—"

Delia cut me off. "You have. We've all been watching your progress."

This didn't make me feel any better. Did they know about the many times I'd tried to transfer before, and failed? "Do I need to bring anything?"

"Just make your wish, and do as we have asked. We will wait here for your return," Faisal said. He traced an area on the map with his thumb slowly, as if his mind was back in that spot. It was the House of Wisdom, on the edge of the palace. He had spent an entire year of his life there.

"How long am I supposed to stay there?" I asked.

"As long as your *shahtabi* lasts." The invisibility wish, which hadn't lasted long the last time. "Now remember: eyes open, mouth closed."

I blinked a few times and sucked in a deep, slow breath. Then I took a last look at my new mark and made my wish.

✦ 8 ✦

ZAYELE

THE CAMEL'S NECK swelled as she walked. Even though her steps were smooth, the motion swayed me in the saddle. It sloshed my stomach, which wasn't comforting, but at least it was a short ride to the canal. My family walked in a line beside me, and I was high enough to see the tops of their heads.

I was convinced they'd put me on the camel so I couldn't run away. I hadn't actually tried to escape, but I might have said something about the mountains being an easy place to disappear into. It was true. I knew the seasons, and how to survive. I hadn't been to the peaks, but it was spring, so I would have had time to make my way over them, even if I'd had to slow down for Yashar.

Yashar wouldn't agree to go. Instead, he told Mother to be careful of letting me slip away. And that was why they put me on the camel while everyone else walked. That is, except for Hashim and his guards. They had their horses.

I wanted to be angry with Yashar, but I couldn't. He had to hold Mother's hand as he walked down the rutted road, not wincing in the sunlight like everyone else. He had to trust Mother with every step. And although he tried to act like he was older, he was still only a boy. His face was smooth.

We were walking in a train down the narrow road alongside the river. The sun delved into the gorge's divide, leaving one wall gleaming so bright I had to look at the water.

The river didn't just flow past us. It ran full speed, tripping over rocks and carrying large bits of trees and some daring ducks. It was white and a foamy green-blue. It belonged somewhere else, not hemmed in by craggy walls.

The morning was dry, shining, and buzzing with flies, but even with all my layers, I was shivering. I forced my hands to stay still. I was just cold. I didn't want anyone to think I was weak.

Finally, the cliffs disappeared into the ground. We walked over a stone bridge, where the horses' hooves clopped and scraped but the camel's padded hooves were silent. Then we stopped beside a canal where three barges lined up along the bank.

Each barge was nearly twenty feet long and made of wood and woven grasses. The center one was to be mine, but there was nothing to signify it would be taking a girl and her companion into Baghdad.

Father had been holding my camel's bridle the entire way, and when we stopped, he clicked his tongue and brought her onto her knees. This was my last chance. The horses were by the barges, and we stood between them and everyone from the village. If I'd turned the camel around and run her off into the mountains, I would have had a head start. Instead, I climbed off and took my father's hand. Our eyes met, and I knew he wanted to say something, but I looked away. I didn't want to argue anymore. It hadn't worked before, and now it was too late. I heard him sigh, and then he walked off to help the vizier dismount from his horse.

Yashar reached out for me and I caught his hand. "Be careful," he said. "Don't forget to pray on your way to the city."

"I doubt the vizier will let me forget," I said.

"Zayele," he said, coming closer. "When you get there, can you see if they have any . . . anything for me to do?" He blinked, but it did nothing to clear his sight. It was always strange, looking at him, knowing he couldn't look back. He couldn't see the uncertainty I felt, but if I wasn't careful, he could hear it in my voice.

My throat got really thick all of a sudden. "Yes," I said, sounding as confident as I could, "I'll find something and then send you a message."

"Thank you," he said. He hugged me then, dropping tears on my shoulders, and stepped back to allow our mother to speak.

"My dear, you've become such a beautiful woman."

"I'm not a woman yet. Remind Father that I am still a child. And he's already shoving me off."

"Zayele," she warned. She glanced back at the men before gripping my wrists. "This is something we all go through. You have no choice because there *isn't any*. Don't you believe that I'd give you one if I could? Don't you think that *he* would have?" She let go of my wrists. "Rahela is going to help you. Trust her. We love you, and we know you'll do well in Baghdad."

There were no tears on her cheeks when she let go.

I stood still while everyone bustled around me. They carried boxes of silks and other goods onto the barges, and they coaxed the vizier's favorite horse onto his personal barge, the one in front. There was a flurry of children running along the water, the guards trading their horses with the village men for other things they wanted, and then the vizier was standing in front of me. He was dressed in black, with his ink-dyed hand outstretched.

"Cousin, let me help you onto your barge," he said. When I didn't reach out to him, he picked my hand up and held it tightly. His palm was dry and callused. Then he took me down the three stone steps to the plank.

I turned and saw Rahela right there, in my shadow. My parents stood together, with Yashar off to the side. Everyone but Yashar watched as we were ushered onto the barge.

"We're going in that?" I asked Hashim. He had taken us to the front, where the sides of the barge rose a few feet off the floor. A door was open in the raised center, showing a dark, gaping hole in the belly of the barge.

"Yes, Zayele."

I crept into the hole. Rahela climbed in and we stood there, looking at the impossibly small space. There was only one sleeping bench and a little bit of floor. Two of our trunks were tucked in beneath the bench. Anything not in the light coming from the door was lost in shadow.

Hashim shut the door in my face and opened a little window with wooden slats.

"You can't lock us up in here!" I pressed my face against the slats, and tried to find a handle. There wasn't one. "It's not like we'd jump off the boat!"

He slid the bolt on the door and locked it, holding up the key for emphasis. Everything inside me froze. "I had hoped to spare us this discussion, but as we are having it, know that if you were allowed to walk about in full view, any man along the way would be sorely tempted. It's for your own safety. It's best if no one knows we have a princess on board."

Then he turned and disappeared from our little window. All I could see was a bit of sky and part of the barge in front of ours. A moment later, I saw him climb on board his own barge and settle down on a bench made of folded rugs. He brushed at the dust on his sleeves, wiping away anything from our village that might have settled there.

"At least leave it unlocked!" I shouted at him. But he didn't seem to hear. Instead, he lifted his arm and waved at the family I couldn't see anymore.

✦ 9 ✦

NAJWA

I BLINKED AND was in the same garden. The sun was eclipsed by the wall opposite from me, and the rays scattered all over the leaves and blossoms. The colors were richer now that there was some shade to contrast. The shadows beneath the bushes bubbled along the tiles, spreading over my feet, but the ground was still warm from the sun.

"*Shahtabi*," I whispered, and I was invisible. Then I bent over and sniffed at one of Janna's roses. The scent was rich and syrupy, and clung to me after I started walking toward the laboratory. It was empty, which was disappointing. I had wanted to catch a glimpse of the prince again. I had been so rushed before, and I needed more details. At least for Shirin's sake.

Since I knew where I was this time, I took more notice of things. The arched doorway that separated the garden from the laboratory wasn't plain, for example. A series of overlapping triangles and stars worked its way up the border and wrapped over the threshold into the room. Inside, the shelves still contained many books, but this time, I noticed the large stone bowls filled with broken crystals and rocks on the floor between them. And from above, a line of colored orbs hung from wires. One was large and yellow, and the rest were of various sizes, set onto their cords so that they spun around the yellow orb.

It was time to try out my new mark. I stared at the orbs and pressed the mark between two fingers. Then I waited, holding my breath, hoping to get some sense that it had worked, but there was nothing. Finally, I let go of my hand and looked away.

The next thing I saw was the selenite sphere the prince had been holding earlier. It lay nestled on a silk pillow, like a prize. Selenite was so ordinary, but in this shape and in the filtered sunlight, it looked completely different. It looked like it hadn't been carved by human hands, but wished into existence by a very creative jinni.

I picked it up with both hands. It was small enough that my fingers could just touch, but it was incredibly heavy. When I rolled it around, I saw that a circle had been cut into the side. I stuck my finger in and found that the inside was hollowed out a little. Why would someone hollow it out like that? Were they going to put something in the sphere?

Quickly, I set it back onto the pillow and sent another image to the Eye. I was wandering toward the other side of the room when the door flung open. The prince strode in, his robe whipping behind him, with his gaze already on the sphere. His face was flushed while he picked up the sphere, tucked it beneath an arm, and turned to go back through the door.

I froze. My heart was in my throat. I'd been so careless. What if he'd come in a minute earlier and seen his sphere held up by invisible hands? He would have known in a heartbeat a jinni was in the palace. I would have disappointed the entire Eyes of Iblis Corps on my first official assignment.

What would have happened if he'd known a jinni had gotten in? Would they have increased the wards? Would they have tried another attack at one of our tunnels? Would it have made any difference?

Breathing easier now, I remembered that the prince had taken the strange object out of the laboratory. If I didn't follow, the Corps wouldn't know what had become of it. Even though I was supposed to stay in the room, I went to the door he'd left open and stepped into the hall.

Besides, although I didn't want to admit it, I couldn't resist following him. He left behind the scent of cinnamon.

The walls of the hall swept up and up until they touched a ceiling covered in sharply angled blue lines. The lines spread along the ceiling like a maze, crossing each other. I ran my fingers along the tiled wall and caught up with the prince.

He hadn't gone far, because another man had stopped him. The man clapped the prince on the back and held him still. The prince nodded once, while a grin spread across the other man's face. I tiptoed closer and pressed myself against the wall.

"Don't," said Prince Kamal. "I'm trying to get out of it."

The other man chuckled. *"Insha'Allah,"* he said. It was a human phrase that meant "God willing." Although I'd heard Faisal say it, it was different hearing a human use it as though he said it all day long, and I grinned despite myself. "I'll see you at prayers. You have half an hour, by the way. Better get moving."

The prince nodded and swept by me. His robes brushed

against my ankles, and he did smell like cinnamon. Somehow he hadn't noticed the jinni squashing herself against the wall. It took me a second after he passed to peel myself off and follow again.

The hall ended in a large, high-ceilinged room. Painted birds and vines climbed up the walls, and ornate plaster relief decorated all that remained. Tall white-and-gold columns divided the space, sprouting up to the ceiling like trees. Between the columns were more men than I wanted to count. They were close together, whispering over each other's shoulders and debating something written on sheets of paper they shook in the air. Boys ran between them bearing trays heavy with copper pots of coffee. The smell, sweet and bitter, wafted through the columns, carrying with it odd spices Faisal hadn't yet had me try. Rich, pungent, and masculine. I pressed the mark on my hand.

At the head of the hall, on a pedestal of rose-colored marble, stood a chair made of gilded peacocks. They reached toward each other, interweaving their necks to create a throne of such metallic poetry that I stared.

I knew that chair. I'd seen a sketch of it in one of Faisal's books. It was the caliph's throne. I laughed, despite the danger of discovery. If there'd been any doubt that I'd gotten into the palace, there wasn't now.

The prince was making his way around the older men. He paused, looked at the throne, and then trotted, faster now, through a set of double doors across the room. Everyone moved to let him pass, bowing their heads.

I wove between the men as quickly as I could and passed through the doors before they closed. I was in another hall now, empty of anyone but the prince, and let out a silent sigh of relief. Any one of those men could have bumped into me.

The prince had stepped into a hall glimmering in gold foil. He stopped at a set of golden doors and knocked twice.

"Kamal? Come in," came a sharp response. I smiled, knowing I'd guessed his identity correctly. The prince reached for the door handle with his free hand and hesitated. Then he shook his head, as if clearing his thoughts, and pulled the door open. I should have stopped there. I should have gone home. Instead, I leaped across the width of the hall into the space behind him.

The air inside was scented with rose syrup, and the room was completely white. The plaster adornments climbing up the walls were the color of milk. The furniture, made of interwoven reeds, was the same color as the walls. And the plants, which hung suspended from the six windows, had been pruned so that only their pale blossoms remained.

A man with a robust black beard lay sprawled on a divan. It had to be the caliph. He matched the descriptions and sketches of him exactly.

"What is it?" he asked. He wore a wide leather belt over his tunic and a ruby-capped dagger. The rubies shone like drops of blood in the blindingly white room.

I didn't dare breathe.

Prince Kamal held out his selenite sphere. "I finally figured it out."

The caliph sighed. "Bring it here."

The prince strode to the caliph and gave him the sphere. The caliph turned it around, then gave it back.

"I don't see how this would work."

"You can't tell at first, of course," Kamal began, "but see how it's hollow? We can put it inside, where it'd be protected."

"But why this kind of rock? Why not a brass tube?"

"Because brass isn't strong enough, and this crystal resists fire. It's almost impervious to heat. In fact, we could use this kind of rock to outfit our soldiers with—"

"How? Have them wear little balls of this hanging on their armor? It's too heavy; it wouldn't be worth it."

Kamal shook his head. "No, Father, we would crush it, then find a way to bind it into the fabric. It would work—"

Crushed-selenite armor? That was brilliant, actually. It would repel our fireballs better than anything they were using now.

"Kamal, I know what you're trying to do." The caliph sat up and faced his son. "I know why you're here."

Kamal straightened, then looked down at the sphere. "I'm trying to help."

"No, you're trying to delay the inevitable."

"Father, please. I have too much work to do."

"Hashim and I talked about this at great length before he left. The girl he is going to bring back with him will be good for you. She is from a tribe whose loyalty we will need in the coming months, and more importantly, she's from Zab. Her presence will give the people in the city more resolve in the coming battles."

My skin prickled, and I didn't know if it was because they were talking about Zab or because I was straining to keep my *shahtabi* going. Zab was where the chain of bloody events that had started the war had begun. It was just a village, but the humans believed we'd murdered two people there, and in a time when fear was running high, that sparked the end of the peace treaty between the races. I had been a baby then, but everyone talked about it like it had just happened.

Kamal swallowed, and when he spoke, his voice was strained. "When are they due to arrive?"

"In a day or two. Until then, you can go back to your rocks."

Kamal's eyes flashed at his father, but he bowed his head. Then he turned around and I had to sidestep to avoid getting run into. He pulled the door open and I followed, afraid to stay behind, alone with the caliph.

He ran down the hall, past the doors to the Court of Honor, and kept going, but I slumped against the wall, releasing the *shahtabi*. The Eyes of Iblis would want to know about this girl from Zab.

✦ 10 ✦

ZAYELE

I GRIPPED THE edge of the bed platform until my fingers ached. The barge had set off, and we were drifting down the canal. Someone was piloting, but I couldn't see who it was. Probably one of Hashim's guards. At least one of his guards had taken a position on the bow. He stood facing downstream, ready in case anyone tried to leap off the shore onto our barge, or come up on us from another boat. As if there was any threat of that happening. The land was flat as bread all around us, and even from the little window, we could see for miles. Not down the canal, though. The view ahead was blocked by Hashim's barge, and I tried to avoid looking at it. The first hour of our trip, he caught me watching him and he just stood there, staring with his river-water eyes until I sank back into the darkness.

Rahela and I had unpacked a few things and set them on the crate beside the bed. She took out her lap loom and began to thread it with yarn, a process that took longer than you'd think. I stretched my legs out. My toes could touch the door.

Our room was too small for two girls, especially on a trip that would take days.

"What does he expect us to do in here?" I asked Rahela.

She shrugged and continued with her loom. She'd gotten one color set into the frame and was selecting a second color.

"How can you do that right now?" I asked.

Rahela wrapped the chosen yarn around her fingers. "There's nothing else to do, and it calms me."

"I thought you were going to do something to the green dress."

"I was, but right now I don't feel like it. I'm still irritated that you ruined the red one."

I pushed my toes into the door, not wanting to talk about the dress. After I had come back with Yashar, Mother and Rahela had ranted at me all afternoon about the dress. They wouldn't stop until I told them I was leaving the next day. Then, when I told Rahela she was coming with me, she turned pale as snow. But she didn't cry or complain. In fact, she didn't say anything for the rest of the night. She just packed her trunk and then helped put the younger children to sleep, as if nothing had changed. I, on the other hand, threw my dresses into my trunk and thought of a dozen reasons why I should run away.

Now we sat, side by side, for what felt like another mile along the canal. "I could help you," I said. I was trying to have a positive attitude. She was stuck, just as I was. We were in it together.

She studied the loom for a moment, then humphed. "Maybe later. The sun is going down soon, and we don't have a lamp."

I hadn't thought of that. So we weren't just locked into a tiny room, where we'd surely drown if the boat took on any measurable amount of water, but we would be in the dark. I stood up and took the one step to the window. The sky to our east was the hazy purple that took over at sunset. Ahead, Hashim was shaking out a prayer rug. Travel wasn't stopped for prayers, even for the caliph's vizier.

When the prayer call came from the barge behind us, Rahela pulled me from the window and made me kneel beside her. I tried to pray, but all I could do was go through the motions and think about how we were like birds in a cage. I snuck a peek at the sky, wishing I could fly out into it.

Later, a hanging lamp was lit on the bow of our boat. Hashim ate a meal served to him by one of the men, and the two laughed. Their voices carried across the water. If a laugh could make it, then surely he could hear me if I yelled.

"Great Vizier," I shouted, "could we have a lamp and oil? It's very dark in here!"

He looked up from his bowl, but it was too dark to see his face clearly. "An open flame would be too dangerous in such an enclosed place," he called back.

"Can we come out for meals?"

"You will get out when we arrive at the palace's dock." He said this like he was stating a fact of nature, like how the sun rises at dawn. Then he got up and disappeared into his cabin, which was set into the center of his barge, like ours. But he didn't share his with anyone, and he wouldn't have been locked in.

I was about to call out again, but a figure appeared on the

other side of the door. "Dinner," the man said. He unlocked the window, which was on a hinge that I hadn't noticed, and passed us two bowls of lentil stew.

I took the food, and we ate in the nearly full darkness.

I looked up through the window into the indigo sky. I could almost feel the wind that blew past our locked door. I wanted to feel the wind. I wanted to be out there in the open, where anything could happen as long as I allowed it to.

I almost wore down the floorboards. I couldn't stop pacing. On the third day of this, we slid out of the canal and into the Tigris River. The water was a deeper green and bubbled with eddies. We moved faster, and the pilot had to work harder to keep us away from the banks. For Rahela and me, though, nothing changed.

That afternoon, we rowed past Samarra, a city squished along the river like weeds against a fence. Once we cleared the city, the guard at the prow seemed more tense than usual. He stood straighter, if that was possible. A series of dark holes, some as wide as a horse, dotted the riverbank, and he kept turning his head to look at them.

"Look at that," I said to Rahela. She put down her loom and I gave her some room at the window. "What are those?"

The holes grew larger. How was the bank not sliding down into the river?

"I think those are tunnels, or caves," she whispered. Rahela rarely whispered, and when she did, you paid attention.

"Jinni tunnels?" I asked. She didn't answer, so I cleared my throat and shouted, "Hey, guard! Are those jinni tunnels?"

He glanced back at me and nodded. He didn't have to tell us to be quiet. Rahela backed into the cabin.

"Zayele," she hissed, "get away from the window."

"It's fine," I said, and I slid my fingers through the slats.

The tunnels were dark and vacant. Either the jinn were hiding from a few poorly defended boats, or they had been driven inward by a battle. Every battle we'd had with the jinn was at the mouth of a tunnel. They were trying to work their way back onto the surface to take our lands. Their numbers had grown and their little cavern wasn't big enough anymore. Also, they were driven by the devil himself. They wanted most to rid the earth of humans.

According to my father, the caliph's army had been able to hold them off, even though the jinn had powerful wishes on their side. The army had positioned itself at the mouth of every cave and tunnel that led to the jinni cavern. So far, the jinn hadn't been able to make it out, and their primary weapons were fireballs, which scorched more than they burned.

I thought of all this while the bank of the river went back to its layered sandstone and clumps of grass. The guard relaxed, but I wasn't able to let go of the window. I turned and looked at Rahela, who sat in the corner of the bench, covered in yards and yards of her woven creation.

"What's wrong?" I asked.

"It's the tunnels. And the jinn. I didn't know—I wasn't expecting—it was surprising to see them," she said.

I left the window and sat beside her, patting the colorful layers piled on her knees. "I didn't realize you were so afraid of jinn."

She nodded. "It's not just jinn. It's the tunnels. They're like anthills, and when we were going by, I kept thinking of thousands of jinn pouring out of the tunnels there, flooding into the river, and overpowering our boat."

I chuckled. "That's not going to happen," I said. "They're not going to risk everything just to catch two girls."

"I know all of this," she sighed. "But I cannot turn away thoughts that come unbidden. This whole time, I've been thinking about jinn. In Zab, we were safe. But in Baghdad, we'll be closer."

"But they've got wards in the palace, and we don't have them in Zab," I countered.

"We don't need them in Zab. They're not interested in a bunch of cliffs and sheep! But they want the palace. Everyone knows that."

I shook my head. "I can't believe you're worried about jinn but don't care at all about how we were practically thrown at the prince. This box of a boat cabin doesn't affect you, and neither does the idea of living forever in another one, in the palace."

"It does affect me," she said quietly. "But one of us needs to be rational. We aren't going to slip away from our obligations."

"Rational," I huffed. "You're the one afraid of some dormant jinni tunnels."

She folded up the weaving and stood with her back to me. "Promise me you'll keep watch for me whenever my head is obstructed by fear, and I will keep it level enough for the both of us when we arrive," she said, and when she turned I saw that half of her mouth had slid into a smile.

"I promise," I said. "But I also promise that if I can find a way for us to get out of here, I'm going to take it."

She rolled her eyes. "Fine. It'll be you against the caliphate, but that wouldn't surprise me."

We laughed, and she sat down on the bench, knocking her bony shoulder into mine.

✦ II ✦

NAJWA

THE RELIEF ON Faisal's face when I came back told me more than anything he could have said. Had he really been worried while I was gone? It wasn't as if I'd gone in without any training.

"How did it go?" he asked. The only people in the room now were Faisal and Delia. The rest of the Eyes of Iblis had gone, and their absence left the room so empty it echoed.

I shrugged and looked at the Eye of Iblis. The caliph's throne filled the entire wall, and it appeared larger than the actual one.

"You left the area," Delia said. Her voice was tight.

I winced, and nodded. "When the prince left the room, I felt like I had to follow."

"You were supposed to follow your orders."

"Delia, she is back, and in one piece. Let's hear what she has to report."

Everything was fine until I told them about the girl from Zab. The air seemed to spark between Delia and Faisal.

"Are you sure the caliph said Zab?" Delia asked. She was as still as a pillar, and as straight.

I nodded. "He said that because she was from there, it would inspire the city." Something I'd said was wrong. The air felt like it was about to combust. "Do you know who she could be?" I asked Faisal.

He closed the space between us and took me by my elbow. "We will take care of it, Najwa. You've done well on this assignment, and I'm sure we will need you to return, so go home and get some rest."

He was ushering me out of the room, and I turned to look at Delia, who had gone to the Eye of Iblis. She was tapping at the image of the throne with her fingernail. "But I'm not tired," I said.

"All your friends have gone home by now," he said. Suddenly, we were out in the hall. I followed him into the circular hall that housed the Lamp.

"There's something about Zab, isn't there?" I asked, and he stopped me, right in front of the Lamp. He had his back to it, like it was nothing more than art.

"We cannot discuss this here, Najwa."

My face flushed in shame. "I'm sorry. I just wanted to know."

Frowning, he nodded, then took me to the entrance. We were standing beside the desk where the copper disks scaled the wall, but a different person was sitting there now, looking bored.

"All of us in the Eyes of Iblis have insatiable curiosity. It's what makes us good. But what makes us *work* is understanding who should know certain things and who should not. Now go back to your mother. You've accomplished more today than ever before. Don't tell her about the palace," he said, pausing to smile. We both knew she wouldn't take that well. "But you can show her the mark. We will see you tomorrow."

I nodded, even though I didn't want to. I wanted the rest of the story. I wanted to know what it was about this girl from Zab that disturbed two seasoned Eyes of Iblis officers. I wanted to know why I wasn't allowed to know. And I wanted to understand why they'd bring me into the Eyes of Iblis and send me to the palace but not trust me completely. If I was the only one who could get there, wouldn't knowing everything about the situation help me?

I didn't dare open my mouth again. Instead, I waved to Faisal and let him pull the door closed behind me. Mindlessly, I made my way across the Cavern, somehow making it over the bridge, past the stores and the library, and up the path that led home.

My house wasn't terribly high up the Cavern's wall. It was one of the stacked buildings littering the cascade of fallen gypsum that had become the foundation in the geode. Most of the homes were decorated using liberal doses of wishes, but none were as gaudy as mine. It was rounded and squashed like a tortoiseshell, with each square of the shell a different crystal. In the center of the roof was a slice of very thin glass that allowed the light in. I had begged my mother to leave it all one color, or just one shape, but it changed every month or so. Everything did in our house, depending on her mood. Somehow, she couldn't get anything to match the image she held in her mind.

I made it home and was about to pull aside one of her woven creations that hung in the doorway when I heard voices. I froze. It was my mother and Irina, her apprentice. Irina was the last person I wanted to run into.

She was the same age as me, but she didn't study at the school. She claimed she was too talented to waste her time there. Apparently, designing clothing was more important than anything else.

"Well, that's it for their relationship, then," Irina said. She couldn't say anything without scorn.

My mother giggled. "I'll be surprised if he comes here tomorrow. He'll have other duties, I suppose." My hand shook the curtain, and I cursed it silently. "Najwa?"

There was nothing to do but go in. Mother and Irina were sitting at the table, each holding a spread of cards in her hand. A bottle stood open between them, half-drunk. Irina's look was smug. She'd gotten close to my mother, and she knew it irritated me.

"Who are you talking about?" I asked. I dropped my empty lunch bag on the shelf.

"Atish, of course," Irina said. Of course. "He made full Shaitan status today. You should see his mark. It's practically glowing. And it's hot to touch too."

"Is it?" I asked, trying not to imagine Irina touching Atish anywhere, much less on his mark. Mother was smiling, but without any sort of smirk. Her thick, straight hair fell behind her, glittering with pink diamonds beaded onto the ends. She had finally chosen a color for her hair, and it was nearly the same as my own. I frowned at the copied diamonds.

"How did your transport test go?" she asked. "I know you passed, since everyone did, but how was it? What sort of flower did you bring back?" Mother was, for once in her life, graciously changing the subject. She had asked me to bring her an earthen flower, and I'd promised. But I was empty-handed, and she could see that.

"I'm sorry, Mother. I had to turn my flower in. To the Eyes of Iblis." She blinked, and I knew I'd never hear the end of that. "But it went well. I was in the most beautiful garden I could have imagined."

"Well, what sort of flower was it, then?" She glanced at Irina, who was adjusting a shawl made of silk and living glowworms. One of the glowworms had detached itself and was making a run for it.

"A rose. Mother, why would Atish not come here tomorrow?" If there was one thing I could count on, it was Atish. He was the definition of routine, and part of his routine was walking with me to school.

"Well, he's in the Shaitan now," she began.

"He's not going to want to walk you down there now that he's not in school anymore," Irina cut in.

The mark on my hand burned, and I wanted to rub it in her face. But I couldn't. Whenever Irina was around, I couldn't find my voice. She treated me as though everything I said was inconsequential, and I usually ended up giving way to her opinions and unwanted advice.

Still, I had my news, and Faisal had said I could share it. "Mother, the transport test went so well, actually, that afterward Faisal brought me to the Eyes of Iblis building." I paused, waiting for the information to sink in, but they just blinked. "And, um, they gave me my mark."

"They *what*?" I had expected Irina to say something like that, but not my mother. She pushed her chair back. "You go to the surface one time, just like everyone else, and he tosses you into the Eyes of Iblis? Just like that?"

"Yes, but—"

"Najwa, that's ridiculous," Irina said. "Where is it?"

I held out my hand to show them. The new mark glittered, and there it was, the truth of what I'd said. The undeniable shift in who I was. In what I was.

My mother's face had paled. "Najwa, I don't know. I hadn't heard they were planning on this. How could he do it so suddenly? To someone so young and—and inexperienced?"

This stung. I had never wanted to tell my mother any secret so badly before. "They gave Atish his mark today. Why not me too?"

"Because you're *you*! And Atish is only going up the ranks in his foolish military organization. But you—you're going to be up there, mingling with *them*. I don't care if it helps us in this idiotic war or not, but having my daughter popping up amongst humans is . . . It's . . ."

"It's disgusting," finished Irina.

"Yes," Mother said, nodding at Irina. "You should be here, where it's safe. Where you won't be tainted."

Her outburst caught me off guard. I had backed up against the shelves. "Why didn't you say something?"

"I did say something, but Faisal wouldn't have anything of it! You know my brother. He's *impossible*. And he was always telling me you were meant for his precious Corps." There were tears in her eyes.

Irina draped an arm over my mother's shoulders. "Maybe you should go out for a bit, Najwa. Let her calm down." She said this with the smile of a snake.

"Fine!" I turned and ran out, practically ripping the flimsy curtain that was our door. I hated them. Both of them.

I ran up the trail that wound behind our house and went as high as I could. There, the gypsum shards bit into each other like the tip of a monster's mouth. I couldn't press on from here—I was at the top, where the ceiling met the wall. As a young child, I could fit between the points almost till the top and bottom melted into one another. I would hide there for hours, soaking in silence.

But now the last few feet were impossible to reach. I stared at the narrow space, squeezing my nails into my palms, and thought of the shock on my mother's face. How had she not known I would end up in the Eyes of Iblis? I was training for it. It had been only a matter of time, and yes, that time had come early, but it shouldn't have shocked her.

Something had changed in me today, though. Maybe that was what scared her. Maybe she could see the garden in me, and the sky. Maybe she could smell the flowers. She had been up there once. Just once, on the day of her own transport test.

I turned and looked at the houses that poured down the Cavern's wall. They stood between the bits of jagged rock, and the lake still curved like a deadly fingernail around the city, flickering here and there. It was all the same as always. None of it was fresh.

The look on Prince Kamal's face when he lifted his selenite ball sprang into my mind. He wasn't sitting in one place, trying to manage. He was doing something, even if his father didn't think it was worth his time. Even if everything in his life pointed to a mysterious girl from Zab.

In fact, it wasn't just *his* life that was being affected by her. She was interfering with mine too. Some human girl, making her way to Baghdad, was going to change things.

And all I ever did was watch.

But that was going to change.

I sucked in a huge breath through my nose, and thought of this girl while I held my breath. I focused my mind on what I knew of her, which was very little. It would be enough. I was ready.

"Shatamana," I whispered.

Then it happened. Tiny grains of sand swirled around my skirt and scratched my cheeks, moving with the air that left my lungs. A wind of limestone bits and musk twisted around and around. The lake rushed past me, a marbled vision of fire and water.

Then I dissolved into smoke the color of my hair and flew up through the Cavern, a burst of flame pushing through the layers of rock and sand.

ZAYELE

"PRINCESS," THE GUARD said. He was knocking on the door. I sat up just as Rahela stood from her spot on the floor. The guard's beard filled the whole window.

"You've come to let us out? That's really too kind," I said, while I checked to make sure I was properly covered.

"No, Princess. The vizier wanted us to tell you to prepare yourself. We will be arriving in Baghdad before the day is over."

It was good I was still sitting down. Somehow, I managed to nod.

"Thank you," Rahela told the guard. She spoke to him about breakfast and needing extra water for me to bathe in, but my focus faded.

Today was the hideous day I'd be let out of my little cabin and brought into the legendary Palace of Baghdad.

After the guard left, Rahela washed my hair and braided it in layers.

"Let's leave my hair like this. It doesn't matter what I look like," I said.

She ignored my complaints and tugged out the knots. "It doesn't matter to them, but it matters to me. I can't walk in looking better than a princess," she said. Then she grinned. "Unless you want *me* to marry the prince and have *you* be the constant companion."

"Would you?" I asked, jerking my hair from her fingers.

She rapped my head lightly with the brush. "Of course not, silly. Besides, Hashim knows what you look like."

"I think I'm going to throw up," I said, resigning myself to her overly elaborate hair design.

At the end of an hour, I had the hair of a princess about to be wed. Then she took out her narrow henna box and painted the soles of my feet and then my palms. She drew diamonds and curlicued flowers across the lines, dipping her brush into the henna pot over and over. The brush tickled and tugged my skin, leaving behind a layer of black goo.

I groaned, pretending not to notice that what she'd done was beautiful. "So I have a few hours left. Then we'll be out of this cage and in another."

Rahela sighed. "The palace won't be a cage. And at any rate, it won't be as small as this place." She stole a glance at the door. We'd leave this cabin and never see it again. "There." She wiped the brush on a bit of cloth and closed the henna pot.

I flapped my hands in the air. As long as the henna was wet, I couldn't touch anything. She reached for my feet and scraped away the dried henna there, revealing swirling flowers coiling around my toes, triangles and pearls on the bottoms of my feet, and bell-shaped flowers curling up my ankle. All of it was red.

It would fade, but by then I'd be a married woman with weeks of experience. I shivered. I didn't want to think about it. I went to my usual spot by the window. Outside, the sun was straight above, so that the guard had no shadow and the water was blinding.

"I'm sure it's dry now," Rahela said behind me. I nodded and turned toward her, but just as I did, something happened. The hairs on my arms rose and a sudden rush of cold swept across me, followed by a wave of heat. I turned back to the window.

A girl was looking through it. I gasped, and in a blink, she was gone.

On instinct, I reached through the window and grabbed at the air. Something caught in my fingers. *Hair.* She hadn't gone. I yanked at it and heard a muffled cry.

She was a jinni. A jinni was *right here.* In my hands. Everything I'd been told about jinn rushed through my mind—invisibility, bejeweled hair, wishes—and when she tried to pull away, I thrust my other hand through the window and touched what had to be her face.

"Got you!"

The jinni gasped, and I felt her shudder. She fell apart and came in through the window like a wave of sand. Then, as quickly as she'd turned to sand, she came together again and fell into me, knocking us both onto the floor. Then her hands pushed at me and she backed up. I reached forward before she could flee, and grabbed her wrist.

She wore a pale gown embroidered in silver stripes, and her hair shimmered with jewels. Her eyes were wide and dark as a gazelle's. And just as nervous. But the strangest thing—even stranger than finding a jinni at my window—was that her face was like my own.

"Zayele!" Rahela shrieked. She backed up in the corner of the cabin, and her nostrils flared.

"She's a jinni," I said.

The jinni froze. "Let me go," she whispered.

"Why do you look like me?" I asked, squeezing her wrist. I was not going to let go.

"Please, let me go."

There had to be a reason a jinni showed up here, right before I reached Baghdad. It couldn't be coincidence. "Grant me a wish."

She tried to pull away, shaking her head. "Please, don't ask that—"

"But those are the rules, aren't they? I know we're at war, but before all that, jinn granted wishes. All we had to do was catch one."

"Don't, Zayele. Let her go."

"I need this wish, Rahela," I said. I gritted my teeth. I had almost given up on escape, but the perfect solution had appeared at my window: if a human caught a jinni, the jinni had to grant that human a wish. It was a rule of nature to keep the jinn from growing too powerful. "You," I said to the jinni girl, "you owe me a wish. Then I won't kill you or call the guards. Is that a deal?"

She balled up her fists. I could feel the tendons in her wrist moving, and was surprised at how human she felt. "Why can't

I wish myself home?" she asked with a strain in her voice. I wasn't sure what she meant, but it didn't matter. I needed this wish.

She looked so much like me. With a change of clothes and a bit of henna, no one would notice. A tingling idea began to form, and I felt the corners of my mouth lifting. I knew what I would wish for. I smiled, and a powerful surge pulsed beneath my fingers.

"Is that normal?" I asked.

She glared at me. "I don't know. I've never had a human hold me prisoner before."

"I'll just say my wish now, then." I breathed. I had to get this right. In all the stories about jinn, the human never said the wish right. I remembered listening to the fables with my cousins and shouting out what the man should have wished for. But it never changed. The man would make his wish and everything would unravel. The rest of the story was always about how he slaved to get everything back to how it'd been before. I was not going to make a greedy mistake. My words were going to be just right.

I looked into her black eyes and felt a stutter in my veins. "I wish for you to take my place and send me home." It was a two-part wish, but I hoped it would work. Rahela cried out behind me.

The jinni shook her head, then ripped her hand out of mine. She turned to the door and tried to beat it down, but she could not slip through it. Crying, she turned back to me, her cheeks flushed and blotchy.

Didn't you have to have a soul to cry?

"What have you done?" Rahela asked. She looked more disappointed than I'd ever seen her look before.

"But—"

A white fire spread across the jinni's skin and then swept over to me. It fell down my shoulders like a desert breeze. The wish was working.

The jinni doubled over and clutched at her stomach. "I shouldn't have come," she said, slumping to the floor and writhing in pain. I watched for a moment before I felt something like butterflies—burning, flurrying butterflies—multiply and spread out through my limbs.

My body fell apart, grain by grain, and turned into a raging fire. I screamed, but the scream didn't come with me.

✦ 13 ✦

NAJWA

MY CHEEK WAS stinging. Someone had just slapped me. I sat up and looked at the woman who had been with the girl who made the wish.

"What happened to Zayele?" she exclaimed, keeping her voice just above a whisper.

My stomach lurched, and I thought I would vomit, but nothing happened. It only turned, along with my head. *What have I done? Faisal will* kill *me.* The girl was gone. Free.

The woman was panting in fear and had drawn back her hand. She held it close, as if afraid I'd hit her back. I couldn't answer her. I had to go home.

"*Mashila,*" I whispered. Instantly, a piercing pain shot through my lungs, and I curled up against the wall of the little room we were in, gasping for air. The woman was looking at me, more curious than concerned.

"*Mashila.*" Again, my lungs were on fire, and the burning spread to my heart, to my stomach, and up my neck. I kept gasping. Each breath caused pain, and I could not take any deep breaths or speak. In desperation, I shook away the *mashila* wish and set Zayele's foremost in my mind. Instantly, the pain and fire dissolved, like ashes in the wind. When I had finally calmed down, I looked over to the woman.

What had the wish done to me? I could barely breathe!

"Keep the noise down, or the guards will come. Now I'll ask again," the woman said. "What happened to Zayele?"

"I don't know," I said. My words were hollow and dry. I couldn't wish myself home. I couldn't stand the pain.

"She turned into a flame and slipped through the window," she said, choking back tears.

Zayele had transferred like a jinni, but why had she turned into fire? I looked up at the woman. "I have to leave," I said. I tried to go through the door, but it was firm as granite, and there was no way to open it from inside.

I couldn't get out! I banged on the door, screaming for it to open.

"They won't open it. Zayele tried that for days." The woman slumped down onto a bed platform. "You look like her."

"I can't stay," I said. I held up my hands and rubbed the owl-eye tattoo. It still glittered. But I didn't press on it. If I managed to escape this strange wish, then any images I sent back would be glaring at me from the Eye. There'd be no way to deny I'd left the Cavern without permission.

How was I going to get out of this if I couldn't open the door and I couldn't wish myself home?

The woman pursed her lips and then said, "So her wish worked." Her gruff voice broke again, and she pressed her hands against her mouth before holding up a clay pot.

"I . . ." I fought back my tears. "Why did she do this to me?"

"Sit." It wasn't a request, so I sat. "What's your name? If jinn have names."

"Najwa." It came out a faded whisper.

"I'm Rahela. I'm Zayele's cousin." She was a few years older than me, with straight hair, narrow shoulders, and a piercing glare. "From now on, I have to refer to you as Zayele. Until she comes back or you find a way to fix all this." Everything I'd been raised to do, all that Faisal had hoped for me, would never come to be unless I escaped. He was going to kill me.

If the humans didn't do it first. Deflated, I let my head fall forward. Rahela picked up one of my hands and spread my palm flat.

"We have to get you ready, and we have very little time."

I shook my head in protest, but Rahela picked up a long, narrow box and set it on her knees. She lifted the lid and pulled out a thin brush. Then she opened a clay pot of henna paste.

I had first seen henna a few months ago, in the artifact room. Shirin and I had drawn swirls and diamonds on our hands, trying to copy human designs. Faisal had been amused. My mother had nearly spat when she'd seen it, and clamored for a jar of the paste, but Faisal wouldn't let it out of the artifact room. She'd simmered for days. None of her wishes matched the intense red the henna had stained into my skin. Now I watched as Rahela took my palm.

She inspected it, flipping it over. She examined my mark and shrugged. "You feel exactly the same, but we will have to cover that up."

"I'm flesh and blood, just like you," I said. A lock of hair fell over her eyebrows, shading them. She nodded, and then expertly sketched out a filigree design on my hand with the brown paste. What if I did look like a human? What if I *could* blend in? My fears eased a little. I was being dressed up like a human princess. I was *in her place.*

Rahela was halfway through with the first hand when the guards rotated their posts. The retiring guard stopped by the door.

"Princess," he said. "We will be there in a few hours." My heart beat quickly, but I managed to look him in the eye and nod. When he left, I started shaking. There was no way anyone would think I was human. They were going to kill me. I was going to die. And then Faisal was going to kill me again.

"Be still, or this will look horrible," Rahela said. "I have to cover up this tattoo." She colored over the owl eye and turned it into a flower petal. Amazingly, the blue didn't show through.

Although everything around me was falling apart, and the mark I'd had for only a day was covered, I was fascinated. She made such small lines. They swirled and joined in what seemed the perfect places. It was nothing at all like what Shirin and I had tried to do. Ours had been childish and random. This was real. I had a *princess* hand.

"Have you done this design before?"

Rahela humphed. "This morning." Of course. She would have to repeat the design. She finished the hand and looked up. "When Zayele disappeared, did she go home?" Her voice was clear, as if the answer didn't matter to her one bit.

"I think so. . . ." I trailed off, looking away. Any other jinni would have kept herself alert, never to be at the mercy of a human. I had let my guard down with this woman. "Why haven't you made a wish from me also?"

"I tried," she said coldly, "but nothing happened. It's good you feel solid and human in my hands. The prince will need to believe, without doubt, that you are the same woman our tribe sent to him. If not, our tribe will lose all honor. And you will be killed." She wiped the brush and picked up the other hand. I held the completed hand palm-up and watched the henna change colors.

Would the prince believe I was human? Would he believe I was Zayele, and play music for me? The thought was disturbing, and I shook it away.

"Are you going to do my feet?" I asked.

"If you *have* feet."

"I have feet," I said weakly.

She huffed, and then paused before dabbing the brush back into the henna and wiping the excess against the rim of the jar. She finished my hand without saying another word. Outside, the barges slid along the river, taking us past fields of grain. The guards stood ready, their swords strapped across their backs and daggers on their waists. What was in the other barges? More women to wait upon the princess?

Rahela pointed at my feet. "You must remove your slippers. I won't do it for you." I nodded and did as asked. "Your toenails are red?"

I blushed. No one, other than my mother, had been this close to my feet before. I had painted them as I'd heard humans sometimes did, but had kept quiet about it. I nodded, pretending it was common for a jinni to have red toenails.

While she decorated my feet, I watched out the window. We traveled on a river as green as jade. The current was slow and thick. The closer we got to Baghdad, the more often we passed groups of farmers bending over in the dirt of the fields, or a mud-brick home set high on the riverbank. Children were everywhere, running around the houses, chasing each other across the small gardens against the walls. Their laughter made it over the water and through the slats in the window. Every time we passed a group of them, they stopped their chasing and stood, mouths gaping, and stared. The adults, too, stopped their work to watch us pass by. They did not bow their heads, smile, or wave. Instead, they kept themselves fully still, only moving their eyes as we glided past.

We had traveled miles from where I had first encountered Zayele and Rahela. Barley field after barley field stood between where I'd first arrived and where we were on the river. If anyone from home had noticed I was missing, by the time they followed my trail to that spot above the river, any impression I might have made would be gone. It would be as if I had dissolved in sunlight.

My stomach dropped. No one would know how to find me. And if they couldn't find me, I would not be saved. But still, I didn't want to send an image. Not until I was certain I wouldn't be able to make my way home. Again, I thought of Kamal and forced myself to think of the sphere he'd shown his father. I needed to stay focused, like Faisal had said. Getting distracted was what had gotten me stuck here.

Rahela finished my feet. "Don't touch anything yet. You can't wear the gown Zayele was meant to wear, as she took it with her, but there is her second-best gown." She stood, stretched her legs, and opened the chest. The inside of the lid was covered with writing, the script moving like water from side to side.

"What's that?" I asked, pointing a paste-covered finger at the lid. She lowered it, so that I couldn't read the words.

"It's nothing," she said. Then she pulled out a gown made of pale green silk embroidered in sky blue at the hem and wrists. The neckline was also embroidered in sky blue, but embedded in the thread were tiny lapis lazuli beads.

I gasped. "It's beautiful." Nothing in Faisal's artifact room, not a single veil or bit of jewelry, compared to this. It was flowers and air and all that lived on the earth—in a dress.

"What do jinni women wear to meet their bridegroom?" It was more of an accusation than a question.

"You don't know about jinni weddings?" I asked.

"It was never my job to know about jinn," she said. Before I could explain how a jinni woman chose her husband, she grabbed one of my hands, checked that it was dry, and then scraped off the paste with a wooden blade.

"Ow!" I said.

"Sorry," she said, but she didn't sound sorry.

My skin was transformed. Roses and swirls of reddish orange covered my palms. I rubbed at them, but the designs weren't just on my skin; they were within it. I rubbed my hands together as she scraped the henna off my feet and put my slippers back on. "If you'd undress, I could help you get into this." She lifted the green gown off the bench.

I hesitated. When I had woken this morning, I had been

eager to fly up to the surface and find a flower for Faisal. I had thrown on my clothes without thinking, choosing my most comfortable gown over my nicer ones. And now, only hours later but in another world entirely, I was going to shed my clothes to dress like a princess. It was as frightening as it was exciting.

I slid off my clothes and let Rahela pull Zayele's gown over my head and tie it at the back of my neck. It went to my ankles, narrowed at my chest, and wrapped around my body as if designed for me. Even my shoulders were Zayele's in shape and size.

Rahela must have been thinking the same. "Fits you just as well. I was worried it wouldn't be the right length, but you've copied her looks well enough." She thought I'd copied the girl's form. What did she think I truly looked like?

"Can you—can you see any differences between us?" I asked. She cocked her head and studied me.

"Yes, but I doubt anyone else would notice it."

"What difference?"

"There's the owl eye on your hand, but we covered it up." Then she gave a sly grin. "Also, you're more anxious."

+ 14 +

ZAYELE

DARK SMOKE SUCKED me out of the cabin, a small whirl of fury, and pulled me away, away, away. I was twisting, a cloud of fire and ember. My stomach flew into my throat, but I wasn't afraid.

I was free. The wish had worked.

When the spinning stopped, I gulped in a deep breath, but the air was too hot and singed my throat. I coughed, and my eyes watered. I brushed some sand off my face and shook it out of my hair. Then I opened my eyes.

In all the stories, there was one place that made me tremble in excitement at the briefest of descriptions. This was the one place my father refused to speak about, which convinced me I needed to hear more about it. It spurred stories, nightmares, and back-and-forth whispering with Rahela and Yashar. And there it was, the nightmare, with all its shining, pointy rocks.

Hell itself. The kingdom of jinn.

A cavern, as huge as a mountain turned inside out, curved up around me. A waterfall fell from a gap in the cavern wall and poured into a canal that ended at a bubbling, flashing lake. Fire twisted in the air above the dark water. In every direction, thousands of tiny homes dotted the cavern's sides, each lit with lamps. The whole place glowed.

I gasped. The jinni kingdom glittered. And it was alive. Hundreds of jinn rushed about, some running along the lake and some walking into golden-framed buildings.

Why was I here? Why hadn't I gone home? Had the second part of the wish not worked?

A thousand feet above, crystal shards and golden spires hung from the ceiling. Birds swooped in the air. Birds with leathery wings and clipping wingbeats. Bats.

I tried not to look at the fires on the lake. It was like watching a campfire—beautiful and mesmerizing. Blinking, I turned my back on the lake and saw that I was in a courtyard. Tall, pillared buildings circled the fountain I stood beside.

There were people all around me. *Jinn.* A group of them were walking past, laughing together.

I froze, almost unable to breathe, until the crowd passed. No one approached and demanded a reason for my presence. No one looked twice at the human standing by the fountain. No one noticed the sweat beading on my forehead.

Jewel-toned robes trailed behind them as they went along tiled walkways. Some jinn were hand in hand and others rushed about, chasing each other. The ones running were short. Children. They had *children.* A few leaned over a narrow bridge that crossed the canal and tossed rocks into the water.

One child ran past, followed by another, who bumped into

me. She turned, flashed a grin, and then chased after her friend. Her eyelids were rimmed in gold, and her hair was braided with ribbons studded with precious stones.

When I found the courage to move, I went as purposefully as I could manage to the bench on the other side of the fountain. When I sat, I looked across the expanse at the buildings, all of various colors, sliding up the cavern's side. There was something at the edges of my memory that had once looked like that, and while I searched the walls for any sign of a way out, I tried to remember. Where had I seen houses like these? Like caves, or birdhouses. Ah, yes. Swallows. The jinn's houses were like so many swallow nests, clinging together.

But they weren't. Right before my eyes, one of them changed shape and color. In seconds, the transformation was over and a jinni stepped out to admire his emerald home. He put his hands on his hips while he did this, then went back inside and shut the door. A minute later, when I still hadn't moved, I saw another house change shape. Its color stayed ocher, but it grew taller and a window of yellow glass grew from the middle. No one came out this time. Maybe they only needed more light. I shivered again. These were the homes of thousands of jinn. As the idea spread, so did my goose bumps.

A mixture of anger and terror washed over me. The wish hadn't worked at all. I was in the wrong place. It was all so wrong, wrong, wrong!

"There you are!" A woman was towering over me, and my stomach dropped. They had found me. "I went to your little hiding place, but you weren't there." Her lips were colored with some sort of crushed gemstone, and she wore a matching shawl with green lines. The lines glowed a little, and wiggled. They were glowworms.

I swallowed back panic. "My hiding place?"

"Najwa," she said, taking a step closer, "I've known about that place for years. Anyway, after Irina left, I went to find you. When you weren't at your usual spot and I couldn't find you anywhere else, I had to go tell Faisal. Where were you? You couldn't have been here the entire time, because I walked past this fountain not ten minutes ago."

I had no idea who Najwa was, but at least this woman didn't know who I was.

"I was just walking around," I lied.

She tilted her head, like a lizard. "What's wrong with your hair? I thought you liked the diamonds." She whined the last few words and held up her own hair, beaded in white-and-pink crystals. Another jinni with hair like that flashed across my mind. The girl in my cabin. The one I wished on. Was she Najwa?

"I was trying something new."

She frowned. "It looks terrible, but we can take care of that later. First, you have some explaining to do. And not just to me. Faisal is concerned now."

I followed the woman and her shawl of woven glowworms and tried not to stare at the pinned-on beasties. They were still alive. She looked back to see if I was coming and caught my gaze.

"Isn't Irina a great designer? She gave it to me for helping her with her last project." She prattled on about a game, and how she'd won round after round. "I know you don't approve, but you haven't the faintest idea how dull my job is. I don't get to go to the surface and get any human thing I want. It isn't fair."

I still had no idea what she was talking about, and the more I followed her, the more my stomach felt like it was going to drop out of me. If I ran off, she'd know something was strange. But the more I stayed with her, the more terrified I felt. I kept looking for a way out—a tunnel, a staircase, anything—but there was nothing. There *had* to be tunnels, though. I followed the woman through a bronze door held open by a male jinni with a bare chest and belted trousers, not knowing what else to do. He led us down a hall and into a torchlit room covered by rugs from different regions. Human-made rugs. They had to be stolen.

The woman clucked at me, and I looked up to see she expected me to bow my head at a man sitting on a cushion in the corner, half in shadow. I hadn't seen him, and his sudden appearance, like that of the jinni girl in my window, made me jump. His wizened bronze face was like an etched pot, round and cut and full of heaviness.

"I'm glad to see you haven't disappeared," he said. He motioned for me to sit beside him, but the woman sat on that cushion. I was left with a thin mat of woven grass. I shifted on it and waited for them to say something.

"She was outside by the fountain, rubbing her feet!" the woman said.

The man pulled at his graying goatee. "Laira, did Najwa tell you she was marked today?" This man thought I was Najwa too. Couldn't they tell I was human?

"Yes," she said. "I had expected a warning before that happened, Faisal."

"There was a development today, and we did not have time to forewarn you."

"What sort of development?" she snapped.

"I can't say, and neither can Najwa, but thank you for finding her. You may go now. I'll send Najwa along in a little while."

Laira's face colored and she shook her head. "Don't tell me what to do, my dear brother. You promised me when—when she was born—that you would not tell me how to raise her."

This man was Najwa's uncle?

Faisal reached for the pot of tea before him and poured himself a cup. "Najwa and I have some Corps business to attend to."

"This late in the evening?" She stood up and pulled me off my mat. "I'm sure it can be taken care of in the morning. Come, Najwa."

"Laira." His voice had an edge. "I need to speak to Najwa now. Alone. If you wish, you can wait outside." He sounded like my father when he was drawing out the details of a trade. Or telling me what I was not allowed to do.

Laira huffed, but she nodded and let go of me. Then she whipped her skirts and fled the room. When I turned around, I found Faisal watching me. His eyes were aflame.

"Where did you go?" he asked. "I know you went up there, Najwa. I can smell the earth on you."

"I didn't go anywhere," I said. I tried to smile, but couldn't manage it.

He sighed and looked down at his cup of tea. "You know better than to lie to me, Najwa." He had gotten very quiet. When he looked up, I saw that there was fire simmering in his round cheeks, just below the skin. Real, liquid fire. "What is the first rule of the Corps?"

"Honesty?" My heart was thumping against my rib cage.

"You cannot go to the surface without permission." He stood up slowly, and I backed against the wall. He was going to kill me. "I never thought I'd be this disappointed in you."

"I'm sorry. I—" I didn't know what to say. What would she have said? I had only known her for a second. How was I supposed to know what to do? I bowed my head, trying to look as apologetic as possible. "I'm sorry, but nothing happened. I won't do it again."

"Shards, Najwa. What if you had been *touched*?" His anger fizzled, leaving him a tired, empty old man. He sank back onto his cushion. I would have felt sorry for him if he hadn't just yelled at me. And if he hadn't been a jinni.

"Well, I wasn't touched." At least that part was true. For me.

"Did you go back to the palace?"

"The palace? No." She had been in the palace? The Baghdad palace?

"Then you must have gone to see the girl from Zab." My face flushed, and there was no denying now that I knew something about that.

"The princess?"

"She wasn't any of your business, but you took matters into your own hands. So tell me, then, what did you see?" His voice brightened, like he wanted to hear how an old friend was doing. But he wasn't any friend of mine.

Something was going on, but Najwa wasn't supposed to know. And so that was why she'd come to my barge. Not because of some Will of Allah. Not because I'd prayed for help. She'd been curious.

"The girl was getting ready for her arrival in Baghdad."

"Did she have her hair braided and her hands hennaed?" My jaw dropped, and I looked at my palms. "Don't think I didn't notice, Najwa. I'm not Master of the Corps for nothing."

I had been holding my breath until he called me Najwa again. "Yes! I mean, I'm sorry. I was so interested in the henna that I had to try it. That's why I was gone so long."

"Get some rest. I have something for you to do tomorrow." Then he waved me away, and I bolted out of the room.

+ 15 +

NAJWA

THICK CLOUDS GATHERED in the sky, and within a few minutes, they fell like a soggy veil. Water pounded the deck and bounced up knee-high. A strip of wood at the base of the door prevented the water from seeping into the cabin, but I reached through the window and let it land on my hennaed palm. It was pure, cold, and real. Rain.

"Don't get the dress wet," Rahela said. The rain was sliding down my wrist, so I pulled my hand back. I kept my face as close to the window as I could without getting wet. Rahela put aside her loom to fold up the gowns we'd left strewn about the cabin.

I dried my hand and helped her, tucking everything into the trunks, but it was unnecessary. The water stayed outside. It ran off the sides of the barge and into the Tigris.

"It's beautiful. It's falling all over, into the river," I said while I shut the second trunk.

Rahela huffed. "You haven't seen rain before?"

I shook my head. "In the Cavern, all the fresh water comes

from one of the cracks in the walls. It falls into a canal, winds through the city, then goes into the lake." I thought for a moment. "We don't have clouds."

She set the loom so it straddled her lap, then passed the shuttle through. "It sounds nicer than I'd thought, but I'm not sure I could live in a rock."

"It doesn't feel small. Or at least, it didn't before."

"Before what?"

"Before I came up here," I said. She chose a different color, and sent that through the warp. The fabric she was weaving was geometric, but she had started adding a bird. "There's so much air here. And the sky doesn't end."

The rain had brought a dampening chill, and I shivered. I'd never been this cold before. Had the rain seeped into my bones and drawn out the fire within?

Rahela put down her loom and rummaged in a trunk, then tossed me a blanket.

"Don't let yourself become ill. The prince wouldn't want a sniffling jinni in his bed."

I pulled the blanket over my shoulders and turned away, not wanting to show how red my cheeks had gotten. She went back to her birds, and I watched the dripping world outside melting into the river.

"My mother is a weaver," I said. When she looked surprised, I added, "She is always making something, planning something. She would have loved what you're making."

"I didn't know jinn needed to weave their clothes." She paused. "I don't think I ever thought about it. Can't you wish your own clothes into being?"

"We can't wish nothing into something. In weaving, my mother knows what it will look like when it's finished. Mostly. Then she sometimes adds things with a wish or two."

She brushed her fingertips across the part she had finished. "I wouldn't add anything to this. Every line is real; every part of this is mine. And though it won't be perfect, neither am I." She looked at me, almost daring me to argue. She didn't know I rarely argued, and the result was that we both stayed quiet.

The rain stopped a few minutes later, without any warning. A wide band of blue swept across the expanse of the sky, pushing away the clouds. The sun, a ball of clean fire, shone along the riverbank and dripped off the shrubs. Each drop of water glittered as it fell into the Tigris. They were quick, disappearing diamonds. Nothing at home gleamed like that, and the more I watched, the more a strange sensation spread through my chest. I was stricken by the beauty of a wet, sparkling world beneath a sun-filled sky.

In the distance, between the sky and the retreating clouds, a rainbow arched in the air. How could that be? There were no prisms large enough to cause such a thing. Then I realized what it was. It was the world—the wet air and shimmering light—that set the rainbow across the sky. They didn't need crystals here.

Rahela had come to the window and looked in the other direction. I was about to point out the rainbow when she took in a sharp breath. Along the curve of the river, two sandstone pillars held up a giant cerulean gate. A wall on each side braced the pillars, keeping the city inside safe from the wind and sand. Beneath the newborn sky, the gate gleamed.

"Is that the gate into Baghdad?" I asked.

"It must be," she whispered. She clutched the window frame with her fingers.

A knot began to twist in my stomach. I tried to ignore it, but it throbbed and tightened into something almost painful. Finally, the first barge reached the gate, and a man called out to a guard posted atop one of the pillars.

"Hashim, Vizier of Baghdad!" the man called out. "Returning from Zab!"

The *vizier*? He was in that barge?

"What's wrong with you?" asked Rahela. "You'd think you were afraid of pretending to be human. Like it might not work out for you."

"I didn't know the vizier was traveling with Zayele," I whispered.

"I might have forgotten to mention that, but yes. He chose Zayele personally."

"Do you think he will be able to tell?"

She shook her head. "Your disguise is almost perfect. Just stop looking like a trapped rabbit."

I nodded and watched the gate slide into the stones, allowing the first barge to slip into the city. Carved silver birds of prey, kestrels, topped each pillar along the wall, facing outward like guardians. Their eyes were yellow topaz, sharp and observant. Our barge slid forward and entered the gate. I pressed my face against the window and watched the gate pass by above. It was all blue tiles and metal teeth.

It had been beautiful from afar, but close up, I couldn't

forget what entering the city meant. This wasn't pretend. If I didn't convince everyone that I was Zayele, I would be killed. Or enslaved, like the jinn long ago.

Inside, the river flowed past buildings so tall they blocked out the sun and cast a charcoal stripe of shadow into our cabin. The river cut through a series of plaster and yellow-brick buildings until another gate, this one green and gold, hung over the water. No one shouted to the guard this time, and the gate slid up just before the vizier's barge approached.

Finer buildings flanked the river on the other side of the green-and-gold gate. Cut-glass mosaics and gilded calligraphy decorated the doors so that the river sparkled, even through the shadow. Another gate lay ahead, but to the right of us stood a wall topped with gold spires, and beside the wall was a stone landing just the right length for three barges.

Rahela mumbled something.

"What did you say?"

"They say there's a city ringing an inner city. We're in the inner city now, I think. And on the other side of that wall is the caliph's palace." Her fingers trembled against the edge of the window.

The barge stopped, and someone tied it to the landing while our guard hopped off the prow. He ran to the gate that led into the caliph's domain. Above the blue gate sat a gold kestrel, sparkling in open sunlight. Its beak opened toward the sky, as if it were calling out to its metal brothers decorating the rim of the city's outer wall.

Rahela left the window. "We're not covered!"

I backed away from the window, deeper into the cabin's shadows, because outside, a throng of people lined the walk between the river and the blue gate. Some held banners of colored cloth, while others were shouting out the vizier's name and that of the caliph.

Rahela lifted the lid of one of the trunks and sifted through the folded silks. She pulled out a sheer peridot-hued veil and handed it to me. "This will match." I set the veil on my head. Then she handed me a beaded headpiece. I studied the colored stones threaded onto the thin wires, then set it over the veil. It was heavy as a blanket, with all the weight pulling at my hair and pressing in my ears.

I was in a cage of beads and cloth.

"Can't you still see me?" I asked.

"Yes, but you're covered enough." She paused. A tight, forced smile appeared on her face. "You're as beautiful as Zayele would have been."

She placed a veil over her face and then sat beside me on the bed, straight-backed and silent.

"What do we do now?" I asked.

Her face was still but strained. "Wait for them to let us out."

Footsteps clicked on the stones and then clomped onto the deck. Someone was coming to open the door. What if they knew right away that I wasn't human? What if they only needed one look? I was not a princess. I was not a human girl, and I was not sure I could act like one.

My hands began to shake, and Rahela gripped one of them. "Ready yourself," she whispered. "If you let on what you are, they'll kill you. Or worse." Her gaze was straight ahead, clear of doubt or fear. If she could pretend I was Zayele, then maybe so could I.

A man in a dark turban, with a long gray beard, appeared on the other side of the window.

"Princess Zayele," he said, "welcome to Baghdad."

✦ 16 ✦

ZAYELE

I BARELY GOT any sleep that night. Laira kept talking about a student of hers while glopping jinni food onto my plate, and then she wouldn't leave me alone until I told her for the third time that I needed to sleep. Jinni beds weren't any different, but they had too many blankets. I kicked them off, and then I couldn't sleep without the weight of them. And it was so *still*. Najwa's bed was carved out of stone and I had spent too many nights on the barge.

Halfway through the night, I woke without knowing I'd fallen asleep. I sat up and stared at the curtain hiding Laira's bed. Her fingertips peeked out from beneath the jeweled hem, and her gold-dust-encrusted nails glittered in the light from the lamp on the table between our beds. Her skin was smooth, never marred by the wind and sun.

I set my feet on the floor and reached across the empty space until my fingers hovered over hers. All I needed to do was press my fingers against her skin and make another wish. If it didn't work because she was asleep, then I would have to try something else. I closed my eyes, made a silent prayer, and then touched her.

"I wish to go home," I whispered. Then I waited for something to happen. A swirling feeling in my stomach, a bolt of lightning, a cloud of sand. Anything. But she mumbled something in her sleep and pulled her hand back behind the curtain, leaving me crouched beside her bed in the weak lamplight. Leaving me in the Cavern.

It didn't work. But I was not going to give up and take Najwa's life as my own. She could have the one forced upon me, but I was going to get home. I was going to get back to what my life should have been.

When I got into Najwa's bed again, I thought of her. She'd be in Baghdad by now, with the prince. They'd be married by now. I pushed the thought away. It wasn't a prison sentence for her. She could use her wishes to make herself more comfortable. And whatever bed she had in the palace, it was certainly more comfortable than this one.

I woke up to the sound of Laira banging a metal spoon against a pot. She was dumping more of her glop into a bowl.

"Najwa," she sang, "time to get up." She set the pot on the table and waved at the sconces on the wall. Their flames grew bigger until the room was filled with the brightness of morning.

I groaned and rubbed at my face. "I really don't want to get up."

"Well, that's new for you." She looked at me sideways while I sat up and took the bowl from her. Najwa's mother was intolerable. She was noisy, didn't brush her hair, and left piles of yarn all over that caught on your heel. My own mother . . . I swallowed. What if I never saw her again?

"There's another thing." She paused. "Atish sent a message this morning. He'll be here soon. I had forgotten that you had a holiday today." I had no idea what she was talking about, but I nodded anyway. "You'd better get dressed."

I tried to copy the way Laira styled her scarf. She looped it around her neck instead of over her hair, letting it drape down her back. I had just finished tying mine when someone rapped hard at the door.

"Go on. Don't make him wait."

I opened the door and found a boy wearing nothing but a leather vest and trousers. He had a strong face, golden-brown eyes, and short-cropped hair. The profile of a golden lion was tattooed on his left shoulder—the emblem of the Shaitan, the most destructive arm of the jinni army, according to my father. They were evil and bloodthirsty. They took their captives to the Cavern—*here*—and dipped their bodies in the Lake of Fire. But he didn't look evil or bloodthirsty.

He leaned into the doorframe, and I sucked in a breath, trying not to give myself away by leaning away from him. "I was going to show it to you last night, but no one knew where you were," he said, turning his tattooed shoulder toward me. Was it new, then?

"That's . . . nice."

"I had always thought it would burn, but it didn't. I don't know why they don't tell us this before we go through it. There's no point to the surprise," he said.

I couldn't think of anything to say in response, but he didn't seem to care. He reached out for my hand and pulled me out of the house.

"I can walk on my own," I said flatly. No man had touched me since I was a child. And he was a *jinni*.

He grinned. "That's not why I hold your hand." It was useless. I'd have to hold his hand if I was pretending to be Najwa. At least his palm wasn't sweaty.

He stepped around a large rock that lay on the path. Had it fallen from somewhere? I looked up, but jagged crystals swept the ceiling, and there weren't any holes. I managed to get my hand out of Atish's as we moved around the rock, and then I wrapped my arms around myself.

"Are you cold?" he asked.

"No."

He looked as though he was going to say something, and then shrugged and smiled. "Good, because you don't want to start today off shivering."

"Why? Are we going somewhere colder?"

"Najwa!" a girl shouted at me as she ran up from a side trail. She hopped over a smaller rock and landed beside me. Her long braided hair, dipped in purple dye, swung behind her. "Where did you go yesterday?"

"Uh . . ."

"Faisal said she was working on something for him," Atish answered.

"Yes," I lied, taking the opportunity to move a step away from them.

She grabbed my arm and pulled me closer. "Well, now you've seen Atish's mark. He was all depressed when he couldn't show it off to you yesterday."

"Shirin, please," he groaned.

She grinned. "You were. Admit it." He glanced at the ceiling. "Anyway," Shirin continued, "can you tell me where you went, or is it a Corps secret?"

Again, I was lost in the dark, so I shrugged.

"Lovely. Between the three of us, I'll be the only one who can talk, and our conversations will be all about wounds and diseases."

Atish chuckled, but I didn't respond. I was trying too hard to figure out what was going to happen next. We wound between jinni houses and ended up in the same courtyard I had arrived in. This time, there were more jinn wandering around, and half of them were our age. It must have been because of the holiday Laira had mentioned.

When Atish and Shirin stopped by the fountain, I thought maybe that was as far as we would go. I didn't want any more surprises. What I needed now was a way to get out of the Cavern before someone noticed I wasn't their Najwa.

Shirin sat on the edge of the fountain and gestured for me to join her. Atish paced like a cat.

"They should get here soon," Shirin said.

"Right." Maybe she wouldn't notice I had no idea who "they" were.

She leaned in close. "You seem more relaxed than I thought you'd be," she whispered.

"Why wouldn't I be relaxed?"

Her eyebrows rose. "I can think of one reason." Clearly, there was something secretive going on between Shirin and Najwa that Atish was not supposed to know about.

Atish turned around and stopped. "When they get here, we'll have to divide into groups. Shirin, you want to go with us or with them?"

"You have to ask?"

"She isn't that bad, you know." Atish sighed, then resumed his pacing, stopping only when a group of boys passed by. One of them separated from the group and approached Atish with an adoring smile. He was short and thin, and looked to be about twelve years old, if jinn aged the same as humans. He looked like the sort of boy Yashar would have played with, before he had to count his steps and hold my hand.

The boy waved. "Atish! I heard you got your mark yesterday." He smacked Atish's shoulder, right where the Shaitan mark was. "I can't wait till I get mine."

Atish crossed his arms, took in the boy, and grinned. "Good to see you, Farhad. I'm sure you'll get yours soon enough."

"So, what are you doing today?" He squared his shoulders in the way boys do when talking to men they want to impress. He did it naturally, without any of the arrogance of Destawan.

"Going out on the lake. Where are you boys off to?"

Farhad cleared his throat. "We're going to climb to the topaz point," he said, gesturing at one of the inward-curving walls of the Cavern. The crystals there were more jagged, and milky white except for one of the longer shards, which ended in a golden-yellow tip. It had to be a hundred feet above the houses. Anyone who climbed that high had to cling to the slick crystal upside down, like a caterpillar beneath a leaf. I looked at the boy, certain that either he was joking or he had lost his mind.

"Are you, then? Be careful," Atish said, bowing his head at Farhad.

"Oh, we're always careful," Farhad said. Then he smiled at Shirin and me before skipping away to join his friends. They disappeared in an alley between two tall buildings.

"They're climbing *that*?" I asked Atish.

He shrugged. "It's not that hard."

Shirin rolled her eyes and bumped her shoulder into mine. "It's easier than dealing with *her*," she said.

"Right," I said, pretending I knew what I was agreeing with.

I didn't have to wait long to find out, because a minute later three jinn walked up to us. Two were men a few years older than Atish, with the same Shaitan mark. The other, a girl, must have been the person Shirin had referred to. She stood like a lioness, ready and watching for prey. She was wearing one of those ridiculous glowworm shawls, and her hair was weighted down by twice as many jewels as Laira's.

"Hello, Atish," the lioness said. She practically purred. "Your mark looks good."

"Uh, thank you," Atish said. He looked to the two Shaitan. "You want to go in the same boat as her? I'll take Najwa and Shirin."

"Sure," the taller of the two men said with a shrug.

"But, Atish, I thought we could go together," the girl said. "I don't really know them that well."

"Oh, um, I . . ."

I stood up. "We already have our group ready, but thank you for being so welcoming." I could tell this girl was not going to be good for Atish. I brushed off my skirt and looked at him. "Should we go?"

The girl's mouth opened, but she said nothing. I led them away from the fountain, even though I didn't know if I was going the right way, and everyone followed. Fortunately, Shirin bounced up and took my arm again. She pulled me away from the courtyard and toward the lake.

"You should talk to Irina like that more often," she whispered. So that was Irina, the girl Laira was teaching. She didn't look half as sweet as Laira had made her out to be. "I heard she can't stand Cyril because he's smarter than her, and she thinks Dabar is boring. She's going to have *such* a wonderful ride."

Shirin grinned the rest of the way to the lake, which wasn't far. When we got there, I realized Atish had said we were getting on boats, and I couldn't help but think of the barge. And Rahela.

I'd left her alone with a jinni. And here I was, surrounded by the rest of them.

Shaking my head, I took in where we'd stopped. We were at a rounded stone that peaked up from the ground. It was covered in moss, but not in a natural way. The moss had been cultured, and spread out in a series of diamonds. I traced over them with my fingers. The moss was spongy.

"You always do that," Atish said. He had gotten too close.

"Oh?" I followed Shirin to a little stone building on top of a wall that lined the lake. We all gathered there, and Irina crossed her arms and glared at me.

"Gal?" Atish called out. A large woman in scarlet and green plodded out from behind the building and smiled.

"Dear, dear, you're here for your boats," she said. She hugged Atish, who nodded and slipped out from underneath her arms. She was as tall as he was, and almost as big around. Her cheeks were circled with crushed, sparkling stone, and I stared until I saw she was coming for me next. I stepped aside.

"Najwa, I must congratulate you too," she said. She took my hand and held it up, inspecting the henna around my thumb. "Why did you cover it up?"

"Cover what up?" Shirin asked. She peered over my shoulder.

Gal smiled, revealing large golden teeth. "Her mark. Faisal marked her for the Corps last night. Right there on her hand."

"He did *what*?" Shirin squealed, and she took my hand, flipping it over to stare at it. "You didn't tell us? And you *covered* it?"

I freed my hand and pulled my sleeves down over my knuckles. "There didn't seem to be a good time to say it," I said. "And it's small." I hoped it was small. I hadn't noticed anything on Najwa, but then, I hadn't been looking.

"You could have told me when I showed up," Atish said. He was glowering. "That would have been a good time."

Gal grabbed a set of oars that had been leaning against her stone building and handed them to Atish, then gave another set to Cyril. "Don't harass Najwa. She needs this holiday at least as much as you do. Now get on your boats and go have a good time." She ushered us down to stone steps that led to a pier set into the enflamed lake. Six rowboats lined the pier, each made of wood. Or something like wood. I hadn't noticed many trees in the Cavern.

Atish jumped down the steps and climbed onto the first boat. The bottom was painted in blue and yellow flowers and streaked with mud.

Gal said to me, "I know it's not your favorite, but that one's already taken out."

"It's beautiful," I said, while Gal helped Shirin and me climb into our boat. Then she helped Irina, Cyril, and Dabar into theirs.

Atish picked up the oars and shoved off. The boat rocked and I felt my stomach lurch. The barge hadn't been as wobbly. I looked out at the lake, which didn't help. It was coated in wisps of flame that danced across the shallow ripples. Some of them lifted up into the air and wavered before disappearing. Others gathered more flames around them, building up into giant swirls of fire that twisted across the surface. I prayed they wouldn't harm the rowboat.

I gripped the edge of the boat, taking comfort in the familiarity of something made of wood. I needed any comfort I could find, because I was sitting in the Lake of Fire, stared at by a boy with a fierceness to him that matched his Shaitan tattoo.

✦ 17 ✦

NAJWA

"BOW YOUR HEAD, Zayele," Rahela said, almost too quietly to hear. I was no longer Najwa. The cloak of Zayele's name tightened around my shoulders, and I bowed both in obedience and to breathe. "That's the vizier," she added.

I looked through the window again in alarm. His gray beard reached his chest, where it met a cloisonné pendant heavy with gold and emeralds. The man had eyes as blue and cold as aquamarine, and they were staring into me. I tried to look away and instead felt myself drawn in.

This was Hashim, the caliph's vizier. He was the second most powerful man in the caliphate, the first and only ambassador to the Cavern, and the one who had started the war. He had hunted jinn ever since, and had been the army's foremost informant on our weaknesses. I knew all this from Faisal, who had never been able to say Hashim's name without spitting afterward.

Hashim handed a key to a servant, who unlocked the door. There was a hint of anticipation in Hashim's face, but it disappeared when he said "Welcome to Baghdad" and stood back to let the servant pull open the door.

Rahela and I climbed out onto the deck. My hands were shaking when I grabbed the railing, and he saw. "You're right to be anxious," he said, frowning. "Your life will change a great deal here. In more ways than you expect."

We followed him off the barge's plank, over the blue-green water, and stepped onto smooth stone. The rain had fallen here too, and the ground was slick and shimmering. Stretched out around us were fifty or so men, all dressed in fine linen. They lined both sides of a white-tiled path and called out their loyalty to the caliph.

Someone shouted, "Allah save the caliph!"

Another said, "Yes, Allah will save him!"

A third man said, "Welcome, Vizier Hashim."

Hashim nodded at them all, raising his arms in salute. Then he picked up his pace and headed toward a looming arched gate with a double door covered in scrolling arabesques of leaves and birds. We stood in the gate's shadow while a pair of guards pulled the doors open.

Hashim studied me curiously while we walked through the gate. It was almost as though he was watching for something, so I forced myself to look confident. I didn't want my first steps into the palace to betray me to this man who knew much about jinn.

We entered a courtyard so immense, it reminded me of the training fields in the Cavern. A long reflecting pool shimmered in the center, flanked by narrower strips of water. Palms, as tall as the courtyard's walls, lined the pools. And everywhere, as if to remind the people of who had built this city, was the caliph's family name: *al-Mansur*. It was hammered into the copper basins holding fruit trees. It was molded into the border, repeating a hundred times around the courtyard.

Benches sat scattered throughout, and the vizier stopped at the first one.

"I have business to attend to," he said. "We will meet again this evening." Then he walked away, leaving us with half a dozen servants who stood like statues behind us.

Rahela perched, rather than sat, on the bench. "This isn't right," she said.

"What's wrong?" I whispered.

We weren't alone, but the nearest people who were not servants were at the other end of the courtyard. They were men, and they were speaking in harsh words and making abrupt gestures. I would have liked to be invisible just then.

"We should have been taken directly to the harem. And given refreshments," she said, keeping her voice low enough that it wouldn't echo. "Not kept here waiting like dogs."

I scanned the courtyard, looking for any sign that someone might have noticed me. Although I might have looked like a human, all covered in wire and beads, I felt like a jinni. But no one paid us any attention. We were just girls who had been dropped off on a bench.

Finally, a woman slipped out of one of the many arches in the courtyard wall and marched toward us. She wore a gown of flowing white silk. The men fell silent and watched her out of the sides of their eyes. She stopped three paces from the bench and motioned for us to rise, so we did.

"Welcome, Princess Zayele." Her face was barely percep-
tible beneath her sheer scarf, but the hollow sound in her voice
came through clearly enough. "I'm Aaliyah, one of the caliph's
wives. I have been asked to welcome you to the palace. Unfortunately, I am also the bearer of sad news."

Rahela's body tightened beside mine, but she nodded, urging me to do the same. We followed the caliph's wife out of the
courtyard and into a small room that reminded me of Faisal's
office. Richly colored carpets and cushions blanketed the floor.
Silks of every color draped down from the central lamp in the
ceiling. Somehow, none of them caught fire.

She ushered us onto the floor, where we knelt, facing each
other. I brushed the carpet with my fingertips like I always did
in Faisal's office. But this wasn't the Cavern. There wasn't a
bare stone in sight, and the carpet was velvety and bent under
my fingernails like moss.

She didn't see that I was a jinni.

"This is my meeting room," Aaliyah said. "We use it to
inspect the women who are brought into the harem, but I
am in no state to perform such duties today. You may remove
your veils." She pulled hers off, showing deep lines between
her eyebrows and a small scar on her chin, but it was the red-
ness spreading across her face that startled me. I took off the
beaded headpiece and veil and held them in my lap. Aaliyah's
lips wavered while she surveyed me. "You will have to excuse us
all today. The palace's peace has been disturbed."

"Disturbed?" I repeated.

She dabbed her eyes with the hem of her sleeve. "Our
caliph was injured a few hours ago." She began crying openly

now, pressing both hands to her face. Rahela coughed into her hand, catching my attention. I was supposed to say something.

"I am very sorry," I said. If the caliph was injured, Faisal needed to know *right now*. I looked down at where my mark was hidden by the henna dye. How could they get to me now, even if I sent them images? I should have let them know before, on the river. I should have sent an image the moment I realized Zayele's wish had imprisoned me. Now it was too late for help, and I couldn't even let them know what I'd just learned.

"The situation is grave," she continued, swallowing back tears and allowing one of her servants to bring her some water. She drank the whole cup and then turned back to us. "He was on a hunt, and somehow he fell. . . ."

A servant girl came forward from her spot in the corner. "Lady, I can take these women to the harem. Would you like to go to the baths? They will refresh you."

Aaliyah picked at a golden bird embroidered onto her dress. "Take them," she said, and shook her head as if shaking away a thought. Her face reddened more, and I rose quickly, eager to leave the room before more tears came. Rahela was right beside me, joining the servant girl at the door, when the woman looked up. "I will see you tomorrow. There will be no wedding until Harun's condition improves."

The servant girl took us out of the room then. Both she and Rahela were stone-faced, and I instinctively wrapped my arms around myself. While the girl went to speak to a male servant who had been posted outside the room, Rahela leaned in to whisper, "This gives us some time."

The male servant led us along a labyrinth of halls, his

sandals clipping against the tiles. He didn't look at or speak to us. Rahela had let me carry the beaded headpiece and wear only the veil, but the headpiece jingled, telling anyone we passed that I was the princess who was *not* going to marry the prince tonight.

Eventually, after another turn, we reached a joining of two hallways. A malachite plinth stood in the center, holding up a golden lamp. *The* Lamp. I grabbed at my mark and pinched, hoping against hope that this would somehow get sent to the Eye.

The Lamp sat there, as big as a lion. I wanted to run my fingers through its flame, but like its twin in the Cavern, it hadn't been lit since the war began. It was only a statue now—a cold reminder of what had been. An Arabic prayer twisted down the plinth and disappeared into the floor, joining the palace with the earth below. When the Lamp had been lit, this was how the jinn most often transferred into the palace. I reached out to trace the carved words and felt the hair on the back of my neck rise. I looked up.

Prince Kamal was standing across the hall, watching me.

✦ 18 ✦

ZAYELE

WHEN THE OTHER boat had left the pier, Atish called out to them, "Devil's Island?"

"Yes!" Dabar said.

"Won't it be crowded?" Shirin asked. She was sitting behind Atish, but he had his back to her while he rowed. He was facing me, and I tried not to look at him while he pulled at the oars.

"Hope not," Atish said.

A gigantic palace loomed over the lake at the end of the wall. It was all edges and points. I didn't want anything to do with it, and was relieved to see it wasn't on an island. We were headed for a bit of land floating out in the middle, surrounded by boats.

Irina's boat pulled up next to ours, and the boys shouted out at each other. Atish winked at me and then pulled, faster. Our boat lurched and soon was ahead of the other one.

Just then, a flicker of flame sprouted from the water ahead, grew like a weed, and flew off into the air. If it hadn't been terrifying, it would have been pretty.

"You should have told me we were going to Devil's Island," Shirin told Atish. "I would have planned something for Irina." A wicked smile spread across her face.

"Like what?" I asked.

"She's always talking down to me. And to you."

"What would you have done to her?" I asked. "Wished her into one of those glowworms?"

"Shards, no!" she laughed. "I just meant I might wish her seams to tighten a little."

"You could still wish *that*," I said, forcing myself to grin. For some reason, I liked the idea that this girl could make Irina just a little more uncomfortable, without her noticing.

"Just stop it, will you?" Atish said. "No one is doing anything to anyone."

I looked behind us to Irina, in her boat. She sat on the backseat, lost in thought.

"My mother wouldn't shut up about her last night," I mumbled.

"I bet," Shirin said.

Before long, Atish had rowed us to the island. It was just a dot of stone rising a few inches above the water, no bigger than a tent. Or a barge.

He pulled the boat along the side and tied it to a piece of rock that jutted from the island. Then he helped us both out onto Devil's Island. It took me a moment to get my bearings. We stood on this small bit of land, in the middle of the Lake of Fire, like a dream that had gone horribly awry. After the other boat arrived, there was barely any room to sit.

"All right," Shirin said. "I'm going in. *Krashish.*" Her gown changed to a long suit of purple cloth that covered her but didn't weigh her down. She spun around to let me see it, and then stopped when Irina snickered.

"*Krashish,*" Irina said. Her gown transformed into something tighter, shorter, and black.

Shirin ignored Irina and her suit, and then jumped into the water. She came back up and floated on her back. "It's cold," she gasped.

Atish was taking off his vest, like Cyril and Dabar, and raised an eyebrow at me. "Are you going to change?" he asked. I had been staring at him, and I looked away quickly.

"I'd like to see what she comes up with," sneered Irina.

I hadn't swum without a hijab around my hair since I was a child, but I pulled it off and stared Irina down. I might not be able to change my clothes with a wish, but I'd grown up swimming in gowns. In a river. Even with the flames licking the surface, this water was more still than a river. I knelt and tested the water by dipping my hand in. It was cooler than I'd expected, and when my skin didn't burn, I decided it was probably safe.

"I'll just swim in this," I said. I shook off my shoes and sucked in a deep breath. Then I dove into the water headfirst.

The water wrapped around me like the hands of winter. It ran through my uncovered hair, down my arms and back, and between my toes. I kicked and brought myself to the surface.

Irina was toeing the water and reaching for Atish, but he was looking at me, grinning. When she pawed the air and got nothing, she gave a sharp sigh and slunk into the water. Then she looked over to me.

"Watch out for that," she said.

A bubble rose beside me. When it breached the surface and spat out a stream of fire, I paddled backward. The movement pulled the flame along with me. It rolled over me, and I shrieked.

The flame passed by, warming me for half a second, and flew up into the air. A moment later, it was gone. The experience had been like passing a finger through a flame. Sheepish now, I looked over at Shirin. She was laughing, and so were the others.

"I haven't seen you jump like that in years," she said. She swam over to me. "You're always so level. And watchful."

"Yes, well, that surprised me," I said.

Irina said, "Why, Najwa, I thought you were never 'surprised.'" She swam like a snake. "Isn't it a requirement for the Corps to always be alert?"

I had to get away from her before I did something I'd regret. I was starting to imagine what it'd be like to pull her down by her hair and hold her there.

"Want to swim around the island?" I asked Shirin.

"Not really," she said. "I pulled a muscle setting a leg splint yesterday, and I didn't realize it was so bad." She rubbed her shoulder and started for the island.

"I'll race you," Atish said.

Yes. That was what I needed. I had spent too many days in the barge, and I still hadn't had much of a chance to move.

"What about you?" I asked Irina. "Are you going to race or just try to look pretty?"

Her nostrils flared. "I'll race."

A minute later we were lined up, along with Cyril and Dabar. Shirin had climbed out and was standing to watch.

"You need something to mark the finish," she said.

"I'll take care of it," Atish said. He pointed at the surface and muttered something, and a line of flames crossed the water before us. "Just swim through it, go around the island, and through it again."

"Brilliant!" I said, a little louder than I'd meant to. I looked at Irina, who treaded water beside me. She was looking at me strangely.

"Ready," said Shirin. "Go!"

I chopped at the water, kicking as hard as I could. It was so smooth. Without any current to fight, it was easy to pull myself around the island. I took a stroke, breathed, and then took four more.

I hadn't moved my body like this in ages, and although the strain was more than it used to be, it felt good to move. In the water, I was free. I didn't have to think about how my father was always waiting for me to do something wrong. I pulled hard at the water until I forgot about jinn, forgot I was in the Lake of Fire, and forgot about Najwa.

I burst through a wall of fire. Atish was beside me, laughing. He splashed my face, and I laughed, splashing back. We had crossed the line at the same time, followed shortly by the others. My heart was beating fast, and I felt more alive than I had in months.

"Najwa, when did you learn to swim like that?" Atish asked. He was incredulous, but there wasn't a trace of suspicion on his face. He just looked happily stunned.

I shrugged and said, "Couldn't let you beat me."

He reached out for my hand, and as he pulled me to the island's edge, I thought of how our bodies were too close in the water. I didn't have my hijab on. I was wet. And he was half-naked.

By the time I crawled out of the water, I was shaking. I couldn't stop, even after Shirin took pity and wished me dry. My hennaed hands were wrinkled, and I held them close, afraid if I let them down, he would take my hand again.

This wouldn't last. Sooner or later, they'd discover the truth, and I needed to be far, far away before that happened. I scanned the walls and saw dark patches that might be tunnel entrances, but were they guarded? Did they go to the surface?

NAJWA

KAMAL WAS CLUTCHING a stack of papers in one hand and a leather bag in the other, but he didn't seem aware of them. While Hashim had made me feel like a cowering rodent, Kamal made me feel *seen*. Neither of us moved, he with his papers and bag, and me with my hand stuck to the Lamp's base, as if I'd grown from it.

Kamal lifted the bag in a wave. "Hello," he said. He was still wearing the white turban I'd seen him in that morning. As he closed the distance between us, I held on to the Lamp for support. Here was the prince, walking toward me, and he was smiling. At me. "You must be Princess Zayele."

"Yes," I said weakly. "And you are Prince Kamal?"

He bowed his head. "I am sorry we were not properly introduced, but everyone is busy at the moment. . . ." He faltered, then continued. "We have had an injury."

"We were just told about your father. I am very sorry." I nearly lifted my hand off the Lamp. Strangely, I felt myself wanting to comfort him, to assure him his father would be well.

This twisted my stomach because I should not have wanted to help. His father was our enemy. *He* was our enemy.

Kamal swallowed and rapped his fingers against the Lamp, making it ring. "He hasn't woken since his fall, but he is alive. My brother Ibrahim is fighting in the south, so it has fallen to me to guide the city until my father wakes up. With the vizier's help, of course."

"I am sure you will do well," I said. Where were these words coming from? I could barely think with him so close to me. I wanted to both step closer and flee.

"Thank you." His expression was flat, but his voice was sincere. "I'm not sure they expected us to meet already, especially since the ceremony has been postponed, but I am glad we did. It lessens some of the anxiety, at least for me." As his gaze traveled over my face, I turned it away. He believed me to be the girl he was going to marry. We would be *together* if I didn't get away soon.

"You were anxious?" I asked, then immediately wanted to take back the words.

He laughed. "Weren't you?"

I opened my mouth to reply, then closed it again and nodded.

"Well then, I'm glad I wasn't the only one," he said, grinning. "Excuse me, though. I am working on something and must return to it. I'm sure I will see you again . . . tomorrow."

His eyes stayed on me while his body bent in a bow, and then he turned and disappeared down the corridor. My mind whirled. Was I supposed to bow? Should I have said anything else? If so, he hadn't waited for it.

I let go of the Lamp and pressed my hands to my cheeks.

"Don't start changing your mind now," Rahela whispered.

"Nothing has changed," I said, but it was a lie. The world was dripping in humanness, and I hadn't touched all of it yet. Also, something had happened when Kamal looked at me. I still wanted to go home, but now that there wasn't going to be a wedding right away, I had some time. I could do what Faisal had trained me for.

I turned toward our escort, Mohammed, and said we were ready to go to our room, trying my best to sound like a princess. He took us directly, and within moments we stood on the public side of the harem's doors. A painted peacock spread its tail feathers across the door, so that a hundred eyes seemed to be watching, daring us to enter.

"You must knock," Mohammed said. "Otherwise they get angry."

I lifted my fist and held it up to the door. So much had happened today, and now I was about to enter the harem. I knocked twice, and noticed that my hands were shaking harder than when I'd first arrived.

The door opened inward, revealing a curtained area billowing with pale silk. I thanked Mohammed and went through the peacock door, followed by Rahela. A girl covered head to toe in scarlet and gold closed the door behind us. She was quick and deft, spinning around and parting the curtains as silently as fire.

The harem was a flurry of colors and sounds, and as busy as the lake wall in the Cavern. Women and children of all ages filled the common space's corners, which were divided by a man-made creek flowing from a fountain in the center.

The fountain sat in the middle of a red-and-white marble-tiled courtyard. It was the most elaborate fountain I'd ever seen, and it spilled into a reflecting pool dotted with pink lotus blossoms. Shallow benches lined the pool, upon which sat half a dozen ladies, some with infants at their breast, others bouncing smaller children on their knees. The older children waded in the creek, splashing each other and shrieking in joy.

Colored silks swooped along a sandstone wall decorated with climbing vines and recessed fountains. Between manicured orange trees, other women lay on thin rugs playing ouds and flutes, while a handful of children chased one another around them. Two women danced behind the musicians, their bodies wrapped in shawls knotted with brass coins. They twisted their hips and jangled the coins, adding a tinkling tune to those of the ouds and flutes.

All this was open to the afternoon sun. Other women sat beside a smaller pool of water, jewelry glinting and hands gesturing in talk, until one of them saw the girl in scarlet bring us out of the curtains. They all turned and the music stopped. The coins clanged on the dancing women's skirts. The young children, however, continued with their play, oblivious to our approach.

The girl in red cleared her throat. "Princess Zayele and her companion have arrived." The women stared, silent, while she led us to a door along the garden's walls and slid it open.

Rahela cast the women a glance before shutting the door. "So kind," she muttered.

The girl showed us that our trunks had been brought in; then she turned and left. Our room wasn't large, but the ceiling rose higher than most trees. Two couches dotted with round pillows and a low table with Rahela's loom upon it were the only furniture. A vine, budding in jasmine, climbed an arched doorway on the other side of the room. It was open, with a sheer curtain for a door, and led to a patio and small garden.

Rahela sat on the floor by the table and tapped her loom. "I have thought of this moment ever since we left home, but it's all wrong."

I hadn't moved more than a step into the room yet, and I wasn't sure if I should go to a couch or sit beside her. She scowled at me, so I went to a couch.

"I shouldn't have left my home today," I said.

"You're right. You shouldn't have," she said. "But maybe Zayele is somewhere she can be happy. There'd been a cloud over her ever since we left. Hashim should have picked someone else." She looked up. "Can you give me that wish?"

I shook my head. "I can't change what has already happened."

She pressed her palms together and touched her lips. "So here we are. She is wherever she is. And you are unable to change anything."

"Yes. Here we are." If I'd been alone, I would have cried.

◆ 20 ◆

ZAYELE

WE SNACKED ON some food Shirin had brought, and then rowed back to the lake wall. Even Irina was smiling, laughing in her boat with Cyril and Dabar.

"Najwa," Shirin said, leaning against her seat and grinning, "I'm so glad you raced."

I raised my eyebrows, but said nothing.

"It was fun," Atish agreed. He hadn't taken his eyes off me since we'd climbed into the boat, and a flush had been slowly creeping up my shoulders. "If you have to best Irina at something, that's a good way to do it. At least it was honorable."

Shirin groaned. "Atish, don't ruin the moment. Najwa, you were amazing. I had no idea you could swim so fast!"

"She was just a little slower than me. That's all," I said.

"Maybe." Shirin didn't look convinced. Then she burst into giggles. "She was so mad, and when you and Atish climbed out of the lake together, she looked like she was trying to digest quartz."

I snorted. I couldn't resist. "Doesn't she always look like that?"

"Not *all* the time," Atish said. There was a slight twitch in the corner of his mouth.

When we arrived at the pier, Atish set down the oars and hopped out, then tied up the boat. He was helping us climb out when we heard a scraping sound, followed by rumbling and creaking. It sounded as if every crystal in the Cavern was pushing past its neighbor. Atish pulled me off the pier and toward the lake wall. I stumbled and he picked me up, making sure I was away from the water. Shirin ran along beside us.

Panic bubbled within me, and I didn't know what for. Shirin gasped, and she looked up. Worry was etched into her forehead. Above us, the crystal shards were swaying.

It was an earthquake. I had felt them at home, but I'd never been through one while I was *inside* the earth. I'd never felt so locked in before. This was worse than the wooden barge. This was all stone, and it was going to crash down on me.

"Get under the awning!" Atish shouted. He pointed at the stone building, where Gal was standing in the door, gesturing for us to come to her. Mutely, I ran, a step behind Shirin, climbing up to the top of the wall.

The earth continued to scrape together. I covered my ears and saw that everyone else was doing the same. Everyone was watching the crystals shift and sway like tree branches in a breeze.

The rumbling stopped as suddenly as it had begun, but no one dared speak. I wasn't sure what would upset the rocks again. What if all it took was one word to send the crystals crashing down? Then the silence shattered with a deafening crack. A shard had split, high above, and dropped. It swooshed for half a second before crashing into the lake. The splash speared up into the air and scattered all the wisps of flame into dizzy sparks.

Atish was crouched beside me when he cursed, "Damn it, Farhad!" As soon as he said it, I remembered: the boys were climbing on the crystals. He hopped out from beneath the awning and spun around to look at the cliff behind us. He pulled at his short-cropped hair and swore.

Then he ran, disappearing behind the building. It took me a second to move, but I did, and found Shirin beside me. We left the safety of the awning and scanned the Cavern's curved walls for any sign of the boys.

One of them had slipped off the topaz crystal and was hanging from a precipice that jutted out from below. Another boy was lying motionless atop the crystal. It looked like a rock had fallen and shattered around him. And a third boy was crouched on a ledge between the two, eyes wide. He was safe, but he wasn't moving at all.

I scanned the crowd around us and noticed that all the jinn were taking care of themselves. No one noticed the boys a hundred feet above. No one but Atish, who was already across the jumble of houses and running up the footpath toward them.

Shirin yelped, and I grabbed her hand. "We have to help. Wish them to safety!"

"We can't transport within the Cavern!" she shouted. "Oh, Atish, run faster!"

Atish leaped into the air and caught one of the lower crystals, then began scaling the cliff, moving from handhold to handhold without looking, as if he'd done this many times. Finally, he reached the third boy, said something to him, and crept over to the precipice. The first boy had not let go, and when I looked closer, his hands seemed to have gone *into* the crystal.

"He wished his hands into the rock!" Shirin said, sounding relieved.

We watched Atish lay his hands over the boy's, causing them to glow. He lifted the boy and set him on the ledge beside the other one. Then he continued to climb swiftly, gripping the rock. His feet slipped, and for one terrible moment, he hung vertically. I froze, terrified that he'd fall trying to save the second boy, but he moved one arm, swung it ahead, and then swung the other. At last, he pulled himself onto the top of the crystal.

"How . . ."

Shirin nodded. "I know. Atish is a really good climber. That's probably why Farhad wanted to climb today."

Atish fell onto his knees beside the boy and swept the broken rocks aside, causing ashy dust to drift from the edge like snow. It had to be Farhad, judging by the way Atish knelt over him and pulled him into his arms.

If jinn couldn't transport within the Cavern, how would he get him down?

Atish stood and settled Farhad, who seemed to be waking, onto his own back. Then he went to the edge of the crystal where it met the wall, and pressed his free hand into the rock. The rock rippled like water in strong wind. When he lifted his hand, he stepped off the edge of the crystal.

I gasped, but Atish did not fall. He had wished a set of

narrow stairs into the wall, and he trudged down them, Farhad heavy on his back. When he reached the other boys, he gestured to them to follow, and they did.

"Come on," Shirin said, tugging me from where I'd grown rooted. She guided me through the other jinn, who had gone back to their business, not knowing a disaster had just been averted. Finally, we reached the start of the footpath and found Atish.

I had expected him to be struggling now, and exhausted, but he was glowing. He was slick with the sheen of sweat, but stood tall and powerful and looked relieved. He smiled at me before setting a squirming Farhad onto his feet.

"Thank you," Farhad said. Whatever awe he'd had for Atish before had been doubled. Atish smacked Farhad lightly on the top of his head.

"I told you to be careful," he said.

The other two boys mumbled their thanks and then ran off, half-carrying Farhad, who kept looking over his shoulder at Atish. We watched them, and then Atish stepped toward me, wiping the sweat off his forehead and making his short hair stand up.

His eyes were burning holes into mine, and for a moment, I didn't mind.

Shirin shifted on her feet. "Um, I'm going to go after them. To make sure they're not hurt." She ran away, easily catching up with the boys.

"That had me worried," Atish said. Then he laughed.

I swallowed. I had to be Najwa, but I could not deny my own self. I was in shock from the earthquake and the terror of watching Atish hanging from a rock, far too high above the ground. Still, there was a heat in my face, and I felt it rising. "That was amazing," I breathed. "You saved the boys. I've never seen someone climb like that. So fast."

"It was just a bit of climbing." *Just a bit of climbing.* I'd climbed shallow cliffs before, so I knew what it was like. But I'd never thought what he did was possible.

I cocked my chin at the ceiling. "What about the rest of the crystals? Will there be another earthquake?"

"You know there's never more than one at a time."

That didn't make me feel any better. "What if you'd fallen while trying to help them?"

"I didn't really think about it. I just reacted. I couldn't leave them up there." He grinned until his whole face was beaming. "It's all part of the Shaitan training. We're pretty tough." Then he stepped closer and put his hand on my shoulder. His touch was hot, searing my skin. But I didn't move away. Instead, I found myself wanting him to come closer. To touch more of me.

Everything had literally been falling down around me, but I had to appear as though it were all normal. Just an earthquake. Just falling crystals. Just a rescue. Just Atish, with his hand on me.

Still, I wasn't supposed to be alone with a man. Even down in this land of jinn, I could feel my father's eyes on me, narrowed with suspicion.

"Najwa," Atish said. His voice had gotten thick. "I don't know what is happening to me, or to you, but something changed." He let go of me and leaned back against a boulder the size of a fattened camel.

"You mean how the Cavern is falling down?" I eyed the boulder, hoping it wouldn't shift, wouldn't roll down the hill, carrying him with it.

He smiled at me. "Not the earthquake. I mean how everyone always assumed we would end up together. I never really thought about it, to be honest. I was just going along with their expectations. But I can't do that anymore."

"What do you mean?" I asked. I crossed my arms. This conversation felt too private.

"You're different. I feel like all these years have gone by and I've never really looked at you before." He looked down at the ground, then back up at me, and his eyes were suddenly bright. "I didn't notice it until I came down from the cliff. You were standing there, with your hair still wet from the lake, and it was like I'd never seen you before, and . . . my stomach flipped."

"I'm sorry—"

"Don't be sorry," he murmured. "All this is making me realize what I've always taken for granted. You." He shook his head. "Now that we're not students anymore, we shouldn't take anything for granted. There's a war going on. I'll be fighting, and you'll be spying. If we don't do something about it, we'll end up pulling apart."

"Or get crushed by a rock," I said, forcing myself to laugh. I looked up and regretted it right away. His eyes were desperate and wide, and a golden fire flickered in his irises. My chest fluttered and my stomach turned over. Was *this* what he had meant when he said his stomach flipped?

"Say something," he whispered.

"I . . ."

"Najwa, we've been friends since we were children, and I just now realized that—that I'm in love with you. You have to say something."

I couldn't swallow. My throat—my entire body—had gotten too tight.

"What's wrong?" he asked. He studied my face, which was growing hotter by the second. I looked aside because I couldn't look at him anymore. He was talking to Najwa, and I wasn't her.

Part of me wanted, just for a second, to be her. But *she* should have been here when he made his declarations—not me.

"Nothing's wrong," I said. What would Najwa have said? Did she love him? "The war won't tear us apart. Not if we care about each other." It was a lie, and the worst part was that I had torn them apart. I had made the wish that changed everything.

He stepped closer, stopping only a few inches away from me, and held his hands over my shoulders. The heat emanating from his palms was like fire—the kind of fire that draws you in, makes you think the air is too cold, so you creep closer until suddenly you're burning.

I waited, expecting him to set his hands on my shoulders, but he never did. Instead, he reached up to my face and into my hair. Then he leaned his face down, and I had just enough time to suck in a quick breath before he pressed his lips against mine.

How they burned. I melted into him, forgetting who I was, forgetting what he was, and letting everything inside me ignite. Finally, when his lips left mine, I felt a chill—the kind that makes you realize how much you needed that fire that had burned you.

Unable to look him in the eyes, I brushed the skin of his shoulder, where his Shaitan mark glowed beneath the surface. It pulsed with a beat different from his own, and I knew this only because his heart was pounding against mine, as rapid as a rabbit's.

I was breathing him in. I was wrapping my arms around a jinni. A Shaitan soldier. And I had only just met him.

He moaned, then kissed me again. This time, I pressed back, giving him as much of myself as he'd given me. I wasn't Najwa, but I wanted this. I wanted *him*. And so I fell into him, wrapping my fingers around the front of his vest and slipping them over the smooth skin of his chest. His hands had fallen to my back and were holding me up in the air. It was like flying.

"Definitely different." He said this with his lips brushing against mine. "I like how spontaneous you've gotten." Then he blinked and looked over my shoulder. "Yes?" He pulled away and stood at attention.

I turned and saw a jinni wearing a bronze-colored vest. He looked like a soldier, but he didn't have the mark of the Shaitan. He nodded at me and snapped his heels together.

"The Master of the Corps requests your attendance."

"Me?" I asked.

The jinni blinked, but didn't move. "Yes," he said. He waved dismissively at Atish. "You must come alone."

"Sounds like you've got an assignment," Atish said. He smiled, but it was wistful, as if he was the one who should have gotten called. I nodded, still shaken from the kiss he'd just given me, and followed the soldier. I left Atish behind at the boulder, but the heat on my lips came away with me.

✦ 21 ✦

NAJWA

THAT EVENING, RAHELA and I were invited to have dinner with the caliph's wife Aaliyah. I hadn't eaten all day, and although I was hungry and excited about trying human food, I grew worried that I would somehow reveal myself. A misspoken phrase, a cultural misstep, and any one of the women at the table might grow suspicious. Rahela, quiet and stoic, raised one eyebrow when I mentioned this.

"Were you not taught the ways of humans?" she asked. I had told her a little about myself. Not enough to betray the Eyes of Iblis Corps, but just enough to indicate that I did know a few things about humans.

"I was," I said. I watched as she brushed her hair. It was as straight as the strands in her little loom. "But I don't know everything. What if they ask me something about Zab? Or the journey?"

"They don't know anything about the place. I think most of them have been here for years, and many have never been out of the city. But if they ask anything specific, I will speak for you. It's not like I can't talk."

When we left for dinner, I was only slightly relieved by her offer to help. I still had a feeling, lodged somewhere in the back of my mind, that someone would notice. Someone would be watching.

Dinner was served on a series of low tables in the harem's courtyard. The sun had set, but cut-brass lamps hung on poles and cast the courtyard in a golden light. The other women were already there, leaning against bolsters and talking.

Aaliyah sat in the center, between two women of apparently high rank, and when she saw us approach, she nodded. "Zayele," she said, "and Rahela. Welcome." She had calmed down since we last saw her. Her face was no longer red, and her voice was steady and strong.

"Yes, welcome," said the woman to her left, and she gestured to a space at an adjoining table.

I sat on a leather cushion beside Rahela, careful not to bump my knees against the table, which was covered with little bowls filled with food. Two other women sat at our table, and they smiled at us.

"Thank you," Rahela said. "It has been a long journey, and we are glad to be here finally."

"How far is it from your little village?" one of the women asked. She sat across from me. She had a long nose, wide-set eyes, and a painted mouth that seemed more used to scowling than smiling.

I glanced at Rahela. We had gone over this. "It's, um, three days."

"It's that close?" she replied, surprised. "I'd expected it to be farther away, considering how different you look from us." She somehow made the word "different" sound sour, and when she winked at the woman beside her, I knew what sort of person she was. I stared at my plate, which was still empty, and reached for a triangular piece of bread. I didn't know what else to do.

"I was thinking the same thing," Rahela said. Her voice had a hint of danger, and the woman shrugged.

I dipped the bread into a yellowy paste and tried it. It tasted of garlic, and something tangy, and I had to have more.

"Zayele, we are all so sorry your wedding has been postponed," another woman said. She was the one sitting to the right of Aaliyah. "I'm sure the caliph will be well soon enough. And then you can send word back to your mother. I remember when I first came here. Don't we all?" She looked around the courtyard and was answered with several nods.

"Yes," said Aaliyah. "Please feel at home here. And enjoy the food, although it may be different from what you're used to."

I suppressed a smile. She had no idea how different it was.

The meal continued, mostly in silence. No one seemed to want to discuss anything but the caliph's fall, and each time it was brought up, Aaliyah looked stricken. It was obvious she cared for him, and I began to wonder about him. Was he like I'd heard in my classes with Faisal? Strong, proud, and shrewd?

Following dinner, when I had filled my stomach with more food than I could remember ever eating, I wandered into the garden. It hadn't taken much to convince Rahela to let me go alone, and for the first time since I'd been caught by Zayele, I *was* alone. More or less. The lamplight didn't reach into every corner, but I was a jinni and comfortable with shadows. I found a gravel path that wound around a clump of bushes and ended at a squat pomegranate tree. I knew the fruit was red, but in the darkness, the pomegranates hung like black orbs, weighing down the branches.

I crouched beneath the tree and looked at the rest of the harem's garden. Most of the women had retreated to their rooms, but a few milled around by the stream crossing the garden. No one, thankfully, was paying attention to me anymore. Alone and unwatched now, I felt the weight of everything press in on me. I was imprisoned in this human life. I was in the very place where none of my friends could save me. And I had foolishly let Rahela cover up my mark with henna, and now it probably didn't work.

I tried to choke back a sob, but it broke through, and I wept. I cried for my disobedience, I cried for the friends I might never see again, and I cried for myself and what would probably happen. Most of all, I cried because even though I was trapped, part of me thrilled to finally be here—tasting their food and wearing their gowns—and because of that, I felt wretched and guilty. I was trapped in a lie, and a horrible part of me wanted it that way.

I looked at the pomegranates hanging above me and their backdrop of stars. The night had gone suddenly to ink, and just like the diamonds in the Command of Iblis, the stars shone. But they were so far away, so remote, that they didn't seem quite real.

This was all real, though, and it had never been meant to happen. I wasn't supposed to run off to the surface. I wasn't that sort of person. I had always obeyed, even if I didn't want to. I had always waited for permission, always done whatever was asked of me, always tried to be my best. But the one time— the first time—I did something wrong, I was caught by Zayele.

I knew I should hate her for what she did, but I couldn't. Something in me felt a bit of sympathy. She had clearly been afraid of coming here.

But I still needed to get home. I still needed to break through her wish. I had broken through the jinni wards and found myself in the palace. Surely I could get myself out of a human girl's desperate wish.

Bracing myself for another bout of pain, I made a wish to go home.

Pain. Horrible, twisting, shredding pain rushed into me the moment I said the word. I couldn't breathe; I couldn't even speak.

I tried again, mouthing the wish.

Fire. A fire raged from the tip of my tongue, down my throat, and to the deepest reaches of my lungs. It burned all the air inside me, and I was hollow. Burning, choking, drowning, and hollow.

I crumpled, convulsing beneath the tree. It was no use. I could not tear myself away from Zayele's wish. All I could do was burn.

Smoke seeped out of my mouth, curled in the air, and smudged the brightness of the stars.

✦   ✦   ✦

Someone was talking, and I managed to crack my eyes open. Rahela was bent over me, saying something, but her words were muffled. Then many hands lifted me in the air, and Rahela was there, squeezing my hand, right over my mark.

"Did she faint?" someone asked.

"Yes," Rahela said.

I knew then that I'd never leave. I'd never be able to fight Zayele's wish if it used fire against me.

♦ 22 ♦

ZAYELE

THE JINNI SOLDIER brought me to a building that stood apart from all the others. It was made of black glass and guarded by two jinn who looked like they could eat babies. I shuffled behind my escort and slipped through the doors into a small waiting area.

A shriveled female jinni sitting behind a desk looked me up and down.

"Najwa." She said the name like it tasted bad, then pulled a copper disk out of a box and put it on a peg on the wall behind her. My escort cleared his throat.

"He is waiting for you in the briefing room," he said. Then he backed out of the building, leaving me alone with the old woman. She was filing some metal points that hung from the ends of her hair. Clearly, she didn't want to deal with me anymore.

There was no turning back now, so I walked forward and ended up in a circular room with an unlit, larger-than-life lamp on a pedestal. On the other side was a dark hall, and somehow I knew that was the way I had to go.

My stomach got tighter with each step. What would the Master want? What did it mean to be a Master of the Corps? Would he know I wasn't Najwa?

Finally, I came to an open door. Inside, a group of jinn stood in half a ring facing a wall of milky glass.

"Oh, Najwa," a familiar voice said. The half circle parted and Faisal walked forward, beckoning me in. "Caspar must have run to get you. Now that we're all here, we can get started."

I was entering a secret circle, and even though it terrified me, my body buzzed with excitement. This was the most interesting moment of my life. And the most dangerous.

The door closed behind me, and the room was dark but for the wall of white glass. Everyone but Faisal turned to face it, so I did too.

"You all know that our newest member managed to get into the palace and capture some images. We've just learned from our analysts that the selenite orb Prince Kamal was carrying is most likely a new form of weaponry." He paused, letting the thought sink in. "Najwa, if you hadn't been there, we might never have known. We wouldn't have had any chance to be prepared. As it is, we are trying to figure out what this orb is meant to do. All we know is that it's meant to harm us."

The woman standing beside Faisal went to the glass wall and pulled part of it out. I nearly fell backward in shock as the wall blinked to a giant image of a white ball on a cushion.

"This is the orb," the woman said. "We need to get this

before the humans can use it against us, and we need to ensure it will be a long time before they can make another. Najwa," she said, smiling at me, "we need you to go back."

Someone asked her a question, but my ears were roaring too loud to hear. Everything in me was sinking toward the floor, and I grabbed the table behind me.

How would I ever get into the palace? And I had already lost everything to stay away from Baghdad. I couldn't wish myself there. I couldn't spy. I was a human.

The jinni's question had been answered, and now everyone was looking at me. If I didn't tread carefully, I'd be found out. And I was in the middle of their nest.

"Sure," I said, forcing myself to look as confident as I could. "When do you want me to go?"

Faisal beamed. "As soon as possible."

"I was wondering," I said, trying to think of something quickly, "aren't there any alternative ways to enter the palace? I mean, in case they've figured out we've been there? What about a tunnel? The wards might be blocking us from going in with our wishes, but maybe they won't work if we just walk in."

The woman's face scrunched up in disbelief. "Why would you want to go any other way? Transporting is untraceable. And safest."

One of the other jinn snickered, but I continued. I needed an alternative route.

"I know, but what if I get stuck?"

Faisal shook his head and came closer. "The wards prevent us from entering in all the ways, including on foot, and the tunnels would take too long. By the time you made it to the city, barring any mishap with directions, the humans would be ready. In fact, they may be ready to use the orb at any moment, so time is of the essence."

"And discretion also," the woman added.

"You want me to go now?" I said. My voice was little more than a squeak.

"In an hour," Faisal responded. "We may have you do something else while you're there, but we need to discuss it. Please wait outside, by the Lamp. I will fetch you in a little while."

I nodded, trying not to show how much I was shaking, and trotted out to the circular room. I couldn't do what they wanted me to do. I couldn't just dissolve into smoke and appear in the palace. I couldn't stay here.

There were tunnels connecting the Cavern with the surface. I had seen them. All I had to do was find one. I didn't care where it ended, as long as there were humans. Somehow, I would get out of the Cavern and find my way home. I would find Yashar again.

I told the woman at the desk I would be right back, and then I ran.

+ 23 +

NAJWA

IT TOOK ME an hour to convince Rahela I would never try that again. But I had to do something, anything, to get information back to Faisal. So after she had fallen asleep, I stayed awake and watched the curtain billowing in from the patio. Lit by a lantern's geometric pattern of light and shadow, it glowed like a wandering spirit, dancing in the open doorway.

I peeled the blanket off my legs and stepped off the couch, setting my bare feet on the cool marble. Without taking a breath, I tiptoed to the courtyard door and pulled it open. It slid quietly into the wall and I stepped through, checking first to see if anyone was still lounging by the pool. The courtyard was deserted, except for a family of peafowl huddling beside the fountain. I'd discovered that their high-pitched call, like that of a marauding cat, could wake a rock. If only I could get past them without their seeing me.

Perhaps, just perhaps, I could still make wishes. Just as long as I wasn't trying to leave the palace. Carefully, I whispered the easiest wish, the one we were taught on the very first day.

"*Shahtabi.*"

Instead of burning me, the wish spread, cool and lacy, across my skin. I could still do it. I had to pretend to be human, but I was still a jinni. Hope and relief filled me and I smiled, despite the darkness, despite the pain I'd felt before.

Invisible now, I passed the fountain and made it to the entrance. In the moonlight, the leaves were silver. The world was asleep, but still it changed its colors. Nothing stayed the same here. I pulled the door open and peeked into the hall. It was darker than it had been before, but dusty oil sconces glowed along the way. The hall was deserted but for a pair of guards facing away from the door. We were guarded at night? Was it to keep us safe, or keep us in?

I shut the door before they had a chance to see it was open and slipped between them. It was only my third *shahtabi* amongst humans, and I was doing rather well. I padded down the cold marble hall to another, and found the Lamp. Servants bustled past it, barely giving it a glance.

At night, the surrounding lamps lit its bronze sides, showing its curvature and grace. I rubbed the metal, imagining how brightly it would have shone when it was lit. It would have illuminated the whole area.

Behind the Lamp lurked a darker hall, guarded by four men, each with a sword as long as my arm. Whatever was down it was twice as important as all the women in the harem. Quietly, I walked around the guards.

Two sconces lit the hall: one where the guards stood and one beside a set of heavy double doors. I slid open a door slightly and saw that the entire room was glowing. Lamps clung to the walls every few feet, and some hung from brass chains suspended from the ceiling. Every one of the four walls was lined with waist-high shelves, which held stacks of paper and bound books, as well as baskets brimming with stones and jars of powder. A young man in a yellow robe, with a head of thick curls, bent over a table, reading from a sheaf of papers and sliding the beads on an abacus. A cat lay curled on the table, stretching over the other half of the man's papers and pawing at a selenite sphere, which was far too heavy for the cat to move. It was identical to the one Kamal had shown his father. The man's quill scratched at the paper while I slid the door open just wide enough to slip in, then shut it again.

The door slapped closed, the man turned around, and I saw it was Kamal, without a turban. He looked at the door, confused, and then wiped his brow with a sleeve and returned to the paper. My heart was beating loud enough that I was sure he could hear it if he stopped scribbling. The cat looked up at me, narrowed his yellow eyes, and then went back to flipping his tail. Kamal shrugged and swept his hand along the cat's back.

This was not the same laboratory he had been in that morning. This one was larger and colder, and didn't have the fragrance from the garden wafting in.

I tiptoed over to the table, across from Kamal, and watched him. He tapped his quill against the paper and rubbed the space between his eyebrows while he reviewed the numbers and circles he had drawn and the red beads of the abacus. A circle had been cut into the sphere, and the removed piece lay beside it. I bent over and peered inside the sphere, careful not to touch anything.

The sphere was empty, but the inside was not completely hollow. A metal bowl half the size of the sphere lay suspended within, and it had a faint dusting of white powder. What was this meant for? With a glance at Kamal, I reached in and wiped gently at the dust. The sphere was heavy enough that it didn't roll when I touched it. He could have used anything, so why selenite?

I rubbed my fingers together. My mind flashed with a series of images Faisal had shown us of all the human creations, and I'd never seen anything like this. Kamal moved two beads on his abacus and an expression of relief came over his face. The crease between his eyebrows disappeared and he leaned back and sighed. Lamplight flickered on his lashes and a lock of hair that had fallen down—it illuminated his skin so that it shone. And through it all, his green eyes stared at the selenite ball.

Whatever he had been working on was done, and he pushed back the chair. It scraped against the floor, and the cat stood up on the desk, arching his back.

"All done," Kamal said to the cat. "I wish I hadn't said I'd do this. If I'm wrong, everyone will know. They'll laugh at me." The cat rubbed his nose against Kamal's hand. "At least *you* don't expect me to save the caliphate, Hamza."

The cat meowed, and Kamal smiled. Then he paced back and forth across the room. I made sure to back up against the wall. The cat could see me, and he tracked me lazily. For some reason, he didn't care that I was there.

"I keep thinking about the princess," he told the cat. My

body flushed. "She's pretty. But there's something there, deeper than that."

Hamza jumped off the desk and sauntered toward me. I froze, hoping he wouldn't come any closer. Just then, the door opened and Hashim strode in, flashing his long robes. The cat ran off and disappeared in the darkness of the hallway.

"Kamal," Hashim said. "Have you solved it yet?"

Kamal shook his head. "No." Was he lying? He had just told the cat he was done.

"We got a report that your brother is in the middle of a battle near Basra. He won't be able to leave until it's over. Apparently, we've taken some losses." Hashim waved a sheet of parchment in the air. "We need good news, Kamal. Surely you have something to tell me?" Hashim strode to the table and ran his fingers over the paper. He picked up the ball and closed the lid, then rolled it between his hands. "If we want the element of surprise, we need to be ready when it's time to send it through the Lamp." The Lamp? But no human could light it. Hashim must have known that, and I studied him, wondering.

Kamal sighed and rubbed his temples. "I'm just not sure if it's a good idea."

"Of course it's a good idea!" Hashim snapped. "You have to put doubt aside and do what you know in your heart to be the best action for all of us. For the caliphate. For Allah."

Kamal sighed and went to the door. "Maybe, but I still don't feel good about it." He was preparing to leave, and I didn't want to be left in the room alone with Hashim. It was too dark, too late. I raced on my toes to the door and stood behind Kamal. He still smelled like cinnamon.

Hashim dropped the ball on the table, letting it fall with a thud, and whipped around. "Doubt is an emotion, Kamal, and you must not let it make you blind."

"Good night, Vizier," Kamal said. He walked through the door, and I followed. Hashim left the room and slammed the door shut behind him. He barreled down the hall, and without thinking, I followed Kamal. The guards at the end of the hall snapped to attention, and he marched through without any acknowledgment.

He went in the direction of the harem, but he passed it, stopping at a white door painted in gold birds and leaves. He paused, and then opened the door and shut it quickly behind him.

I leaned my ear against the door but could hear nothing, and after a minute passed, I went back to the harem. Once within, I went past the peafowl, who hadn't budged, and slipped into my room.

The moonlight was gone. I felt my way to my couch, let myself become visible again, and crawled between the sheets of a princess's bed. It was another hour before my heart settled.

+ 24 +

ZAYELE

I THOUGHT I was going to vomit. I ran out of the Corps building, past the fountain, and spun around. Somewhere in this Cavern were tunnels that led to the surface. I needed to find one. Now.

I took a breath and decided to run into the city, which was on the other side of the canal. Beyond the city, the wall was darker. It could just indicate darkened crystal buildings, or maybe there were tunnels. I took off, not caring now what anyone thought. I had to move fast. I had to get out of sight before the Corps realized I was gone.

I dashed over a stone bridge that went across the canal, and almost ran into a pair of cane sticks that had moved out in front of me. I skidded, grabbed a lamppost, and looked up the sticks to see that a man was standing on the top. His feet were tied to the ends, making the canes an extension of his legs.

He reached up to the top of the lamppost and lifted off a glass cloche, whispered to the flame, and put the cloche back on. Then he looked down and saw me.

"Sorry if I scared you there," he called down. "It was almost out. Had to wish it back." I nodded knowingly, noticing now that some of the lamps weren't lit. So they had to wish their fires into existence. Some of them anyway. And the wishes weren't permanent. I was about to move on, then hesitated.

"Sir? Do you know where an unguarded tunnel might be?"

"What do you need to know that for?" he asked, scratching his forehead.

"I'm supposed to do a study. For the Corps. Just got a little lost."

"Well, I do think there's a tunnel behind the waterfall. It goes up to a place that's hidden from humans. Or so they tell us. Maybe it's just to keep us happy," he said. He shrugged.

"Oh!" I smiled widely. "That's right."

"Glad to help the Corps," he said, then pointed to the next lamp, indicating he had to get on with his work. I looked behind to see if anyone had come out to follow me, but the guards were standing in place. The Corps building was halfway across the Cavern now.

I exhaled in relief and ran along the canal toward the waterfall, passing a group of small children and their moth-ers. When I reached the waterfall, I paused. It fell from a split in the crystal wall and poured into a pool, where it stirred up blue-green foam. There was a space behind the waterfall just wide enough for a person. I snuck behind, careful not to slip on the wet stone.

There was no one there. It was like being on the edge of the cliff overlooking the valley at home—only I was hidden and saw nothing but clear water and stone. There was a break in the waterfall only a few inches wide, where the water split, cascading down two sides of a crystal that poked out ten feet above me. Through the break, I could see a strip of the jinn's city. Jeweled homes studded the land beyond and along the canal that led to the lake.

I turned and took the last few steps to a narrow gap in the wall. On the ground beside it lay an old rock lamp filled with oil. It was almost too simple, like someone had known I'd need it.

I lit the lamp with a flint that dangled from the handle and then stepped into the tunnel.

"Hello?" I whispered. The sound started small but echoed, stronger, until it grew louder than the waterfall. How deep did the tunnel go?

I took two more steps. A strand of hanging lichen brushed against my hair, and when I wiped it away, it fell into my hand. It was spongy and gray, as if it hadn't seen light before. I waited, letting my eyes adjust to the lamp in the darkness.

But I couldn't adjust to blankness or see past the lamplight. The waterfall and the tunnel blocked the light from the Cavern, leaving me alone with my single flame. My mind raced with all the things that could go wrong. I could get lost. I could get caught. I could fall into a pit full of spiders.

I shook the thoughts away. This was going to be exciting, not frightening. I had survived a sandstorm. I'd manage *this*.

Last autumn, we'd snuck off on one of my father's camels, riding her down the gorge and past the barely green fields. I'd never seen the desert, and this was the time of year it came the closest. Because it was my birthday, it hadn't been hard to convince Yashar to ride with me. Borrowing a camel was forgivable, but I would have gotten whipped if I'd gone alone, so I brought my younger brother. It was the first, and last, time I'd gotten away from my father's scrutiny.

We left the foothills and raced the camel over the dead tufts of grass, around monster-sized boulders flung off the mountains, and into the windswept golden realm of the desert. We ran until the camel stopped. The desert spread all the way west to the horizon, where it met up with the bluest blue sky and turned into a dark, churning cloud.

"What is that?" I asked Yashar. He had been here before, with Father, so I thought he'd seen everything.

He stiffened. "I don't know. A storm?"

"Should we go back?"

"Yes. Quick."

He turned the camel around, and she suddenly picked up her speed. But the wind was faster, and in minutes we were surrounded by a cloud of stinging sand. The camel stopped and settled down onto the ground. Baffled, I tried to grab the reins from Yashar.

"Get off the camel!" he screamed through the trailing bit of his turban that he held to his face. Quickly, we climbed down and curled up against the camel, away from the wind. With my face shielded from the sand, I could see a little further ahead. A huge boulder stood there, braced against the storm.

"There!" I shouted. "Better than a camel!"

Yashar shook his head, and through the tiny crack in his turban, which was now pulled down over his face, I could see he did not want to move.

"Come on!" I could barely hear myself over the roaring

wind, so I grabbed him, and he came with me. We stumbled toward the boulder, leaving the camel behind.

I should have listened to Yashar. I should have trusted him and Father's camel. Instead, I dragged us out into the open sand and we lost our way after ten steps. The sand was too thick, too fast, and dug its way through the fabric we had pressed against our faces. I could taste blood on my lips where it'd torn the skin away, but I kept pushing forward, holding Yashar's arm tight against me.

"Zayele!" he screamed. "Back!"

It was too late to turn around. We had to keep going forward. Then I slipped in the sand and we were down. A wave of sand blew over us, pulling our clothes away with it. My hijab was gone, and my face was bare, but I couldn't stay there. I was not going to let the sand bury me, so I stood and pulled Yashar off the ground. We climbed over the deepening sand as fast as we could.

I smacked my nose into the boulder. I'd found it! I squeezed Yashar's arm tighter and brought him around to the other side. The sand was still blowing, still strong and biting, but we could breathe there.

Yashar pulled off his outer robe and wrapped it around us, and together we huddled, crouched against the storm. It wasn't till the roaring stopped that I heard Yashar's cries.

The sand had ripped his eyes to pieces.

When the storm passed, I found the camel—she was unhurt—and rode her home with Yashar clinging to my back, crying in my ear.

Now, in the dark tunnel, I could almost hear his whimpers. They were like the echoes of spirits, slipping along the damp stone walls. I had to push on. I had to get back to Yashar.

I held the lamp out and reached for the walls with my other hand. I walked with trepidation at first. And then I was enchanted. Walking in nothingness, surrounded by stone and the light of the lamp—it was like being inside a golden bubble of fire.

I picked up speed and felt cool, moist air on my face. And then I stepped down. It was just half a step, but it was jarring. The tunnel sloped downhill and then back up again. Going up was good, since I was supposed to be heading to the surface. I pressed on, careful of the floor. The tunnel was big enough for me to walk upright, but not so big that it felt like another cavern.

Eventually, I lost track of time. I could sense my heartbeat, my throat when it became thirsty, the sensation of the cool water I drank hitting my stomach, and the slight warmth of the flame in the lamp. The air smelled astringent, with the tang of the lamp oil surrounding me most thickly.

The tunnel divided into three parts. I stopped. Each opening had the same darkness, the same air, the same gray rock walls. My pulse quickened. How would I know which one to take? I had to make the correct choice. I had to, or I'd be lost in the earth. I closed my eyes and shut off all sensations from outside my body, trying to feel which was the right one. If there was a hint of a breeze, I'd know.

No matter which way the side tunnels went, the one in the

middle was wider and seemed like the way to go. How could it go anywhere but up? I checked it out one last time and then entered it, holding the lamp before me.

The tunnel sloped upward. I drank once more from my flask, just a sip. And then the tunnel split into two. I had to feel my way forward, hoping that somehow, deep within myself, I'd make the right choice.

I went left because when I headed to the right, a coldness struck me in the very pit of my stomach. Nothing could make me go that way. The left tunnel had an inscription on the wall, just inside it, that gave me greater confidence. It was written in jinni, but it had to mean I was going the right way. And I had made the proper choice earlier too.

Breathing deeply, I picked up my pace. My legs were growing tired, but I would not rest until I saw the sun. Or the stars, at least.

Eventually, I got hungry and tired. The darkness before and behind me was suffocating. I was in the middle of the earth, and it was the most frightening thing in the world.

I sat down with my back against the tunnel wall and rested, cursing myself for not bringing anything to eat. The wall was rougher than I'd expected. Just as I was about to rise, the lamp started smoking. The flame was half the size it had been, and the color changed from gold to pale blue.

If the light went out . . . I jumped up and ran, cradling the tiny flame. But I tripped over a stone and slammed into the ground. The lamp arced in the air. As it did, I got a glimpse of the area around me. A cavern half as big as the jinni one swelled up and around. The rocky ground slipped down like a stone waterfall before disappearing into the earth. The lamp crashed halfway down on the stone and cracked.

My eyes were open but I couldn't see anything. I blinked, hoping something would happen. Maybe I would see a crack in the ceiling above, a bit of light filtering down. But there was only darkness, as thick as the earth itself. I instantly thought of Yashar and felt sick. This was what his life had been like every day since he'd gone blind.

My lip stung and throbbed, filling my mouth with the metallic taste of blood. I tore off my scarf and pressed it against my face as I sat up. Then I felt for the walls, panicking. I crawled around, desperate to find something to hold on to, but there was nothing but air. Somewhere beyond my arms were the walls, and not far away was where the ground fell in a waterfall of stone.

"No!" My voice echoed, sounding more frightened than it should have. "This cannot happen." Talking hurt my jaw, so I cradled it and cried angry tears.

It wasn't supposed to end like this.

I WAS DREAMING of the Palace Lamp. It floated in the middle of my room, screaming out that I wasn't Zayele, that I wasn't human, that I was going to kill the prince. All the caliph's men came running into the harem and broke down my door. I was unable to move a muscle while they ran across the floor and impaled me with every weapon in the armory.

When I woke, I was shivering. I had kicked off the blanket, and it was curled into my arms like a dead mouse. The first rays of sunlight were pressing on the patio curtain, lighting up a corner of the room. It was the second day.

Everyone would know I was missing by now. I rubbed at my mark, but it was hidden by the thick layer of henna Rahela had put over it. The only thing I could do now was find a way out. But first, I had to find something worth coming here for. I had to learn the orb's purpose.

I sat up, and Rahela stretched. "You're awake?" she asked.

"Yes," I said, standing up and going to the chest of clothing.

"You don't have to dress so soon."

"I do, I think," I said. I sifted through the gowns, but nothing was right. They were either too delicate or too long.

"I put up the peach-colored one last night for you, after you fell asleep." She pointed at the gown draped over a cushion. It flowed onto the floor and reached out for the encroaching sunbeam. It was one of the more delicate gowns.

"But . . ."

"But what? Jinn don't wear that color?" she snapped.

"No. I mean, yes. I just don't think it's right for me." I ran my hand over the silk. Where had Zayele's tribe come across this fabric? My mother would die for it.

"You're a princess, remember, *Zayele*? If you act like one, you won't harm the gown." She was out of her bed now, riffling through her own stack of gowns. She yanked out a brown shift. "Zayele loved that peach dress."

"It's beautiful." But it wasn't what I had in mind for today. I was going to find a way out. And the dress wasn't something anyone could easily escape in. Rahela pulled her dress over her head with one swoosh and then took mine and shook it.

"Put up your arms." When I didn't move immediately, she gave me a look that reminded me of Faisal when he caught me daydreaming. I put up my arms and she slipped the dress on. It was as delicate as the rose I'd picked the day before. Janna's rose. I shook away her attempt to do my hair and ran my fingers through it. In a minute, I had it braided as usual, but without gems. We had buried them in a potted plant the night before, afraid they'd make the servants suspicious.

Rahela opened our door to peek and then shut it quickly. "They are coming with trays of food. That's good, because I don't feel like eating my breakfast out there."

"You'd rather eat with me than with them?" I asked. She snorted softly and then opened the door again just as a servant was about to knock. Two women carried a tray laden with fruit and yogurt. Once they set it down, they left without saying a word.

"They're not all bad, but a few of them are ignorant and superior. I don't want to stomach that first thing in the morning, do you?"

"No."

Rahela sat down. "You're a jinni, so of course I don't trust you," she said, spooning the yogurt onto her plate. "But I can't help liking you. So far, you've done nothing nearly as fearsome as what I'd been led to believe a jinni would do." She motioned for me to sit across from her. "You didn't choose this. She did, and she left me behind with a jinni who looks—well, like her. And you turned out to be not that unusual. You aren't disappearing into smoke, I mean. You haven't killed me, or taken my soul, or any of that."

I sat down and tried to copy the way she mixed the fruit with the yogurt. "This war between us . . . it isn't personal. We are only trying to survive."

"I don't want to talk about the war. That's outside of this room. Tell me what you can do about this wish Zayele made."

I looked down at the spoon for a long time before I spoke. "I'm trapped. Last night, I tried to go home, but this wish burns. It's not a normal wish. And no one can rescue me, because I'm the only one who can get through the jinni wards." I was about to mention the first two times I saw Kamal, but it didn't seem like the right thing to do. She wasn't in the Corps. She wasn't even jinni.

"I'm trapped too, you know." She tasted the yogurt. "I can't tell them who you are, or they'll blame our tribe. They'll say it was some sort of trick. So I'm a traitor instead."

I took a bite of yogurt. It was slippery, sour, and delicious. "But you're keeping the honor of your tribe."

"My tribe, my family, over the caliphate. Over other *humans*. What does that say about me?" Rahela pushed the food aside and rubbed her temples. "You know, Zayele would have loved it here, if she'd given it a chance. I was looking forward to living here with her. I wanted to be part of a harem, where I could blend in and be safe. It was going to be far better than staying in Zab. For both of us. She was just so worried about Yashar."

"Who?"

"Her brother. She didn't want to leave him behind. In a way, she's as much a child as he is."

"And they expect her to have children now? With the prince?" As soon as the words came out of my mouth, I blushed. "I couldn't imagine having a child now."

Rahela laughed and her cynical grin returned. It was as if she hadn't opened up about herself. "If you cannot find a way out, you'll have to get over that. They expect Zayele to provide a child within a year of getting married, I'm sure."

"But I'm only fifteen and a half."

She had been tying on a scarf but stopped. "When were you born?"

"Fifteen years ago."

"When during the year?" she asked. "What season?"

"We don't have seasons, but—"

"Of course you don't." She was grinning, like this was some sort of game.

"Six months ago. That season."

"Interesting," she said, then finished with her scarf. Before I could ask what she meant, the door slid open, and the girl who had first let us into the harem bowed.

"Prince Kamal would like you to meet with him in the garden."

Rahela stood. "We'll be ready in a moment."

We left behind the food on the table, the unmade beds, and Rahela's musings.

26

ZAYELE

MY HEAD ACHED like I'd been kicked by a camel, and my lip stung where it had broken open. I kept closing and opening my eyes, hoping I would see something. Hoping the blackness would retreat. But all I could sense was a constant roaring. It wasn't rain. Not in a cave. And it couldn't be in my mind.

I felt around for the edges of the tunnel, inching my fingers across the gritty floor. The ground sloped. This must have been the way the lantern fell. Slowly, I reached forward and found the edge of the floor where it dropped off into nothingness. I lay on my stomach and reached down, finding a flat place only a foot below. Beneath that another, and yet another. It was a staircase of stone. I slid down feetfirst into the never-ending night.

Anything could have been creeping on me. I shivered, thinking of crawling things with too many legs climbing into my hair, and fought off the urge to scratch at my neck. What would live in darkness?

What hunted down here?

My neck was tingling. *This is just a tunnel,* I thought. *It's dark. That's it.* I was like Yashar now, lost in the dark. He had found his way around the village after a while, and if he could do that, I could find my way out.

I slid down another step. On the eighth one, my foot landed in something wet. It was cold as ice and rushed over the step. Using one hand to prop myself on the stairs, I felt around for its source. It poured out from a gash in the rock.

I placed a few drops on my tongue. It was pure, stone-cold water. My throat demanded more, so I cupped my hand beneath the step and drank from the water. It was the best I'd had in ages. Quickly, I reached down again, but everything was wet and I slipped. I scrabbled at the rocks, but couldn't get a grip and fell into the water.

I was caught in a current, grabbing at the steps, but they were slippery. I tumbled down one step after the other until my foot got stuck between two rocks. I was underwater, pinned beneath the current.

I couldn't breathe, and I couldn't get a hold on anything. The water raced over my head, pulling my dress and hair with it. The dress tugged on my throat and tightened.

I was going to die.

Using everything I had, I pushed up from the ground. The water dragged the dress sideways and flowed over me. My nose, then the rest of my face, broke through the surface. Coughing, I spat out water. My foot was still stuck in the rocks, and I kicked with my other foot and found something to press against. I twisted, pulling as hard as I could, and one of the rocks slid to the side. I was free, and then the current took me again. I fell down, down, down into a deep, still pool of water.

I came up for air, grabbing at it as if it were a solid thing that would save me, and then sank back down. The water tasted of tears, thousands of tears. Again, I pulled myself up to the air, churning the water over and over again, grasping for anything.

My fingers scraped against something rough. Rock. Wide, flat, and at the water's edge. I pinched my nails into it, pulled myself out of the water, and collapsed on the stone. I breathed in the blindness, not caring that it was cold. Too cold.

"So dark," I gasped. I had spoken into nothingness and the echoes returned, one by one, to tease me. "I wish it wasn't so dark."

A strange feeling spread from the center of my spine, up and out of my arms. I blinked, amazed. My *skin* was glowing. The light spread, and with it came exhaustion. I curled up on my side and watched the rim of the water, that bit of darkness lapping the rock. Besides the rock and the water, I could see the bruises spreading across my ankle in the light from my skin.

Something wasn't right, but I was too tired to do anything. I pressed my cheek into my hand and let my aching body shut down, starting with my eyes.

27

NAJWA

A BIRD WITH gossamer blue wings trailed behind us while we followed the girl across the harem. Rahela walked at my side, ever my shadow. We wound through the roses, under an arbor, and to a gazebo against the wall of the palace. The girl motioned for us to enter and then disappeared through a set of white doors. The bird, disappointed that we didn't have any seeds, flew off.

A rectangular window, set with a lattice, opened between the gazebo and the palace's interior. I sat beneath it on a bench and leaned my head against the lattice, feeling a soft breeze flowing between the two spaces.

A voice whispered in my ear, "Hello again." I jumped and turned to find Kamal on the other side of the window. He was smiling and pressing his face into the lattice.

"Hello," I said, leaning away from the wall. I felt my face grow hot.

"Should I leave you?" Rahela asked. She stood up from the bench.

"No. Please stay," I said, trying to cover the desperation in my voice. I needed her there with me.

"Yes. I'm sure they would insist," Kamal said. Then he pulled off his turban and ran his fingers through his thick hair. I stared, remembering how he had done that the previous morning, when he didn't know I was watching.

"But you did want to talk to me?" I asked.

"Yes." He frowned. "I am supposed to ask what you thought of your journey, but I'm sure it was long and boring. Am I right?" I nodded. "And Hashim wanted me to ask if you were feeling homesick, or sick in any way. I was surprised he cared. What I really want to know is what you are like. Do you enjoy art?"

I glanced at Rahela, but her face was blank. "A little," I said. What I'd seen of human art was interesting, but it didn't speak to me. It was the stories that drew me in.

"What about jewels?"

"I—uh—yes. I like them." He was so close. My field of vision held nothing but the white of the lattice and the green and gold of his eyes. I blinked and looked away, along the palace wall. A vine climbed up the stones and I focused on that. "But I also like gardens," I said. "And I like stories. Finding out why people do things."

"What kind of stories?"

"Human stories." I said it before I thought about it. "I mean—" I had met his gaze but now looked away again while a flush spread across my cheeks.

"Stories that show what people are like? Not what they pretend to be?" he asked.

"Yes," I said, recovering. "But also, the choices they make when strange things happen." Such as, what would a human girl do in this situation? And what should a jinni girl do?

He laughed and reached his fingers through the lattice, curling them over the edges. "Nothing strange should happen to you here. If anything, the hard part will be keeping yourself from getting bored. For a girl used to the mountains, the walls might make this feel more like a cave than a palace."

I smiled. "I doubt that." I glanced at Rahela, who was grinning like the devil.

"Zayele," he said, testing the name, "after I saw you yesterday, I . . ." His head dropped, and I saw he was flustered.

"Yes?"

"Here." He pushed a tiny linen bag through one of the holes in the lattice. "It's for you."

"Thank you." Our fingertips touched as I took the bag, and a jolt shot through my arm. His hand shook, as if he had felt it too. Quickly, I opened the linen bag. Inside lay a small pendant strung on a leather cord.

"I made it for you last night."

The pendant was silver, with an arched arabesque window holding a teardrop-shaped crystal. It was as iridescent as the moon, which had given this stone its name.

"Moonstone," I whispered. Jinn lived surrounded by rocks, but never moonstone. It leached wishes and life right out of our veins. My hand was shaking, and I wrapped my fingers around it, trying to show I wasn't afraid. The stone was cold, and froze the skin of my palm where it lay.

"I work with it so much that sometimes I forget it's not . . ." He swallowed and then said with effort, "You reminded me it can also be beautiful."

I had made him think such a stone was beautiful? I opened my hand again, now that my nerves had settled. It hadn't killed me, and I didn't feel anything other than the biting-cold thing lying there. Maybe the moonstone had to be swallowed first.

"Do you like it?" His voice was whispery again. He pressed his fingers into the lattice. "If you don't, I can get you something else."

"No, don't do that. I like it very much." And it didn't feel like a lie. The pendant shone, a drop of milk and silver on my hand, and I held it against my chest and tied it around my neck.

Within seconds, the spot of skin beneath the pendant was tingling and cold.

Concern rose in his voice. "Are you sure you like it?"

"Yes," I said. My voice had cracked.

"It looks good with your gown," Rahela said. She plucked a red hibiscus blossom off the bush beside her and sniffed it, hiding half of her face.

"I'm sorry I don't have anything—"

"No, don't be. Besides, your father is sending men for the army, so my father will be pleased when he wakes up. Everything is ready and we will just wait for him." He was blushing now, fidgeting behind the wall.

"May I ask you a question?" I asked. He nodded. "Why moonstone? Why do you work with it so much?"

He shook his head. "That, Princess, is a secret. Besides, it wouldn't interest you anyway."

"It wouldn't? Let me guess." His mouth twitched, and I continued, choosing my words carefully. "There isn't enough to give to everyone in the army, so . . ."

He chuckled in surprise. "If I'd ever doubted you were the vizier's cousin, I don't now. You sound like him. Logical and curious. But I still can't answer you. It's a secret that isn't mine to share."

I'd nearly gone too far already, so I smiled as sweetly as I could and nodded, trying not to think too much about the vizier. I was not like that man. Rahela still hid her face behind her flower, and I wanted to cast knives at her.

"Then what else do you do?"

He flashed me a grin and I forgot all about the vizier. "Do you like pomegranates?"

"Yes." I had seen one opened once. The seeds looked like tiny red rocks, and I couldn't imagine what they tasted like.

"Then I will bring you some, if I can convince Hashim to let me out of the palace for a while. He's been keeping me here. In fact, I must go. I told him I'd meet with him after breakfast. I wanted to give you that first." With a nod at my necklace, he smiled and was gone, disappearing into the palace's shadows.

I watched after him until Rahela spoke.

"I wasn't expecting any of *this*," she said. "He is romantic, even if he gave you poison."

I stood up. I would not let her sour the moment. "Can we go back to our room?"

"What about your garden?" We had found a small garden behind our patio but hadn't been in it yet.

I'd forgotten all about it. "Yes. Let's go. And it's not mine. Nothing here is truly mine."

"I know." She tossed the hibiscus onto the bench and led the way.

28

ZAYELE

SOMEONE WAS SQUEEZING my shoulder. I tried to lift my eyelids, but they were swollen and heavy. I was only able to peek. Atish was holding a lamp, and he was frowning.

"Are you hurt?" Was I? Yes, my foot had been stuck in the rocks. It ached and ached.

"My ankle," I croaked. I pulled it to my chest and gasped when I touched the side.

"We can get a physician to look at it. What were you doing here, Najwa?" I'd forgotten I was Najwa now. "Everyone is looking for you."

My head was going to fall in on itself. It hurt nearly as bad as my ankle. "Can't you wish my ankle fixed?"

He frowned. "Only physicians should do that. It's good I found you. Why were you here?" He pulled me up onto his lap, and I rested my throbbing head against his chest.

"I was trying to get to the surface, like Faisal wanted me to."

"But this tunnel opens into the sea."

"How do you know?"

He sighed. "You *have* lost your mind. Come on. I'll help you."

"I can do it," I said. I tried to stand, but pain shot up through my leg and I fell back down, moaning. Atish huffed, hooked an arm under my left one, and guided me up. The climb was difficult, but not as bad as I'd feared. Beside the wet stone was a path, smooth and dry. Of course I had completely missed that on my way down.

"How did you end up in the water?" he asked.

I was hopping on one foot. Each time I landed, the pain grew more unbearable, and hopping only increased the throbbing in my head. "It was dark," I grunted. "I fell in."

"What happened to your lamp?"

"I dropped it."

"What about wishing for some light?" So, a jinni would never get lost in the dark. How was I supposed to know that?

"I was having some problems," I mumbled.

"Something is going on, Najwa. You can't just run away. We've been scouring every shadow and alcove looking for you. They were ready to start looking in the lake! And you can't— shards, Najwa!" He pinched the bridge of his nose, like Rahela did when she was frustrated.

"I—"

His jaw twitched. "I thought something had happened to you. I didn't know what it could have been—maybe some new weaponry that could snatch us from the Cavern—but no. You were just sneaking away." He paused, stopping mid-stride, and brought the lantern up higher, so that his features were sharper. "Today, I thought you'd finally opened up to me. You were more spontaneous. I thought you were that part of me I'd always felt was missing. And then, when we kissed . . ." He stopped and picked up my hand. "But none of that is worth anything if you walk away from the horrors we face. We're in a war, Najwa. You can't just run off whenever you feel like it."

I glared at him. "You don't know what I've been going through." My throat was thick and I tasted copper. He didn't know. He could fight his enemy, and everyone would cheer him on for doing so. But my enemy wasn't so clear. I wasn't even sure what it was.

His arm dropped, and when he lowered the lantern, shadows shifted and stretched along the tunnel. "Then tell me. How can I help if you keep secrets? You've got to trust me or we've got nothing."

"It's just . . . I'm sorry. This was my own fault. I should have been more careful."

He tightened his grip on me. "You don't need to do everything alone, Najwa. No matter what the reason is." He shook his head, then froze. He was staring at my hand, confused. I slid it behind my back, but he had seen. His eyes narrowed. "Hold out your hand," he commanded. When I hesitated, he grabbed it and held it up to the lamp. "Where in Iblis's name is your mark? Gal said Faisal had marked you, but I don't see it."

I pulled my hand free. The henna had worn off a bit in the water, leaving the design looking like shredded embroidery. "I don't know. It faded."

"Marks don't fade." Atish's skin turned to gold and lit up, the light rippling like a raging current across his arms and face.

His eyes shone like coals, and they were huge, and I pulled, scrambling to get away. This must be what the Shaitan looked like in battle. "I can tell you're lying, Najwa."

His skin burned, brighter than the lamp, and I stepped back, shielding my face. The tunnel walls were bare in the brightness, with only the cracks and rough patches holding on to the darkness. The cracks were too small, and my ankle was too weak. There was nowhere to go, and I could not outrun a Shaitan.

"I'm not Najwa." There was no point in hiding anymore. Not in this light.

His fists tightened and released, slowly. "What are you talking about?"

"My name is Zayele." In this tunnel, in the land of jinn, the word sounded more like an echo of someone else, not my name.

He blinked in confusion. "If you're not Najwa, then where is she?" The lamp was inches from my eyes, but I didn't dare turn away. I stared back at him, as defiant as I could pretend to be.

"She's in Baghdad. In the palace."

His jaw twitched. "Jinn can't get into the palace."

"Apparently, she can, because Faisal just ordered me— her—to go back. She's been there before."

"*What?* Who *are* you? Are you even from the Cavern?"

He still didn't know? I thought about making up a story about being from a different group of jinn, but he looked so concerned, and the brightness was fading into a glow now. I couldn't lie to him anymore.

"I'm not from . . . here. I traded places with Najwa."

He swore, cursing the tunnel, the Cavern, and everyone in it. "You're not jinni?"

"No, but I wasn't going to hurt anyone!" I said. "I just want to go home."

"When did you trade places with her?" He leaned closer. His irises were golden-brown again, as if the anger had consumed itself. I couldn't look away from them, remembering how only this morning he'd looked at me with hunger. Seeing the difference was like finding a knife in my chest.

"Yesterday," I said. "I caught her, and made a wish."

"You *wished* on her? What did you think, that you could just change places? That her life was easier?" He rubbed at the back of his neck and then peeled away from me.

"I didn't want her life," I said, hobbling closer to him. "I only wanted to go home. And I'd never seen a jinni before. I didn't even know you were *people*. I thought jinn were . . ."

"Soulless? Mindless demons, alive just to give humans whatever they want?" He swung the lamp away and dropped it by his side. "You're right. We're people, and we have lives. Lives that humans are so quick to take."

"I didn't know I was taking a life! I was just trying to get home. It's all I want."

His lips curled up in a sour smile. "So this was your plan? Kiss me and then run off to the tunnels?"

"I . . . no." My ankle hurt more than anything I'd felt before, but I couldn't let him see the pain. If he tried to help—if he touched me—I'd melt into him again. And the thought that he wouldn't help was more than I wanted to face now. "You weren't part of any plan."

He shook his head and sighed. "I can't believe my first kiss was with a human."

Najwa hadn't kissed him before? A blush spread across my face and I turned to the wall to hide it. I wanted him to know I'd never kissed anyone either, but anything I could say would sound childish or desperate.

Besides, he knew who I was now. He could bring me to the Shaitan, and they'd kill me on the spot.

"So now what? Are you going to take me back or kill me right here?"

The lamp began to waver, and when he whispered, it flashed back into life.

"I don't know what to do with you," he muttered. He stared at me for a long time.

The wall was cool against my cheek, and I welcomed it because it was solid, and real, and just as I'd expect. Everything else in my life had been turned upside down. There wasn't anything I could do to help myself now. I couldn't talk my way out of it. I couldn't even walk.

"I kissed you. A human."

"You had never kissed Najwa before?"

"No," he said. His face was a mixture of curiosity and frustration, which probably mirrored my own. "I never really wanted to."

"And you're a jinni. In the Shaitan, even," I said. My heart was pounding in my chest. All of a sudden, I didn't want him to leave me. Not only because I was stuck in a tunnel. I wanted him to forget I was human. I brushed my fingers over my lips, remembering.

He was staring at my fingers, at my lips, before he curled his hands into fists. "I can't—I have to go." He thrust the lamp into my hands, careful not to touch my skin, and ran down the tunnel until he was nothing but shadow.

I was alone with only the bubble of light he'd left behind. I sank to the floor, set the lamp beside me, and cried into my knees. The world hadn't wronged me this time. Everything—all of it, even Atish—had been my fault. I had ruined someone's life to avoid a marriage. Even still, I didn't want to go to Baghdad.

It didn't matter anymore. I was unable to walk, and the flame would go out eventually. I would die here, in the coming darkness.

❖ 29 ❖

NAJWA

IT WASN'T DIFFICULT slipping out of the harem. When Rahela decided to take a nap, I turned myself invisible, ducked behind the curtains that shielded the door, then skipped past the guards. Because it was midafternoon, they were barely paying attention to the harem door anyway.

Even so, the thrill of slinking down the corridor buzzed in my veins. I still hadn't found a way out of Zayele's wish yet, but I was able to do something. I didn't have to stay locked up with the other women. I could do what I was trained to do.

I remembered a little of the map Delia had shown me, so I knew which direction to go, even if I didn't know which hall to take. As long as I was back before the *shahtabi* wish wore off, I would be fine.

I ran down the corridor, around the darkened jinni Lamp, and down the opposite hall. I passed the laboratory Kamal had been in the night before, then kept going. Twice, I slowed down, careful not to disturb the air around people who were walking along.

A giant door of interlocking stars and triangles stood at the end of the corridor. It was closed, but after I waited a moment, the door swung inward. A gray-bearded man walked out with his arms overloaded with books, so I took the chance and darted in. I was getting good at sneaking through doors.

I had been hearing about the House of Wisdom my entire life. Faisal had been a student there prior to the war, and he had clearly fallen in love with it. He said that in the House of Wisdom, there were more books than I could count. More educated men than anywhere else in the world. More minds willing to see both sides to an argument. And there had never been anywhere else where humans and jinn worked side by side.

Before the war, the sciences had blossomed, and a large part of that was due to the open discussions between our races. According to Faisal, if it weren't for his brother and Jafar al-Jabr, one of the caliphate's best mathematicians, we'd be lost in a world of confusing numbers. And since the day the jinn left, there hadn't been any new discoveries.

The door closed behind me and a puff of air blew my skirt, but I barely noticed. I was in the House of Wisdom, and all I could think about was that no jinni had been there in ages, and a female jinni had never been allowed to enter. I was the first.

Thousands of books, with spines of red leather or black or brown linen, sat on shelves two stories high and a hundred feet long. The scents of ink and glue laced the air, and I breathed them in deep. At least thirty men, all in long robes, were in the library. Some sat at low tables, bent over opened volumes. Others stood in a small group, listening to two men discuss something. A few roamed along the walls, pulling books off the shelves and tucking them beneath their arms. The room was heavy with stories, and I ached to read them.

Faisal had once been one of these men, with access to all these books. All these minds. No wonder we built the Lamps—the bridge between the worlds. No wonder we gave the humans cartloads of jewels to set foot in it. No wonder Faisal fell in love with this place.

I spun around, taking in the sight of so many books. Where would I begin? Where *could* I begin? Scanning the spines of the books would take too long, and I couldn't go up to one of the men and ask him for their books on jinn.

But there was a map of the library. It sat propped up on a tall, skinny table and outlined different areas of interest, showing where the books were located. I ran my finger over the ink, but none of the descriptions pertained to jinn. Then I saw that there was a tiny section on the second floor labeled "People of the Lamp." I almost pressed my nail through the paper when I found it. That had to be about us.

Quickly, I found a set of narrow stairs and climbed to the second story of bookshelves, then braced myself before looking over the railing. The men below me were oblivious that a jinni was practically floating in the air above them. Thankful for my invisibility, I stepped along the balcony and found the corner I'd come to see.

One shelf, on the bottom of a bookcase. That was all they had set aside for my people, and it had only four books. A brass lamp held them up against the side of the shelf, and I couldn't help but grin at that. It was something Faisal would have done.

I knelt and read the spines of the books, but none of them looked like they could help me. Most were just records of what the jinn had studied while they were in the House of Wisdom. I pulled one out and flipped through the yellowed pages, then tucked it into the pocket in my gown.

That was when I saw them. A row of Memory Crystals, individually tied with a strange twine. These crystals were how we recorded our histories and honored our dead. But how had they gotten here? They were supposed to be kept in a special place in the Cavern, never removed. I picked up a dark green one with equally dark smoke that swirled, suspended, within.

My nose started to itch, and before I could try to prevent it, I sneezed. Then I gasped, because the sneeze echoed across the open space. I leaned into the bookcase and away from the railing, hoping no one would look up, because for a moment, I forgot they couldn't see me anyway. Maybe they would assume the noise I'd made had come from someone downstairs.

But then I heard a man ask, "Is someone up there?" He must have been pointing, because another man answered him.

"I didn't see anyone. What books are up there anyway?"

I could feel the blood draining from my face. If they came up here, there'd be nowhere for me to go. I couldn't slip around them, because the balcony was too narrow, and by then it wouldn't matter if I was invisible or not. I couldn't turn myself into a book.

The men's voices were getting louder.

"The map says it's where they keep the old records," said the first man.

"Let's go. Maybe there's a kitchen boy hiding up there,"

said the second. I could hear the scowl on his lips, and I started to panic. I stood up, looked over the railing again, and held my breath. I couldn't climb down, and it was too far to jump. But there was a window at the end of the balcony, by the stairs. Maybe I could stand on the windowsill while they passed.

I sprinted to the end and climbed into the window just as they crested the stairs. The sill was barely six inches wide, but it was enough. I clung to the top and held my breath as two men with long dark beards walked past. They didn't stop to look out the window.

I was like a lizard, crouching between sky and house. Outside lay a dirt field pocked with scrubs of grass and one long trough for horses. At the other side of the field was a fence, and it was swinging open. At that moment, a horde of horsemen trotted in. Their weary faces were striped with sand and blood, and their armor showed signs of fire damage. One man fell off his horse and landed on his side. Another man dropped his spear, then ran to help the fallen man get to his feet.

These weren't just ordinary horsemen. They were soldiers, coming back from a battle with my people. The scorch marks on their round shields proved that.

I knew I should not feel any sort of pity, but I did. The man who had fallen was now being carried off by two men, and many others were climbing off their horses and limping across the field. A man in a clean, unbloodied blue tunic helped some men guide the horses to the water. He called out to another man dressed in black, and when that man turned, I almost let go. It was the vizier, Hashim. Even from afar, he frightened me.

My skin was starting to tingle, which meant I had only a

few minutes before my wish faded. What would he think if he saw me sitting up in a window, in the House of Wisdom?

I bolted down the stairs and ran, not caring now if anyone felt the gust of wind. I made it to the curtains behind the harem door before my *shahtabi* wish was gone, and by then being invisible would not have made a difference, because my pulse was loud enough that one of the peacocks tilted his head at me.

I took a breath and stepped into the harem's garden, and that was when I realized I still had the Memory Crystal in my hand. How had anyone not seen it?

ZAYELE

HE CAME BACK. I was crying and crawling on my hands and knees when a glow came from down the tunnel. Then I saw his face. He still looked angry, but he crouched down and swooped me into his arms as if I were a child.

My throat burned, and I tried to stop crying, hiccupping with my temple against his chest. His arms were warm, and finally I relaxed into him.

He had come back.

"Everything I know tells me I should just walk away," he said. "But I can't. I don't want to."

I nodded, unable to speak. He had come back. He knew what I was now. He knew I'd been lying and what I'd done to Najwa. But he didn't know why. He didn't know about Yashar, or the barge I'd been locked in with Rahela, or how empty I'd been in the tunnel's darkness. He didn't know that I had nowhere to go.

He carried me out of the tunnel, moving swiftly. We emerged behind the waterfall, and he stopped. Mist billowed around, making the hairs on my arms slick. I dug my fingers into his vest, afraid I'd slip off and tumble down into the water. He tightened his grip on me.

"Honestly, I don't know where to go. I can't take you to Faisal or Laira. And I can't take you home."

He was betraying himself for me. I couldn't understand it. I sobbed again.

"I know," he said. "Shirin."

"She'll be so mad."

He nodded once. "No madder than I am. She wasn't ..." He didn't finish the sentence. Instead, he carried me out from behind the waterfall and took a path to a house near a tree-lined avenue. Behind the house, Shirin was painting on an easel as if it was the most natural thing in the world. She flicked the paint into the air from her brush and, with a nod, sent it flying. It smacked onto the paper as hard as hail. The picture was a series of overlying dots and drips—a stark contrast to the precise weaving I'd grown up learning. And strangely enough, it made me think of Rahela. She was afraid of jinn, and I'd left her with one.

When Shirin lifted her brush the second time, Atish cleared his throat. She looked up, her jaw slackened, and she ran to us.

"What happened?" she shrieked. Atish shushed her. I looked away. I couldn't watch her face. "What happened?" she repeated.

Atish nodded at the house. "Is your mother home?" She shook her head. "Then let's go in."

She led the way, opening the door. Her face was scrunched up in concern. "Najwa, what happened?"

Atish laid me on one of the beds and sat on another one. "Her ankle's broken."

"Let me see." Shirin reached for my ankle and I rasped in pain, pulling it away from her.

"It really hurts," I croaked.

"You've been crying." She looked at Atish. "Where did you find her?"

"In the tunnel." He could not have made his voice any darker.

"Why did you go there?" She shook her head at me. "Never mind. Let me fix you. Then we'll talk." Her hands hovered over my ankle and she whispered something. The air between her hands and my ankle glowed green. In seconds, the pain was gone. I tested my ankle by squeezing it.

"How did you do that?"

"What do you mean?" she asked.

Atish grumbled, "She's not Najwa. She's not even *jinni*."

Shirin's eyes narrowed and she studied me. "Of course she's Najwa." She waited for me to say something, but I didn't, and when the silence had gone on too long, she frowned. "Aren't you?"

I could not answer her. Not with words.

"She's human," Atish said. "She was on her way to Baghdad when she ran into Najwa—"

Shirin twisted around to face him. "What was Najwa doing—"

"I don't know. But she caught Najwa and wished on her," he explained.

Shirin's hands started to shake and she backed away from

me. "You have to explain yourself. What have you done to our friend? When did you take her?"

"The vizier came to our village," I said, then explained how I had been chosen to go to Baghdad. "The day we were supposed to arrive in the city, a jinni appeared at my window. I didn't even think. I just reached out and caught her."

Shirin gasped. "You forced a wish from her?"

"Yes. I needed to get back home. And she looked just like me. I thought it was a sign, a way for me to get out of there. I mean, I was desperate, and there she was! With my own face! So I wished that she take my place and send me home."

Shirin's voice rose. "And you came *here*?"

"Obviously," Atish said. Shirin ignored him.

"It doesn't make any sense!" she exclaimed. "It's one thing—a horrible thing—to force a jinni to grant a wish for you, but it's quite another to force her to take your life. And look at you! You're a mirror image of Najwa."

"I know," Atish said. "If it weren't for the missing tattoo, I would have just thought Najwa had lost her mind."

"At the time, I thought it was a disguise," I explained, "or some effect of a jinni being so close to me." They weren't yelling at me anymore. Shirin sat beside Atish on the bed, staring at me. Atish was fiddling with the latch on his dagger's sheath.

"It's eerie," Shirin said. She reached over to the table between the beds, pulled open the drawer, and removed a hand mirror. She held it out to me. "You've always looked like this?"

"Yes."

"Then it's not part of the wish." She took the mirror back

and dropped it in the drawer, then slammed the drawer shut. "Atish, you're not going to turn her in, are you?"

"It's too late, and we need her to get Najwa back." He pulled the dagger out of the sheath and rolled it between his hands. Then he looked at me, which he hadn't done since we'd gotten to Shirin's house. "You're going to help us."

"How?" I said.

Shirin rubbed her hands together. "We will solve this, somehow. First, where are you from?"

"Zab, near the mountains."

She turned to Atish. "Wasn't that where the murders happened?" When he nodded, she continued, "This is making my head spin. You look like Najwa, and you always have. Then, at a time when you're most troubled, you come upon her. You switch places—against her will—and end up here, of all places, after you wished to go home." She paused, and a smile spread across her face. "I don't think you're really from Zab," she said. When I started to protest, she held up her hand to silence me. "Just a minute. Atish, you didn't turn her over to the Shaitan. Why not?"

"It didn't feel like the right thing to do," he said. "Although I wanted to."

"You wanted to tell them about me?"

"Shh," Shirin said. "You aren't Najwa. I understand that, and it makes what happened earlier with Irina make sense. Najwa is always too polite with her because she doesn't want to upset her mother. But I have this feeling. Maybe it's the same one Atish has—"

"It's not," he cut in.

She rolled her eyes at him, then told me, "Well, I don't think Najwa can come back unless you go to her. You're the only one who can undo the wish, and if you die, she might be stuck in your place forever."

I drew my knees up to my chin and covered my face with my hands. Hot tears pooled in the spaces between my fingers.

"I'm sorry," I said, but not to them. The words barely made it past the lump in my throat. "Just tell me how to fix it. What do I wish to get her back here?"

"You have to go there," Atish said. He stopped fiddling with his dagger and put it away. "But we can't get in there, because of the wards. I have no idea how Najwa got in there in the first place."

"She *what*?" Shirin asked.

"That's what Zayele said," Atish said, gesturing at me. "Najwa had gotten into the palace, and Faisal was asking her, Zayele, to go back."

"I knew something big had happened," Shirin said. "And something made Najwa seek you out, Zayele."

I looked up from my knees and wiped the tears off my face. "What?"

"I don't know, but there's someone who does. Atish, we have to tell Faisal."

"Absolutely not."

"He will kill me!" I said.

"No, he won't. He's too wise to make such rash decisions, and he will want Najwa back as much as we do." She got up and paced between the beds, turning around every two steps. "Let me go talk to him. I'll tell him I know where Najwa is, and when I've got his attention, I'll explain everything to him as gently as I can."

"I should do that," Atish said.

"No. You're too involved emotionally."

"I am not!"

"Atish," she warned. "Stay here with Zayele. I will be right back. Don't let anyone in."

She leaned forward and hugged me. "It will be all right." Then she whirled around and slipped out the door, shutting it with a nod.

After she was gone, it was just Atish and me, alone in the house. He reached down to his dagger's sheath.

"Please," I said, "don't play with that anymore. I keep thinking you're going to throw it at me."

He looked genuinely surprised. "I would never. Besides, like Shirin said, we need you to get Najwa back."

A moment passed, and neither of us said anything. I didn't like the silence and the waiting. Shirin was on her way to tell one of the most important jinn in the Cavern what I had done to Najwa, and I didn't have as much faith in him as she did.

I watched Atish, who kept avoiding my gaze. His lips were pressed tightly together, like he was trying to keep something inside.

"Why didn't you leave me there, in the tunnel?"

"I already told you, I don't know. I just couldn't, all right?"

"But I hurt the girl you love."

He shook his head. "I don't love her. I tried to, but there wasn't . . . I don't want to talk about this right now."

Whatever had prompted him to kiss me had never happened

with Najwa. Only with me. Suddenly, a prickle spread down from my neck. I looked up at him and saw that his eyes were on me, questioning. He shifted so that we sat across from each other, knees to knees, and although the space between us appeared empty, it was full of something living, something very much like what had just spread down my shoulders.

I could not look away, and I didn't want to. He was seeing me now for who I really was, and although I knew he would find me lacking in whatever trait only jinni girls could have, I didn't want to be lacking. In that moment, alone with him in the tiny space that was Shirin's house, I felt a closeness I'd never felt with anyone. Not even with Yashar. And with each beat of my heart and each blink of my lashes, I wanted him closer still.

He was about to say something else when the door burst open and hit the wall. A throng of guards rushed in, their Shai-tan shields and daggers blazing. Atish stood up and tried to get between them and me, but they brushed him aside without a word. One of the men bound my wrists behind my back and dragged me out the door, careful not to let me touch him with my hands.

Irina stood outside with her arms crossed. She wore a shawl in the Baghdad style, but her eyes were glowing jinni-bright, her irises red as lava.

"Irina!" Atish shouted behind me. "You did this?"

She huffed. "Of course I did. As you should have." She took two steps toward me. The guard thrust me forward until she was only a few inches from me. "I knew you couldn't be her. Najwa wouldn't have dared to do half the things you did."

She turned her head and I saw that Shirin was behind her, also held by guards. Tears streamed down her cheeks.

"She was spying on us!" she shouted. "She called the guards before I even left the house."

The guards lifted me off my feet and carried me behind Irina. Shirin continued to shout until one of the guards released her. Atish was being held back by two other guards. His face was dark, but his eyes stared straight into mine. I knew without doubt he would find me.

❖ 31 ❖

NAJWA

THAT AFTERNOON, WHILE Rahela was in the harem's garden, I pulled out the Memory Crystal I had hidden beneath my mattress. I untied the twine and lifted the crystal up to the sunlight that streamed in from the garden. It was just as deeply green as it had been in the House of Wisdom. The darker the crystal, the higher the rank of the jinni whose memory it contained. This must have been the memory of someone very high. I'd never held one so dark.

Inside the crystal, the memory swirled like incense smoke, ever bending and twirling over itself. The crystal kept it safe and unaltered. All I had to do was hold it before me and concentrate, urging my mind to go inside. I'd done it many times in my studies with Faisal, and just as before, I held it out and stared, waiting for it to pull me in.

A moment later, I was looking through the eyes of someone grimacing at a bowl of slime-covered water. A foot kicked out and turned it over, and the water spread across sandstone bricks and seeped into the mortar. The person whose memory I was experiencing tried to move his arms, but they were tied to an iron bar in the wall.

I was feeling the memory now as though it were my own, and in it, I was wearing nothing but a loincloth in a room with one iron door and no windows. I was leaning against the wall, feeling the chill and damp seep into my bones. My wrists burned.

"That was all you were going to get today, so I hope you're truly sorry," a man said from the other side of the small cell. I looked at him, taking in his immaculately white turban, his jewels, and his golden robe, then spat in his direction. "You are mine now, Melchior, and I expect all my jinn to behave. You will do as I *wish,*" the man said with a sneer.

"I will do nothing," I said. My voice was deep and resonated off the walls.

The man snapped his fingers, and two men in military uniform stepped through the door. They pressed knives against the twine while the man in the turban touched my forearm with the tip of his finger.

"When they release the twine, you will have your powers back. However, I am touching you. My guards will be holding you perfectly still, so you will not be able to shake yourself free of my touch." The man nodded at his guards, who slit the twine around my wrists. As the pieces fell, I saw they were braided with long strips of paper inscribed with intricate calligraphy. Whatever was written on those strips of paper was keeping me from wishing myself free.

"My other jinn are wasted," the man continued. "They

cannot grant wishes greater than a small bead of gold at a time. But you are fresh and strong. It's fortunate we caught you." He pushed his finger hard into my arm until his nail bit into my skin. "I wish for ten pounds of gold."

"No," my heavy voice said.

The man smiled, revealing a line of polished, crooked teeth. "Oh, I'm sure you'll change your mind. You jinn always do. It's in your blood. You cannot resist a human wish, especially mine."

I felt the wish spread outward in my rib cage, like a tumor. It stole my breath, squeezing my lungs tight. My lungs felt as if they were being twisted, and I understood then why a human's wish was impossible to refuse. I had imagined it to be painful, but I'd never *known*. My lungs wouldn't release until I breathed out the wish.

I would rather suffocate than grant this man his wish.

I was not going to give in. I was a trained member of the Corps. I *ran* the Corps. I couldn't disappoint them.

But it hurt. It burned. Great Crystals, it burned like fire, like the lava of the deep. My lungs were peeling apart, layer by layer. It burned. It burned. It burned.

I couldn't. I couldn't do it.

I looked the man in the eye and mouthed, "Granted." The wish unwound itself from my lungs, ripping itself out like a serrated splinter. Pain, mixed with sweet air, pulsed through me, and I felt the wish take form, pulling the energy it needed from me.

I slumped in the guards' arms just as something golden flashed behind the man.

It had taken everything to resist, and even so, it had not been enough.

I looked at the man, whose face gleamed. "It's always the hardest the first time, because you try to resist. But as you now know, you are mine to control. I, Caliph Mohammed al-Mahdi, thank you for your service to the caliphate."

It had taken too much to fight his wish, and darkness pooled in. A darkness I couldn't shake.

I dropped the Memory Crystal on the floor and rubbed my eyes, trying to get the image out of my mind. I knew who Melchior was. He had been the Master of the Corps before Faisal. And now he was one of the last magi left. In the memory, though, he was a slave! He was being controlled by the caliph, but humans hadn't had jinni slaves since the treaty had been signed twenty years ago. How long ago was this memory from?

The pain he felt was horrible, but it was nothing to what I'd felt when trying to break away from Zayele's wish. The wish commanded by the caliph had seared this jinni's lungs, but it hadn't filled them with fire.

I couldn't shake away the burning memory in my own lungs, and I ran to the small garden behind my room to breathe in the fragrant air. It was more of a courtyard than a garden, surrounded by a high stone wall, but it had a bench, a small fountain, and a trellis covered with white jasmine. A shape matching my new silver-and-moonstone pendant was cut into the wall at the opposite end, the hole barely big enough to fit my hand through. When I looked in, I saw a mirror image of my garden, down to the simple fountain bubbling in the middle. Whose garden was that? Whose room would back onto mine?

But it didn't matter. I had just been in the mind of someone who was trapped in far worse conditions than my own. I breathed in deeply while a lark landed on the bench beside me. It sang at me, its tone demanding and sharp, as if to say there was more to see.

It was just a bird, but maybe it was right. Maybe I needed to see more.

Reluctantly, I retrieved the crystal and brought it outside, where the fresh air would continue to soothe me. Then I looked into the swirling smoke within it, letting myself be pulled in.

I was Melchior again, in the same stone room. Another man was shoving liquefied food down my throat in swift, forceful moves. I gagged, but it stayed down. After a minute or two, when the man was convinced I wouldn't throw it up, he released me. I pulled at the twine, wincing as it dug into my shredded wrists.

The man knocked on the door. It opened and the caliph stepped in, this time in a sapphire turban and matching robe. He clapped his hands in one loud burst, and the guard behind me began to untie my bindings. He was rough, not caring how it chafed my skin, or that my blood oozed around the twine.

"I see you're ready for the next wish," the caliph said. He strode over to me and gripped my chin. I tried to turn my head but he held firm. "I'll be quick. This time, I'm not asking you for gold or riches. I need something no one else can give me. My wife Janna wishes for a special kind of flower, one my gardeners have not been able to produce. She has painted the blossom for you to see. Oh, you didn't realize my wives would know of your existence? All of Baghdad knows, my jinni. And they clamor for more." He reached into his sleeve and pulled out a sheet of paper with a rose blossom painted across it. The rose was pale pink, with white chevrons sprouting from the yellow center. "See it? This is what she wants. Exactly this. I wish for you to make me a garden of roses such as these."

He wanted roses. He was keeping me as his personal slave, keeping me apart from my own wife and daughter, to build himself a garden.

"Bastard," I managed, before the wish flew out of my throat and I fell into the darkness.

I was still Melchior, waking to someone shaking my shoulder. Because he hadn't brought a lamp, I couldn't see who had come to wake me. It wasn't the physician to check if I'd revived, and it wasn't a guard to see that my wrists were securely bound.

"Don't move," a young man whispered in my ear. He had a different dialect, from the north. "I have taken a great risk to come to you. I have an offer to make."

"What is it?" I asked. If he was here just to get a wish from the caliph's personal jinni, I was going to kill him. With my knees if I had to.

"I will set you free if you grant me a wish." When I said nothing, he added, "Please. I beg you. My parents are dying. There's a drought, and my family is starving. If my father dies, my entire tribe will suffer. I need you to save them."

I grunted. I wasn't going to save this young man's human family. Humans had caught me, imprisoned me for months, kept me from my own family, and forced me to live with both a physical and an emotional pain that were reawakened every day. I had been granting the caliph enough gold for everyone in the caliphate. Why would any of his subjects be starving? I had done enough for them.

But this young man was going to let me go. He didn't need to know I had only enough energy now for one wish. One wish that would take me home.

"I will do this," I lied. I was gruff, but the young man didn't seem to care.

"Thank you," he said. "My tribe, the al-Rahman of Zab, thank you a thousand times over. And we will pray for your soul."

After months serving the caliph, I wasn't sure I had a soul left to pray for.

The man pulled out a knife and sliced my bonds. Then he did the foolish thing I was counting on: he stepped back and bowed in thanks.

I didn't wait. I wished myself home.

The crystal turned cold, and I set it down on my lap. Melchior had gotten free. He had tricked the man who released him. Even though I was relieved for him, I felt a pang of guilt, as if I were responsible for what he had done. The human had clearly risked something to sneak in and free a jinni, and he got nothing in return. His parents might have died. His whole tribe, from Zab— I gasped.

Al-Rahman. Zab. That was Zayele's tribe. But who would have been here before the time of the treaty? Who would have known how to sneak into the palace's prisons? Who would have dared to free the caliph's most treasured jinni?

My blood turned cold, and I knew. It had to have been Hashim. He was from Zayele's tribe. He had been here in the dark days before the treaty. And he had been invited, years later, by someone in the Corps to serve as the first, and last, human ambassador to the Cavern.

The jinni he'd set free had repaid him, but it must have been too late.

Suddenly the sound of laughter came to me from the other side of the wall, through the cutout. Another person laughed in response, although his tone was lower.

Slowly, I moved to the hole and peeked in, then felt a rush flood my body when I saw who was on the other side. Quickly, I whispered, *"Shahtabi."* I couldn't let them see me.

Kamal and another young man had entered the garden. The other man was wearing a green robe, like the ones I'd seen the palace scholars wearing. He was tall but thin, and moved quickly to a bench, where he flopped down.

Kamal's room backed onto mine. It had to have been planned. The harem's private gardens must back onto those of the caliph and his sons. I looked more closely at the wall and noticed a faint arched line, where it looked as if someone had filled in an opening. There had been a door here once, and the cutout was all that was left open between our spaces. Would they break it open once we were married?

"I don't want to imagine it, Ahmed," Kamal said. He stood

with his arms crossed, glowering. "I mean, what would he do, really?"

Ahmed leaned forward, resting his elbows on his knees. His voice was bright and full of laughter. "First, the House of Wisdom would be turned into a martial arts hall, and all the books would be used as targets."

Kamal groaned, but he was smiling. "It's awful, but that's not even a joke. Ibrahim *would* do that."

"You know what else your brother would do as the caliph?" The other boy grinned. "He'd get rid of the black-market wine. Oh, and he'd make it mandatory that everyone go for a 'light run' first thing after morning prayers. Followed by two hours of sword practice."

The stone was pressing into my cheeks while I strained against it, watching them. I'd never seen young human men joking before. It wasn't that different from how jinni men were, except one of these men had given me a necklace. And I was supposed to marry him. And he was human.

"The women would have to run too," Kamal added. "And they wouldn't be allowed to cover their hair."

"Or their chests," Ahmed said, laughing. Kamal looked at Ahmed, who added, "Well, maybe not that."

"No, that's what *you'd* do." Kamal walked around the fountain, dragging his fingers in the water. "Ibrahim would want her, you know."

"Who? Your wife?"

"She's not my wife," he hissed.

Ahmed's eyebrows rose, and he leaned backward, away from Kamal.

"Not yet anyway," Kamal said.

"I was just trying to—"

"I know. For a moment, I did forget about what happened to my father." He flicked the water off his fingertips and sat down beside his friend.

"So what do you think of her?" Ahmed asked.

Kamal shrugged. "I don't know yet. But it doesn't matter what I think, does it?"

"You must feel something, or you wouldn't be afraid of Ibrahim taking her."

Kamal rubbed at his face. "I don't want him to take her, but I don't know why. I mean, it never bothered me before when he married other girls. But it doesn't matter, because right now I'm too busy. Hashim wants me to do something—no, don't ask—and my father is out of commission. Ibrahim is coming back, and there's a girl here who—" He shook his head. "Never mind. Let's go. I have to get out of here."

Ahmed nodded. "To the stables, then?"

"To the stables," Kamal said. He stood and ushered Ahmed out of the garden. Before he left, he looked back at the fountain, then up at the cutout in the wall. He stared at it, then sighed before turning back to his room.

He hadn't seen me. I was sure of that.

♦ 32 ♦

ZAYELE

THEY THRUST ME into a stone cell and slammed the iron door shut. Everything in the room was covered in ash, as if this were where the world had burned to dust. The place was lit by a single lamp outside the door's tiny window, and a weak light spread across the floor. Hot tears rolled down my cheeks and splattered my tattered dress. I wiped them away.

I was more angry and broken than when my father had handed me over to Hashim. And this time, it was my own fault. I sniffed, determined not to cry anymore, but then I thought of Yashar. I was going to die here, and he would never know what happened to me. He was waiting to hear if I'd found a place for him in the palace, and I hadn't even tried. All I'd managed to do was get myself mixed up in the war. Yashar was stuck at home without anyone. But at least he was at home. Rahela wasn't. Najwa wasn't.

My chest shuddered, and I pushed myself backward until the wall stopped me. Then I curled up and tucked my chin, holding back the sobs that were building up.

Dust floated in the broken beams of light, rising up. I watched it, to calm my nerves. If I could only transfer back, like a jinni, I could change things. I would marry the prince, even though the thought still made me sick. I'd give Najwa everything back. She deserved her friends, while I did not.

I was lost in the dust and light when someone rattled the door and pushed it open. I scrambled upright as Faisal rushed in, followed by Atish and Shirin. He stopped in front of me, with worry spreading across his face.

"Zayele," he said. I nodded. He sighed, put his hands together as if in prayer, and shook them. "I knew your mother."

"Know," I corrected, but the slight tremor in his lips said otherwise. "What are you getting at?"

"Come with me. I'm going to take you out of here. I need to speak with you. With all three of you," he said.

Faisal had spoken with the Captain of the Shaitan before he came to my cell, and whatever they'd discussed must have been interesting, because I was out of there only a few minutes later. A few of the guards raised their eyebrows when they saw me escorted out, but Faisal ignored them and ushered us out of the small prison, across the jinni city, and to the school. I was flanked on each side by Atish and Shirin.

In his office, Faisal took a chunk of frankincense off a shelf and put it on a thin sheet of metal set above burning char-coal. A sliver of white smoke rose and curled in the air. Faisal squinted through the smoke, looking into my eyes.

I didn't want him to look at me like that, and I fidgeted.

It was as if he could see inside me. Was he using a sort of jinni magic to read my mind?

"What do you want to tell me? Do you know how to get me home?" I asked.

He took one of my hands, turning it over so that my thumb was at the top. That was the place Najwa had her mark, I guessed, but on my hand there was only a bit of worn-off henna.

"What are you doing?" I asked. I meant to sound stronger, but he had unnerved me, and my voice came out cracking, unable to hold itself together. Even though they'd taken me out of the stone prison room, I was still on edge.

"There can be no other explanation." He dropped my hand and ushered me to one of the floor cushions. I sat between Atish and Shirin and watched him go to his desk and bring out a shard of green crystal the length of my arm. "I never thought I'd see you again." Then he sat across from me and laid the crystal on his lap. "Why don't you tell me how you got here. And where you've put Najwa."

The incense was growing thick, and the smell made me woozy. I fanned it away and said, as nicely as I could, "She came to me when I was in the barge—"

He cursed under his breath, and I paused until he motioned me to go on.

"Anyway, I didn't want to be there, and suddenly there was a jinni. I thought it was a gift."

"Did you wish on her?" His words became fire in the air, and I backed away, almost falling off my cushion.

"Yes," I squeaked. "But she was a jinni, and I needed to get out of there. I didn't know—"

"What did you wish?" Faisal had grown red-faced, glaring at the crystal.

"That she take my place and send me home." His eyes were so hot I could feel them heating up the room. "I didn't want to marry the prince," I said lamely.

"I don't think Najwa wanted to, either," Shirin said.

Faisal looked grim. "No matter your reasons, you had absolutely no right to make a wish on your sister."

The room was silent. I shook my head and stared at the flame beneath the incense, trying not to look at the others. I was afraid of what I might see in their faces. "You said Najwa is my sister," I said as softly as I could. I waited for him to correct himself, but he only stared, tight-lipped.

"Najwa is your twin." I opened my mouth to protest and he held up a hand, silencing me. His face was changing—the skin was turning dark blue across his cheekbones. "Your mother and I—"

"You haven't met my mother," I said. "Have you?" I couldn't imagine my mother consorting with a jinni, but so much had happened since I left home that I didn't know what to believe anymore.

He rubbed at his wrist and frowned, as if he'd expected something to be there. "The woman you think is your mother is, indeed, not your mother."

"Yes, she is." I'd been with her my whole life! And I didn't have a twin. Rahela had known me when I was a baby. She would have said something about that.

"I think it's time you looked at this," he said, holding up the crystal. "I meant to show Najwa first, but she isn't here. You will have to be the first, come what may." He pressed his hand over his heart and looked at the floor.

"You've just said I have a jinni for a sister and my mother is some other woman, and you want me to—look at a crystal?"

Two tears ran down his cheeks, leaving shining streaks as they fell. He nodded and held out the crystal. "Take it, Zayele. It's one of my memories, and it's about your mother."

I held back, staring at the green shard, realizing now it wasn't entirely solid. The crystal was clear, and something greenish swirled inside, as the frankincense was doing in the room.

"What is it?" I whispered.

"It's a memory," Shirin whispered, her voice full of awe.

"We look at these to learn about our history," Atish added. He moved closer, sitting only an inch away from me. "It won't hurt you."

"Watch and listen to what it has to say," Faisal said. His voice reminded me of my mother's. It was soothing, lilting, and made me ache for home.

33

NAJWA

BY THAT EVENING, I still hadn't had a chance to read the book I'd taken from the library, so I waited until Rahela was asleep, then went back into my garden. I couldn't bear to pick up the Memory Crystal, so I carried only the book with me, then stood in the middle of the courtyard, waiting for the moon to rise. So far, I had seen the sun, felt rain on my fingers, and found out what peacocks did when startled, but I hadn't seen a moonrise.

In the Cavern, one of the bridges over the canal was made of alabaster bricks. It had been there for centuries, but the bricks were older than that. They had been used for something else, something no one remembered. Each brick had a tiny moon carved into a bottom corner. Some of the bricks had full moons, some had crescents, and some had half-moons. When they built the bridge, they paid attention to that and put them in order, even though we didn't have the moon. When I was much younger, I never stepped on the bricks with the full moons, because they were darker than the others.

Now I would see the real moon hanging in the sky, and I didn't even know which phase to expect.

A sliver peeked above the stone wall, slippery and silent. Then I heard footsteps on the other side of the wall, in Kamal's garden.

Whoever was on the other side thumped a hollow object and began plucking at the strings of an instrument. It had to be Kamal, with his oud. He tested the strings, then began playing. The music was delicate and haunting, like night. I sat on my bench, set the book aside, and twisted a feather on my lap while I listened.

He played faster now, and a tingling feeling spread down my arms. I was sitting in a human palace, listening to a prince play music beneath the moon. There was nothing real about my situation.

The song ended, and he began playing another. The notes clashed, and he sighed. He started the song three more times, then stopped. He had been silent for a while when he called out tentatively, "Zayele, is that you?"

I cleared my throat. "Yes?"

He must have heard me, even though I was sure my voice hadn't been louder than a mouse's, because in the next second, his face appeared in the cutout in the wall. His eyes swept over me and I checked to make sure my veil was in place. He held up the oud to the hole in the wall.

"They told me your room was that one, but I wasn't sure if I believed them. Anyway, did you hear?"

"Yes. It was beautiful."

He shrugged. "It wasn't as good as it should be. I've been

playing for a year now and I sound like I just started. But that's not the point." He bowed his head.

I stood up and went to the wall. "Then why do you play?"

"When I'm playing, I have to pay attention. I can't think of anything else or I'll make a mistake. So it takes my mind off things."

"Do you play in front of other people?" I asked. It wouldn't matter how much I paid attention; playing for others would make me too nervous. I'd mess everything up.

He laughed, shaking his head. "I can't imagine what they'd say if I held a concert, out in public. No. It's just for me." The moon lifted off the wall and hung in the air. "And for those who listen in," he said, grinning at me.

My face was burning. "I'm sorry. I was out here waiting for the moon—"

"Waiting for the moon?"

"Ye-e-s," I said, drawing out the word while I thought of an excuse. "I hadn't seen it in Baghdad yet."

"Is this something you do often?"

"Yes," I lied. "And we always had music while we looked at it."

"Right. And I suppose you all sang 'My Mother's Garden'?"

How did he know that song? It was one every schoolchild in the Cavern knew. It was the type of song that tiptoed into your soul and danced on it while you slept—lilting, romantic, and a little sad. "That song," I whispered, "I haven't heard it in a very long time."

He looked surprised. "I think I can play it." He picked up the oud. "Want me to?"

I wasn't sure I did. What if it wasn't the same? What if it *was?* "You don't have to."

"No, it's fine. Just don't laugh when I mess up." He went to the bench, sat down, and bent over the oud.

The song was the same. I shivered, feeling the same ache in my heart that it had always given me. He was humming the tune, keeping his lips pressed together. They were thoughtful lips, full of the tune but not willing yet to let the words out.

When the music slowed, he glanced at me. The music and moonlight had left me open, and something dove into me and squeezed my heart.

"Sing," he whispered.

I would never have agreed to it before, but something in me wanted to hear the words, so I sang, clutching my fingers around the cutout's frame:

"He left me at the well,
saying his soul was dry.
I grew, I breathed,
I danced, I cried.
The sun hid behind the moon.
The water turned blue.
He came home with pockets of silk
but his soul was dry.
I took him to my mother's garden,
gave him hope to drink."

I sang the last line three times, and was done. The oud lay still on his lap, and I stared at the carvings on its body. They swirled, like the carvings along the palace walls. I could feel his eyes on me.

"That was beautiful."

I shook my head. "Is it the same as you sing it?"

"Yes, but we say 'love' instead of 'hope.'" He tapped the strings, and they shook, making a rich sound. Then he stood up and spun on his heels. "I think I better go now. See you in the morning?"

I nodded automatically, and he bowed and retreated to his room. I sat back down on the bench while the rhythm of the song pulsed inside me.

Gave him love to drink.

The words echoed in my mind till long after I had climbed into my bed.

+ 34 +

ZAYELE

"I DON'T REMEMBER when I met your mother. She—Mariam—was always there," Faisal said. "We were a Dyad—a bonded pair, united to multiply our power. She was the Shaitan, and I was the magus. They had paired us up even before we took our first transport test. Then, when that day came, we were all supposed to find a plant and return with a part of it. But something happened to Mariam that first trip, and she kept returning. After a while, she admitted she had fallen in love with a human. She swore me to secrecy, and of course I agreed." He smiled, wistful. "When she told her father about the human, he banished her to the surface. I visited her whenever I got the chance, and this is what I want you to see. Look into the shard. Remember, you will be in my memory, so you will be watching as though you were me."

I was pulled into the crystal. Faisal's voice lulled me until all I could hear was a woman humming.

I listened, listened, listened. And then I blinked and I *was* Faisal.

+ + +

A woman leaned back against a bolster with an infant in her arms. She had tumbling black hair, a straight nose, and wide green eyes. Mariam. I was sitting in front of her, also holding an infant. My hands were larger, callused, and tattooed with an owl eye between my thumb and forefinger.

We were in a tent, and she was cooing to the babe in her arms. The infant in my arms was tightly wrapped in a blanket and was asleep. She had pomegranate cheeks and long lashes, just like her mother.

"I wish he would at least look at them," Mariam said. She was talking about her father, who had scorned her daughters before they were even born.

I shook my head. "You need to wait. At least until the caliph dies and his son takes his place."

Mariam bounced her baby, who had started to twist and pull against the blanket. "They'll be grown by then."

"Perhaps. But it is better for them to grow here, don't you think? No one will know what they are."

She nodded, then started to sing to the fussing baby.

"*The sun hid behind the moon,*" she sang. "*The water turned blue.*" She continued, and I stared in awe and love. She was the most beautiful woman I had ever seen, and even though she loved a human, I still loved her. I hadn't expected that when I'd arrived, but it was a pleasant surprise. More surprising still was that the moment I held her daughters in my arms, they felt like extensions of me. I was not their father, of course, but was something more than an uncle.

Mariam kept singing until Najwa was asleep and I grew drowsy, cuddling the child she had named Zayele.

Then the mist returned.

When I opened my eyes, they were wet, and so were the wrinkled ones looking into mine.

"You were so tiny," Faisal said. "And after everything, I couldn't give up this memory. I had to keep it for myself."

"That was me," I said. "And Najwa . . ."

Shirin sniffed. "You should have warned us," she said, wiping at her cheeks.

I was holding back tears, biting my lip as hard as I could bear. "What happened to her?"

"I have kept only a few memories from Mariam herself," Faisal said. He held out another crystal, but this one was heavier, and blue as the sky. "Look into it, but be warned it does not end well. These were the last memories I was able to get from her."

"Why doesn't it end well?"

"What you have heard, about the night your village was attacked, has never been the truth."

"You mean Hashim didn't save me?"

Faisal spat on the ground. "Hashim didn't save you. I saved you. Look into the crystal, and watch."

I took the crystal. It was heavy and cold. "Is everyone watching, or just me?"

"I will," Atish said. He reached over and placed his hand on mine. "You shouldn't do this alone."

"Atish, I can understand why you want to accompany her, but I don't think it's a good idea," Faisal said.

Atish nodded and looked down at his lap, but he didn't let go of my hand. "We'll be here when you're done, Zayele."

A moment later, I was twirling around in an orange grove, breathing in the scent of young blossoms. My skirts were a full circle, swirling with me, catching on the weeds between the trees. I ran along a row of trees, reaching out as I passed to brush the blossoms. A trail of loose petals followed me, dropping like flakes of snow.

I ran like this until a man came around the last tree in the row and stopped in his tracks. I halted, breathing heavily. Then I turned away and tried to run, but he called out to me.

"Wait!" he shouted. "Don't run."

I looked over my shoulder.

"I know what you are," he said. "But I won't hurt you. I won't even touch you." He reached out to one of the trees and picked a handful of orange blossoms. With a tentative step forward, he held them up to me.

The image blurred, then was clear again. I was with the man somewhere else, but this time I knew his name. Evindar. I leaned in his arms, watching the village men make a fire. My dress rounded out in front, revealing my pregnant belly. Evindar whispered in my ear and smiled, then pulled me into the darkness of a tent.

Again, the image shifted, but now everything was rushed. I was wrapping a child in a blanket when a woman came in with worry lines etched into the corners of her mouth. A little girl, Rahela, had followed her into the tent, and she pushed her back outside.

"You don't have to go," Rahela's mother said to me.

"I *do* have to," I said. I laid Zayele on the floor along a wall and went to a pile of blankets. Najwa was there, wiggling free. She began to whimper, and I lifted her up to my breast. The whimpering stopped. "Hashim is coming tonight. Last time, he *saw* me. If he touches me, then—"

"Just go away for a little while. Till he's gone back to Baghdad. I'll watch the babes."

"I won't leave them. No."

"Then let me go talk to my sister. I won't tell her what you are. Just that Hashim has made . . . advances."

I nodded, and Rahela's mother disappeared out the door.

Alone now, I looked at my daughters. One was nestled in my arms, nursing, and the other lay on the floor, asleep. How could I leave them behind?

Just then, Evindar rushed in, flushed and sweating. "He's here. Now."

I felt faint. "But—"

He picked up a bag and handed it to me. "Go, Mariam. Take the girls, and go."

"Evindar," I said with a croak. I had frozen in place, staring at the man behind Evindar.

Hashim stood there, holding the flap open. He held a sword in the air and knocked Evindar to the ground with the blunt side of it. His eyes were bright and glaring, and when he looked from me to the baby in my arms, he growled.

Evindar struggled to his feet, but Hashim slashed at him with his sword and he fell again, clutching at his side.

I screamed and backed up against the wall. Najwa slipped

off my breast and was crying now, clutching at the strands of hair that fell across my face.

"I came back to check on you, Mariam," Hashim snarled. "I thought we had agreed you would not bring these abominations into the world."

"No," I said, standing up straight. "We did not agree."

"Then I will have them," he said, holding out his hand.

"I'm going home. You won't have to see us ever again." I looked at Evindar, who lay on his side. Blood flowed freely onto the rug, faster than the weaving could soak it up. My nostrils flared, and I swallowed. "Please."

He shook his head. "I can't let that happen. Allah would not approve of me letting you live."

"Who are you to say what Allah approves of? You aren't his messenger." I turned toward Zayele, asleep on the floor. "You will not have us."

The air between us glimmered. A lick of fire flashed across the room, and Faisal stood with his blade drawn, poised above Hashim's head. He looked tired, but seeing him flooded me with hope.

"Faisal!" I cried. He nodded and swung at Hashim, who had taken a step back.

"Another jinni? Oh, your dyad. Of course. How good of you to come," he said, bowing his head a fraction of an inch. Then he swept his sword at Faisal, who blocked it with his long dagger. The blades struck, each sliding down to the hilt of the other, and the men pressed hard until they were face to face. "I've been waiting for this moment ever since I was betrayed by Mariam's father. I was the one who freed him, you know."

"Let. Mariam. Go," Faisal grunted.

"I will. But she must give me both of her children first."

Evindar had pushed himself up off the ground and crawled toward Hashim, who was busy with Faisal. I stood still, afraid that if I moved, Hashim would notice. Evindar lunged with the last of his strength and stabbed a small knife into Hashim's foot.

Hashim wailed in pain and backed out of the tent. In a second, he was gone, and Faisal and I stared at each other in shock before I ran to Evindar and lifted him onto my lap, cradling Najwa.

He was already gone when I got to him, and my heart splintered. He couldn't be gone. Not like this.

"No! Evindar, I just can't. I can't!" I wailed.

"We need to go," Faisal said, watching the door. "He is going to come back." I ignored him. "Your husband is dead, Mariam, but your daughters are alive. You need to save them."

I looked up at him. "Take them, Faisal." I handed Najwa to him and pointed to Zayele, asleep on the floor.

"I will take you all," he said. He pulled me off Evindar and was reaching for Zayele when Hashim burst through the door with two other men behind him. Their swords glinted like lion teeth in the air.

"There's the jinni!" Hashim shouted, pointing at Faisal. "He murdered Evindar!" Faisal's eyes widened in surprise, but he jumped to his feet and braced himself. Hashim rushed at him, sword held straight at Faisal's heart. But he was holding Najwa.

"No!" I pushed myself into the space between the men,

right before Hashim's sword came forward. The blade sank in before I felt anything. And then pain. Indescribable pain. And silence.

Hashim pulled his blade free, and I fell. I couldn't hold myself up, and I knew. I knew what was happening. I looked over to Faisal. I tried to speak, but I couldn't. As a Shaitan, I'd been trained for this, but I'd forgotten. I'd forgotten all of it the moment I saw Evindar.

Hashim made another rush at Faisal, and he disappeared with Najwa.

This time, the blade sliced into a whirlwind. Hashim shouted out in anger, but I didn't care. I only had eyes for the baby left behind. I was leaving her too now. Zayele slept on, but my blood reached out to her.

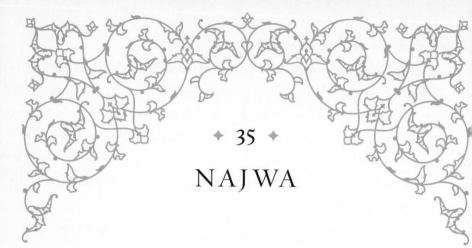

✦ 35 ✦

NAJWA

RAHELA AND I stood against the wall just inside the harem doors, waiting for our escort to the welcoming feast. We had received notification earlier that they were holding a celebration to welcome me to the palace, in lieu of the wedding feast. I was wearing my sleeves pulled down low because I had accidentally scrubbed off some of the henna that morning and a corner of the eye was peeking out. We hadn't had time to reapply the henna. Rahela had started chewing on her bottom lip when we noticed my mark, and she hadn't stopped. I could see it through her sheer veil.

There was a knock on the door, and I opened it. Prince Kamal was on the other side. He bowed his head, keeping his eyes on me. His lashes were thick and shadowed his green irises. He had a cream-colored turban wrapped around his head, and with the folds perfectly placed and hiding his hair, he looked so different from the boy he'd been last night, playing his oud. This was the prince, one of the most important men in the caliphate. This was not a boy.

"If you don't mind, I'd like to be your escort," he said.

"Of course." I tried to keep my face as neutral as possible, and took Rahela's hand, pulling her out of the harem. I needed her there to remind me of who I was trying to be. I forgot whenever Kamal was nearby. "I didn't realize we would be eating with you today."

Kamal looked sideways at me. "It won't be the average meal. We're celebrating a small victory in battle. And Hashim wanted you there." Facing forward now, he took us down the corridor, away from the Lamp and the House of Wisdom.

We walked past a line of windows covered in wooden screens. The latticework was a merging of eight-pointed stars and triangles in a pattern that seemed designed by nature, like the salt crystals growing in one of the Cavern's tunnels. Each window was identical to the others, so I was able to study the details while we walked. I was trying to distract myself, because soon I'd be sitting with Kamal, Hashim, and some men who had had a victory—probably against my own people.

Kamal didn't speak again until we reached the end of the corridor and a set of opened doors. String music and drumming streamed out.

"Don't be alarmed by the soldiers. They've had a rough ride today, and several are wounded. They won't speak to us, so don't worry about having to interact with them," he said, standing still and straight. "They may, however, stare at you."

"Why?" I asked.

"Most of us have never seen a princess like you before."

His words held something in them, something I couldn't decipher. Rahela snickered quietly behind me, and I worried there was something wrong with my appearance. Had I not dressed appropriately? No, she wouldn't have let that happen. Why had she snickered? When he didn't elaborate, I pulled my sleeves down to my knuckles and followed him across the threshold.

Walking into the dining hall was like stepping into very cold water. All my senses were on alert, because most of the people in the room turned to watch us.

Along two walls with opened windows, on dozens of bolsters, sat the entire court and a good many soldiers. Most of them were men, lounging on their sides and laughing with their neighbors, but there were a few women I recognized from the harem, more by the colors of their veils than by their faces.

In the center of the room, propped up on a shallow platform, sat five men with a few ouds and a set of drums. They were the source of the music I'd heard down the corridor. They were playing just loud enough to be heard over the many voices echoing in the room.

Kamal turned and urged us to follow him past the people on the floor, past the platform with musicians, to a set of bolsters at the opposite end of the hall. As we made our way across, I felt too many eyes on me. I looked up to avoid them and found myself beneath a sky of glass lanterns. They hung from the mosaic ceiling like spiders from their webs. Glowing, smoking spiders.

"Beautiful, isn't it?" Rahela whispered, and I realized she had probably never seen anything like it either.

When I looked back down, I saw Hashim and a man dressed in leather armor watching me. Kamal sat beside the vizier and gestured for me to sit on the other side of him. Grateful that I wouldn't have to sit beside Hashim, I sank as gracefully as I could manage onto a red silk cushion.

Before me stretched the hall and its many hanging lights, its low tables filled with strangers, and the musicians. Many had stopped talking, and they turned to face where Kamal and I sat.

Hashim leaned forward and looked at me. "Princess Zayele," he said, just loud enough for our table to hear, "I hope you do not mind that we've paired your welcome celebration with that of our army." He didn't sound like I was allowed to mind.

"Thank you for inviting me," I replied. Then I looked to Kamal. He was only a few inches away, sitting cross-legged and leaning back against the wall.

Hashim looked out across the hall, and lifted a cup. "Friends, we're here to celebrate the future union of Prince Kamal and this princess from Zab." Applause and whistles filled the air. "But we are also here to share some much-needed good news. Our esteemed *qaa'ed*," he said, pointing at the man to his left, "has returned with a message from Prince Ibrahim. The army has broken through a jinni guard, killing several of their precious Shaitan. Prince Ibrahim's soldiers are holding their position at the mouth of the Basra Tunnel."

This time, the applause and whistles were so loud the windows shook in their frames. But I couldn't clap. I had frozen, gripping the edge of my cushion, when he said some Shaitan had been killed. It was like I'd been hit in the stomach. *Atish.* I hadn't thought of him all day. I'd been too preoccupied with pretending to be Zayele, and with trying to find something in the book I'd taken. I'd been too distracted by Kamal. By a human.

"Are you all right?" Kamal whispered. He placed his hand beside mine till they were almost touching.

"Yes," I whispered. "I'm just nervous. There are so many people here."

"Let the food be served," Hashim called out. His voice was like sandpaper on my nerves. "We shall celebrate, because tomorrow, our great prince will return. And he may have some jinn with him."

The musicians picked up their instruments and erased the silence with the rhythm of a flowing river, of birds in the air, and of the wind blowing across a garden. This was music we'd never be able to make in the Cavern.

A side door opened, and a stream of servants entered carrying huge platters of rice, lentils, and roasted lamb. My stomach, an iron knot of nerves, practically cried in relief when one of the lamb platters was set down before me.

I had never eaten this sort of food. It was richer and tastier than grilled blindfish, and it got better with each bite. Even the rice, fragrant and golden, was like something from another world.

For a few minutes, our table was quiet while we ate. Rahela was moaning in pleasure each time she took a bite, and I laughed at her.

"I can't help it," she whispered. "This is better than anything I've ever had. What did they add to the rice?"

Kamal leaned across me, and I pressed myself against the

wall. "Saffron. It comes from near your region. Are you certain you've never had any?"

Rahela shook her head. "Never, Prince Kamal. It must be secretly guarded by—"

"It is protected," Hashim cut in, raising his embroidered cuff. "It requires a special guard just to transport it. The guard skirts around Zab, which is why you do not hear of it. I, too, had not known of it before arriving in Baghdad."

"Why is it not shared?" I asked.

"It's too precious for sharing. Just as jinn do not wish to share their jewels, the cultivators of saffron do not share except with a handful of houses." Hashim rubbed his thumb in a circle over the molding on his cup. I noticed with a start that it was emblazoned with a lion in the same style as the mark of the Shaitan.

It was as if he knew, somehow, what I was. I looked down to check on my mark, but it was still just a speck of blue, and I'd kept it hidden so far.

"Well, it's delicious. I'm sorry you haven't had it before," Kamal said. Then he turned to Hashim. "Is it true Ibrahim will arrive tomorrow?"

"I believe so," Hashim replied. Then, without looking at the man beside him, he asked, "*Qaa'ed,* can you tell us more?"

"Yes, Vizier. Prince Ibrahim fought valiantly. Everyone in the regiment did, although we suffered more casualties than we would have liked. The Shaitan were not brought down until the end."

"But they were brought down," Hashim said.

"Yes. And when we have the new weapon, it will happen at the start of battle."

Kamal set down a leg of lamb and wiped his hand on a cloth. "*Qaa'ed,* how is it you've heard of this? It is still a secret."

The *qaa'ed* smiled faintly. "I heard from Prince Ibrahim himself, last night. He said that you, Prince Kamal, were developing something. He told the entire regiment, saying it might be our last battle in which we had the lower ground."

"Hashim," Kamal hissed, "we weren't going to tell Ibrahim yet. It isn't ready."

"But it is, my boy. Or it will be by the time Ibrahim arrives."

Curiosity was burning through me, and I could not resist all the years of training I'd had in gathering information. I put my fingertips on the sleeve of Kamal's tunic.

"Prince Kamal, what weapon is this you speak of?" I asked. I forced my face to appear calm. "Will it help us defeat the jinn?"

He turned and looked shaken, as if he'd forgotten I was there. "I can't speak of it. I shouldn't. But yes, it will help. My greatest hope is that it will end the fighting, once and for all." He looked down at his plate, but didn't touch the food.

"Princess Zayele," Hashim added, "it will not only end the fighting. It will end the possibility of any future wars as well. Your prince here has developed the perfect weapon."

The perfect weapon. Kamal had been working on a *weapon* when I first saw him, not just playing around with rocks. And although his father had dismissed his idea, Hashim clearly thought it was a good one.

The jinn's only hope was that the image of the selenite

orb I had obtained would help them counter the effects of the weapon. The problem was, the effects were still a mystery. And I was stuck in the palace, playing princess.

I didn't know what to say in response, so I filled my cup with water and drank it. It did nothing to wash away the fear building up in my throat.

Hashim and the *qaa'ed* began discussing something in hushed tones, and while I tried to listen in, Kamal leaned closer to me.

"Zayele, please don't look so upset. We've spent too much time and too many resources on the war with the jinn. So many, actually, that the caliphate is at risk of falling. This weapon will help us get into the Cavern, and if we can get to the jinn, we can force an end to the war. We'll prevent future deaths."

I twisted the napkin on my lap, watching the oils from the lamb soak into the fibers. "What will this weapon do to the jinn?"

"Let's not talk about this now," he said. He took my hand in his, but kept it below the table. "Can we meet again in the garden tonight?"

I tried to concentrate on Atish, on Faisal, on this mysterious weapon, but all I could think of was his hand on mine. On my mark. My skin tingled like he was pouring all the power of a wish into the bones of my hand.

"I promise we won't talk about the war," he said. His voice was deeper than it'd been a moment ago. Was he feeling something too? "Just music, and maybe you can recite for me some of the poems from your homeland."

"Yes," I said, watching as a man scurried into the hall. His face was dark and strained, and he was heading to our table.

Kamal dropped my hand and stood up. "Is it my father?" he asked the man.

"Yes. Prince Kamal, you need to come. He is failing."

The music stopped, and the entire hall took a breath. Kamal stood up and ran past the platform of musicians, past the stunned faces of the court, and out the door.

✦ 36 ✦

ZAYELE

I PUSHED THE crystal off my lap, and it hit the ground with a thud. I pinched my arm, just to make sure I was back in Faisal's office and not in some memory, and then shut my eyes.

"Zayele?" Faisal asked. His voice was gentle, and in it I could feel the pain he'd felt when he left Mariam on the ground, dying. When he left me behind.

I looked up. "You didn't come back for me."

He shook his head. "I did, but they were expecting me. The women never took their eyes off you, not even at night. I was going to wait until they calmed down, but then word came of the attack in the House of Wisdom." He clenched his fist. "My brother died in retaliation for what the humans thought I had done. They slit his throat while he was translating Aristotle. After that night, everything changed. We retreated, snuffed the flames of the Lamps, and waited."

He reached for the crystal and I picked it up and handed it to him, passing my mother's last memories into his hand. A few minutes ago, I had known who I was. Now everything had changed. I wasn't *me*.

"While you were in the memory, I told Shirin and Atish what it contained." Faisal turned the crystal shard around in his hands, studying the blue swirls of smoke inside. "I went back for her, after they had buried her."

"You dug her up?" Shirin asked, incredulous.

"No. I returned to make this." He gestured at the crystal.

He hung his head. My mind raced, remembering my parents' deaths. No one should see that. I wrapped my arms around myself. I wanted to stop the image of my parents' blood staining the rugs in the tent.

"Why didn't they tell me I wasn't their child?" I whispered. "My mother. She was my aunt. And my father." Then it dawned on me. "He must have known I was half-jinni, and he sent me to Baghdad." I stood up too fast and had to hold myself against the wall until my body stopped shaking. I was going to vomit. "I can't stay here."

Shirin jumped up. "But you have to help Najwa. She's your—she's your *sister*. Right, Atish?"

Atish had a strange look on his face, as if he'd tasted something he wasn't sure about. "Yeah," he said tonelessly.

"Faisal," I said, "if Hashim hated my mother so much—"

"He didn't hate her. He was in love with her. Everyone was."

"But he—"

"He was angry she was a jinni, and even angrier when he found out who her father was."

"Who was her father?" I asked.

"An official. It's not . . . I will explain that later."

"Fine. But if Hashim was so upset, why did he come back to Zab? Why did he choose me for the prince?"

Faisal froze. "*Hashim* chose you for Prince Kamal?"

"He wanted someone from our tribe. He came out himself, the first time since—" The words caught in my throat. "Since that night. He picked me."

Faisal stood up quickly. "Atish, go get Captain Rashid." Atish nodded, but moved slowly, like he was half-asleep. "Don't just stand there. Hurry. Hashim has something planned. Something he needs jinni blood for."

After Atish left, I stared at the frankincense curling in the air. Everything was different now. I wasn't who I'd always thought I was. I was half-jinni. I had a twin sister. And I had sent her straight to the man who killed our parents.

Atish returned with another jinni, who wore a leather vest studded with obsidian points. His face was carved in a permanent scowl, and his belt held two daggers. He was broader than Atish and had a long scar that stretched over his left shoulder, over the lion mark of the Shaitan. He was holding a map clamped on a piece of slate, and I noticed that his knuckles were white with scars. From training or from fighting humans?

Faisal spoke first. "This is Rashid, Captain of the Shaitan. This is Mariam's daughter Zayele." Rashid was exactly what I'd always thought the Shaitan would look like. Fierce, determined, and bloodthirsty. He grunted a hello, then pointed at the map, showing it to Faisal and Atish.

"She'll have to go in. They are there, there, and there."
Faisal nodded each time Rashid's finger jabbed the map.

"Who will go in?" I asked. "Me?"

Atish nodded solemnly. "You're the only one who can.
You're part human—"

"I'm more human than jinni," I said bitterly.

Faisal placed a hand on my shoulder. "Zayele, the truth is,
we need you. You can get past the jinni wards, just as Najwa
did." His voice had gone dry, and he swallowed.

"I know the wards keep jinn out of the palace. But what *are*
they, exactly?"

Atish sounded very tired. "Hashim put them in place after
he murdered Mariam. We don't know what's on them, but
we've gotten intelligence that tells us where they are."

"They're just paper," Rashid said, "but they're powerful.
They have a holy mark on them that blocks anything made by
the devil."

"So, jinn *were* made by the devil?" I had heard rumors about
jinn, but I'd never paid attention to that part. I had only cared
about the wishes.

Shirin took my hand. "It's not as bad as it sounds. We aren't
demons, you know."

"The first jinni was a human," Atish said.

"Iblis?" I asked, throwing out the one name I knew.

Shirin nodded. "He found an angel lying broken on the
ground. Fearing it was a test, he helped the angel, and then—"

"The angel offered to give Iblis a gift," Faisal cut in. "But
Iblis declared he did not need any gift from an angel. The

angel laughed and said he could not resist such a gift—and he gave Iblis what we now call 'wishpower.'"

"And it changed everything," Atish said.

"How?"

Faisal smiled grimly. "Human bodies can't handle the power needed to grant wishes, so it changed his body. He twisted into a being of fire and sand. A jinni. Then the angel showed Iblis where he could take his tribe, to start a new race. They followed a tunnel that led here. It wasn't until later that Iblis discovered he'd helped the first of the fallen angels, and by then it was too late."

"Iblis built the Cavern out of wishes?" I asked.

Faisal and Rashid eyed each other. "We don't have time for this," Rashid said. "Jinn are as evil, and as good, as humans. That's all you need to know. We need to take down the wards."

Faisal nodded. "Zayele, whatever the wards are, they stop us from going anywhere near them. I don't know how Najwa got there the first time, but she did. And I believe you can too. It must be your human blood."

"But I don't know her. Not like my brother—" I stopped. Yashar wasn't my little brother. Not anymore. Something cold went through me as I thought of how nothing had been real. "I just took a wish from her. That was it." I looked again at the map that showed the palace. She was in there, somewhere.

"It was a Fire Wish," Atish said. He sounded grave. "When a jinni demands a wish from another jinni, that's what it's called. It's the worst thing you can do to a jinni."

Shirin cut in. "But she didn't know she was a jinni. She didn't know about Fire Wishes."

Atish looked at Rashid. "So what happens?"

"Zayele," Rashid said, looking me squarely in the face, "when you made the wish, you took away Najwa's choice, and most of her power."

"She can make everything right again," Faisal said, stepping between us. "She can go back, and she can expose Hashim. She can save her sister."

"How?" I asked. "No one listens to me. I was nothing but a bride."

"Let's go outside," Faisal said. He motioned for me to follow, and I did. We left the school building, and for the first time, I looked at the Cavern's ceiling, at the jutting crystals and the ever-changing homes, and knew my mother, Mariam, had lived here. Part of me was from this place.

Faisal walked toward the wall that stretched along the lake. He held his arms behind his back while he strolled. He was at ease, the opposite of everything inside me. Finally, he stopped.

The lamplighter walked past, high on his stilts, and Faisal gestured toward him.

"Zayele, if that man can wish a light out of empty air, you can find a way to show the world the truth."

I leaned forward and pressed my hands into the coarse stone of the wall. "I can't."

"But you must. You're able to slip through the wards, so it *has* to be you. You've got to save her. You're the only one who can undo what you did, as much as that is possible." He frowned. "A Fire Wish is the most devastating thing one jinni can do to another. A long time ago, when we first came to the Cavern and we were learning about our power, there were a few who commanded wishes from the others. They stole their free will, just as you took Najwa's. Whenever she tries to defy your wish, and I'm sure she will, it will be excruciating."

Again, I'd done too much. "I didn't know."

"We know you didn't mean to harm Najwa, but what is disturbing is that you so freely took from someone else."

There wasn't anything to say to this. What could I do now?

Atish, Shirin, and Rashid came toward us. Rashid was holding his map rolled up like a scroll, and he held it toward me.

"We need to focus on what's most important. We need to get in there and take down the wards. You're the only one who can do that, other than Najwa," Rashid said. "You are as much a jinni, and a human, as Najwa." He had gotten even more intense, and I found myself backing away from him.

"We can help you," Shirin said, placing her hands on my shoulders and gripping me firmly. "After you take down the wards, we'll come."

"And after that? Where do I go?" I couldn't go home. I couldn't face my father—my adoptive father. And the Cavern, even with its jewels dripping from the ceiling, was too alien. I didn't belong anywhere.

"It's up to you," Faisal said. I watched the flames on the lake while I thought about it. They twirled around each other, no two alike.

"All right. Show me how," I said.

◆ 37 ◆

NAJWA

I SLICED THE lemon in half and squeezed the juice over the back of my hand, right over where the henna hid my mark. It stung, and I gasped. I had been rubbing at the skin for several minutes, and it was already raw. The lemon juice was like a poison, seeping into the cracks of my skin, but it was nothing like the burning in my lungs when I tried to resist Zayele's wish. That had been *real* pain.

"I told you it would hurt," Rahela said. She was sitting across from me, rolling another lemon in circles on the tabletop, pressing it beneath her flattened hand to make it juicier. "Is it fading?"

It was, but only because I was scrubbing off a few layers of skin. "Yes," I said, wincing. The Eyes of Iblis mark was almost whole, although it was a little redder than it should have been. "I don't know if it will work, but what else can we do?"

We had decided not to hide it anymore as soon as we'd gotten back to the room. If the caliph was dying, we didn't have much time before they'd decide to marry me to the prince, and I needed someone to find Zayele before that happened.

The lemon's acidity worked better than my scrubbing alone, but I couldn't sit still. It stung, and I flapped my hand in the air, trying to get it to stop.

"Maybe you should do something else for a while. Like read that book you found," Rahela suggested. "I'm afraid you'll rub all the skin off."

I picked up the book with my non-stinging hand. "Good idea," I said. "I'll try a distraction." I tucked it under my arm and went out onto the patio. Kamal had said he'd meet me here tonight, but I wasn't sure he would come now that his father's condition had gotten worse.

The sky above was the bruised color of a dying day. On the other side of the palace, the sun was setting, but there was still enough light to read by. I sat on the bench, took a look at the cutout between my garden and Kamal's, and opened the book I'd taken from the House of Wisdom.

It wasn't long before I discovered it was a journal. The charts and lists of names had thrown me before, but now I realized it was organized by date, and each entry began with some activity that had happened that day. I flipped through the pages and came to an entry I had to read twice.

I've told Faisal, but he doesn't believe me. He trusts Hashim too much, and I think it's because he helped Melchior bring Hashim into the Cavern. He never wants to admit he could have been wrong. I have sent a letter to his supervisor, but have not yet heard back.

Faisal and Hashim were friends? He had *never* told me this. Everything he'd ever said about the man concerned his betrayal and his hand in the start of the war. He'd never said he knew him.

I flipped to the end, but it was blank. The last entry was halfway through the book, and hurried. It was darker now, and I could barely make out the words:

> Someone attacked a human village, and they're blaming Faisal. Hashim was there and is due back tonight with more details, but I cannot bring myself to believe a word he says. He wants more than the ambassadorship. He wants the caliphate, the Cavern, and a jinni to command.
> Delia says I should return before Hashim arrives, but someone must stay and defend Faisal. Someone must keep the flame going. I will continue in my translation work until I hear from Faisal himself.

Faisal had told me once that his brother had been working in the House of Wisdom. He had been a translator, but had died during the first wave of attacks the humans made on the jinn. This had to be his journal.

I swiped my thumb over the last of his words. They'd been written just before the war began. If he had left the palace like Delia suggested, he wouldn't have been killed.

Saddened, I laid the journal on my lap and glanced up at the moon. It seemed I could only get my hands on tragic stories, whether recorded with pen or with crystal.

"Hello," someone said, and I jumped. The voice had come

from the wall, and I saw Kamal's face peering through. "You looked very absorbed. I almost didn't want to disturb you."

"It's very engrossing," I said, sighing.

"What is it?"

Quickly, I snapped the book shut and held it behind me. "It's just an old journal."

He raised his eyebrows and smiled. "Interesting. May I see it?"

I didn't know what to do. I couldn't exactly run back into my room. That would raise too many suspicions. But what if he saw who had written this, and it made him even more curious? "I found it lying around," I said, holding it up. His eyes darted to the leather.

"Is that a jinni journal?"

"Uh—yes," I said. "That's why it's so fascinating."

He smiled. "May I see it?"

Maybe if he read it, he'd discover the truth about Hashim. Maybe he wouldn't suspect me at all. I hesitated, then went to the wall and passed the book through the cutout. "Of course."

Just before our fingers touched, a tiny spark flashed between them. I dropped the book, and he caught it. "Are you all right?" he asked.

"Yes. Are you?"

He was still holding the book between our gardens, like it was the one solid link between us. He kept it there, until I asked, "How is your father?"

The book slid through the cutout into his garden, and he frowned. He looked away, then up at the darkening sky. "His heartbeat is weak, and the physician is having trouble getting any water in him." He pressed against the wall. "I'm afraid, Zayele. If he dies, I won't be the only one affected."

"You mean, because he is the caliph?"

"Yes. My brother wants to be caliph next, and I don't think Baghdad is ready for him."

"Why?" I asked. I had heard his brother was a soldier, the kind who thought of nothing but battles and sieges, but I hadn't heard anyone say he wasn't a good man.

"It's the war. He and Hashim had been pushing my father to take the next step—"

"The next step?" Finally, I would learn something.

He shook his head. "I don't want to talk about it," he said, sighing. "The truth is, Ibrahim wants this war to continue. He wants to keep fighting the jinn. He wants to bury them."

"And—and you don't?"

He hesitated. "Well, I don't want them to destroy us, but I would like it all to end. I barely remember it, but before the war, they were here, in the House of Wisdom. *Jinn.* We learned so much, working side by side. Even Hashim has to admit that." He brushed his fingers over the journal, as if pining for a lost friend. "If Ibrahim becomes caliph, he will never stop fighting them."

His words chilled me. And not even the moon could soothe my own fears. If Ibrahim became caliph, and if he discovered me, it'd be all over. He'd have a jinni to command, and I would have to attack my own people if he so wished.

"Then your father mustn't die," I said.

"Yes. I will pray throughout the night for him. Will you?" he asked.

"Yes."

"And if you are not offended at the idea," he said, still looking at the journal, "would you also pray that the jinn will once
again be our friends, rather than our enemies?" Then he looked
up, right into my eyes.

My insides were in a flurry, like a spinning cloud. Right
there, on the other side of a very thick wall, was a human who
did not want the war. I felt an urge to run my fingers across
his sharp cheekbones, feeling the face of someone who thought
differently. Someone who, like me, was not put off by differences in race or power. The moment I realized I wanted this,
I pulled my hand back abruptly, scraping it against the edge of
the cutout. Now both of my hands were raw and reddened.

"I'm not offended by peace," I said.

"Of course not," he said, smiling. "War brings only death
and lies. But when people work together, they can do great
things. When the jinn were here, mathematics was advancing
faster than ever before. And, strangely, so was our music."

I looked behind him, trying to climb out of his gaze. "Have
you brought your oud?"

"It's always here," he said. He went to his room and came
back with the oud, then sat down. He set the instrument on his
lap and laid his hand on the strings before turning to face me.
"I wish you could sit by me."

Then he ran his fingers over the strings and played. I was
instantly saddened. The music pulled out all the parts of me
that had been afraid, or lost, or hidden, and my heart grew
heavy in my chest. He bent his head further over the strings
and furrowed his brow while the pain I'd felt slipped down

my cheeks in two streams of tears. My life had been stolen by Zayele, and I had no way yet to get home. I'd disobeyed Faisal by seeking her out. I had caused all this trouble. I thought of the man who'd written the book, the man who had stayed back to keep the flame going. He'd given his life for nothing. No one had listened to his warnings, and the Lamps had been snuffed out anyway. I thought of the caliph, and how his death might give greater power to a bloodthirsty prince. I thought of how Kamal had been meant for Zayele, of how he only knew me by her name—if I told him who I was, he would never look at me again like he had tonight. Even if he claimed he wanted friend-ship with jinn, it did not mean he wanted me.

He slowed his fingers and looked up, then stopped. "You're crying," he said.

I wiped away my tears, but he had already seen. Quickly, I pointed at one of the stars that shone so brightly beneath the moon. "Does that star have a name?"

He smiled, and it was like he'd been transformed. The darkness within him dissolved, and he put down the oud and came over to the wall beside me.

"That's not a star," he said, grinning. "It's the planet Zuhra. She's one of the brightest."

"A planet." I had heard of there being other worlds, but I'd never looked at one before. I'd never known it was possible. "What sort of planet is Zuhra?"

He blinked. "I don't know. It's bright, and it's close, but that's all I know. The reddish one below it, just to the right? That's Merrikh. The Greeks associated them with their gods. Zuhra was the goddess of love, and Merrikh was the god of war. War always chases love," he said. His voice faded, like he'd just thought of something.

This was what I had always yearned for—the stories behind the real things in the world—and for the first time, I was with a person who knew about these things. "And that one? It's not as bright." I was pointing at a star halfway between the planets, but off to the left.

"That one *is* a star. It's al-Dabaran, part of a constellation."

"They look so much alike," I said. "How can you tell it's not a planet? And how are they different?"

"That's what I've always wanted to know," he said, looking up at the stars and planets. The crescent hung over them, leading them in a line up the sky, surrounded by a wash of dimmer stars. "What are stars, exactly? I've been discussing it with the astronomers in the House of Wisdom, but no one knows. They just want to know exactly when each star will rise so they can set the clocks by them. I understand the importance of that, but I want to know more. Unfortunately," he added, "Hashim doesn't think I should spend much time on it. He has me working on other things."

"I know how you feel."

"You do?" He turned back to me, surprised.

"I have an interest that people have always told me to ignore," I admitted.

"I suppose it doesn't have to do with the stars," he said slyly, "or you'd have known their names."

I laughed. "No, not stars, but stories. My entire life, I've been fascinated with stories. To everyone else, it seemed like the story itself was enough. But I wanted to know *why* someone told the story in the first place. Had something happened? Or were they only wishing for something to happen? But when I started asking this, everyone told me there wasn't any need to know. Stories just were, and that was that."

"Like the stars," he breathed. He wasn't looking at the stars anymore, though. He was only a few inches away, with his eyes locked on mine. "Everyone says, 'They're just stars, leave it at that, and go calculate their locations.' But I want to know why they're there, and what they're made of. I want to know why they move like they do, not just that they move."

"Yes," I said. I was smiling now. No one had understood this before. Not Atish. He had been amongst those telling me to forget it, that I should focus on the problems in the world instead of the world's discarded dreams. But Kamal, this prince from Baghdad, this human boy, understood. "Just like the stars."

In that moment, with his eyes reflecting the light from above us, I knew. I was in love with him. And like the pain of Zayele's wish, it was suffocating. I could never be loved by him. Not truly. Not if he knew who I was.

"Zayele," he murmured. He started to reach for my hands, but I tore myself away from the wall, stumbled over the bench, and slipped past my billowing curtain, where I could cry without him watching.

✦ 38 ✦

ZAYELE

"THE FIRST THING you need to know about wishes is that there are two sorts," Faisal said. We were in a large garden behind the school, with walls of granite blocks studded with rubies. There weren't any actual plants in the garden, only sculptures covered in white moss. Shirin and Atish had come with me, while Rashid had gone off to ready the Shaitan. "The first kind is the easiest to make, but it requires that you memorize certain words. The second kind is more difficult, because you have to translate words into an image in your mind, and push it out into the world to make it so."

"I have no idea what that means," I said, biting at my thumbnail. "So there are magical words that make some things happen, but you can also make things happen just by thinking them?"

"More or less. Today, we will work on teaching you a primary wish. I believe that once we get you to the palace, this is the one you'll need the most," Faisal said. He gestured for Shirin to come closer. "Shirin, will you show Zayele the wish?"

Shirin grinned, waved at me to back up, and whispered, *"Shahtabi."* She vanished.

I gasped. "Where did she go?"

Atish chuckled beside me. "She's right there, unless she moves fast."

"I didn't go anywhere," Shirin's voice said. It came from the empty air right in front of me.

"We can *do* that?" I asked.

Faisal cleared his throat. "It's a simple wish, if you can remember the word, pronounce it correctly, and maintain your focus," he said. "The only weakness of this wish is that once it has been made, you cannot make the wish again until the wishpower has been replenished. For some, it can take an hour or more. Shirin, you can reappear now."

"Rashatab," she said. The air wavered, and then she was there, winking at me.

"That's amazing! I think Najwa used that spell, but it must have worn off. Otherwise—"

"That's another important difference between the two kinds of spells. The first kind is temporary. It's weaker, but it requires less energy to use. The second kind is permanent, but it can leave you exhausted."

My mouth went dry. "Like the wish I made with Najwa?"

Faisal's face was grim. "A Fire Wish is permanent until the one who made the wish recalls it."

"Then why don't I just undo the wish right now?"

Faisal set his hand on my shoulder and squeezed. "Zayele, for you to recall the Fire Wish, you must be in the same place as Najwa. To do it here would be too much of a risk. You could both end up trapped somewhere between the palace and the Cavern."

"In the earth?" I asked. He nodded, then took his hand away. "So if you're going to teach me just this invisibility wish, how am I going to get there?"

Shirin squealed. "The Lamps! You're going to light them, aren't you?"

"I will try. But first, we must teach her how to go unseen in the palace. If she cannot do that, there is no reason to send her there." He motioned for me to stand apart from the others. "Now, before you try making this wish, you must clear your mind. It will be difficult at first, but you can do it. You've made a wish before, even though you didn't realize all it entailed." He paused, then asked, "Is your mind clear?"

"I don't know. Maybe," I said.

"Crystals above, Zayele! Just calm your mind, and think of only one thing."

I had been keeping my eyes closed, but opened one to look at him. "What?"

"*Shahtabi.* Invisibility. Say it now."

I shut my eye again and tried to think of nothing. Of emptiness. "*Shah-tabi,*" I said. Nothing felt different, and when I looked around, I could see they were all staring at me. Shirin fidgeted. "Did it work?"

"You didn't say it right." Atish looked amused.

I sighed. "It feels strange in my mouth. Is it a jinni word?"

"You don't want to know what language it is," Shirin said. "It's creepy. But it works."

"Let me try again." This time, I tried to think of something see-through, like an icicle. *"Shahtabi."*

"Whoa!" Atish said. "You're not quite invisible."

I looked down. I could see through my hands. "What do you mean?"

"You are clear, but visible. Like water," Faisal said. He tugged on his beard. "I've seen worse on the first day of lessons, so do not be discouraged. A few more times, and I think you'll have it."

I didn't want this to take forever. *"Shahtabi."*

"You got it!" Shirin said, and she jumped and clapped. "That was quick. Just like Najwa. She always got this stuff before anyone else did."

"Now you've got to undo it," Faisal said. The creases in his forehead had gotten smoother. Could he actually be *proud* of me? Or relieved? My father—my uncle—had never once looked at me with pride. He was always watching for something. Now, I realized, he must have been watching for some sign of my mother's blood in me. No wonder he'd hovered over me.

"Rashatab." I had remembered the counter-wish.

"You're all there," Atish said. He had started to smile, but it faded fast. "Like Najwa."

"So now I can do this. Is there anything else I should know?"

"Yes, but we don't have time. This will have to do," Faisal said. "Now I must take you to the Eyes of Iblis Hall."

"You're going to show us the Lamp?" Shirin asked. She rushed to Faisal's side and wrapped her arm around his. "Right? Please let us help."

Atish stepped up to them. "Yes, Faisal. We should help Najwa."

Faisal looked like he was about to disappoint them, but then he sighed. "Very well. I may have use for you after all. Zayele," he said, "you learn quickly, and I thank the crystals for that."

We left the garden, four abreast. For the first time since I'd left Yashar, I felt like I belonged.

✦ 39 ✦

NAJWA

I HAD JUST finished the dawn prayer and had crawled back into bed, yawning, when the door to our room slid open and four men in uniform rushed in. They were closely followed by one of the older ladies of the harem, who was screaming at them. I sat up and blinked away the sleep.

"You cannot come in here!" the woman shouted.

One of the men gestured for her to move aside. The other guard pointed at me. "Get up!" he said. "You're coming with us to see the vizier."

Had someone figured out who I was? I looked over at Rahela's bed, but it was empty. She was already at the chest of clothes, throwing a dress over her undergarments.

"Now!" the guard barked.

Rahela slipped between the guards and me, spreading her arms wide. "There is no need to talk to the princess Zayele like this," she said. Her voice was shaky, but firm. "She will get dressed and come with you. But first, you must let her dress. And she cannot do this with you *watching* her!"

One of the guards blushed and muttered something to the others. I took that moment to regain my composure and stand up, keeping the blanket pressed against me.

"Would you please step out into my patio? I will only be a moment," I said. The words came out much calmer than I felt.

The guard who convinced the woman to move frowned at me before taking the others behind the curtained partition. The moment they were out of sight, Rahela thrust a gown into my arms, while the older woman pulled my hair into a braid.

"What is happening?" I whispered. Rahela shrugged, waited for the woman to finish, and then pulled the gown over my shoulders. It was red, the color of confidence. Then she wrapped a matching hijab over my hair, pinning it at the nape of my neck.

"Whatever happens, remember that you are a *princess*." She said this loud enough that the guards could hear, and then she whispered, "If you run, make sure they can't follow."

"This is taking too long," the first guard said, then pulled aside the curtain and stepped back into my room. When he saw I was dressed, he had one of the others open the door to the harem garden. "Come. The vizier is waiting."

My body flooded with panic. I couldn't run because there was nowhere to go. Zayele's wish had grounded me in Baghdad, like a tree at the mercy of the gardener's shears. I left my room surrounded by the guards, grateful that so many of the harem women had returned to their beds after prayer. Only the peafowl watched me. They blinked in protest and backed away from the men.

The woman pressed a cloth into my hand, then stepped

away from the door. By the time I looked down to see what it was, she was gone. It was an embroidered piece of silk, probably to wipe my eyes with after the vizier was done with me.

What did she think I had done to warrant this?

A moment later, we were in the corridor. To keep up with the guards, I had to take steps so wide that they pulled at the hem of my gown. Rahela had snuck along, and when one of the guards began to protest her presence, she gave him a look that would have cut quartz.

They took us to the Court of Honor, which was filled with the men of the court. They parted, showing Hashim on the caliph's throne, tapping his knee with his long fingers. The men of the court turned to face us, and with their backs against the marble pillars, they looked like they had grown straight out of the tiled floor, permanent features with etched lines of worry and doubt.

Hashim cleared his throat. "Princess Zayele, I apologize for not giving you much time following our morning prayers, but I'd come to a realization that could not wait." He smiled, and every hair on my arms rose in fear. "After I found you in Zab, amongst my cousins, I was pleased to see that you carried with you so many of our fine traditions, as well as our faith." He gestured to the men, as if inviting them closer. "As you can see, this young woman is a sight to behold. She not only exudes beauty, but she has power. Power that most of you have never dreamed of."

Someone ran into the court, from around the side of the raised platform that held the throne. It was Kamal, and he ran up the two steps to stand beside the vizier. His face was red with anger, and he bent over to whisper something in his ear.

Instead of responding to the prince, Hashim chuckled. "The prince has found fault with me sitting on his father's throne." The audience responded with nervous laughter. "I apologize, Prince Kamal. I was merely acting in your father's stead since you were not present. But I am glad you've appeared, for what I have to say affects you more than most of us here."

"And what is that?" Kamal said, standing up straight. He saw me, and confusion spread across his face. "Why have you brought Zayele here?"

Rahela gripped my hand. She was choosing to stand by me, to support me, even though she knew what I was. She could have told everyone there, right then, but instead she held my hand.

Hashim stood up from the throne, took a step, and pointed straight at me.

"Because, young prince, she is a threat."

"What?" Kamal stepped off the platform, shaking his head. "She is harmless."

"No, Kamal, she is a jinni."

The crowd gasped, but I couldn't make a sound. I stood still, my blood hard and cold as glass. It was all I could do to look Kamal in the eyes.

"That isn't possible," he said, growling. He turned to face Hashim. "You chose her, Hashim; you should know. She's as human as any of us."

"Yes, I chose her," Hashim said smoothly, "but I learned in prayer today that she is not the young Zayele." I managed to swallow, but my throat was a geode, sharp and hollow. How did he know? How could he have learned this in prayer? "This woman is a jinni, and she murdered the princess Zayele on her route to Baghdad. We discovered Zayele's swollen body in a canal outside the city. She had been dead for days."

Rahela started to slump, and I pulled her up to me. "I didn't kill her!" I said. My voice echoed throughout the chamber.

"'Her'?" Kamal asked. He was facing me, and he looked weighed down by his turban. "You're not Zayele?"

"Of course she's not!" Hashim hissed, and his declaration was repeated by the men of the court, who began to move away from me. The circle around me grew wider, but it still felt like a noose. Kamal was staring at me, waiting for me to counter Hashim's attack.

But I couldn't speak. I couldn't say anything to defend myself. Rahela and I were surrounded by men, none of whom would understand what had happened in the barge between Zayele and me. I'd had time to live with it, and even I didn't fully understand her binding wish.

As the men backed away, a space opened up between them, and Rahela's suggestion earlier sprang into my mind.

I was tearing up as I looked at Kamal and whispered, *"Shahtabi."*

Then I sprinted for the opening, flew past the men, and left Rahela to stand alone in the midst of them.

❖ 40 ❖

ZAYELE

AFTER A SHORT period in which I was told to rest so that my wishpower would build up again, and after a longer argument with the lady at the entrance with the bronze-tipped hair, Faisal got us into the Eyes of Iblis building. We stood in a circle around the Lamp, which was the size of a plump cat.

The woman named Delia joined us, her face a mix of solemnity and excitement. She bowed her head at Faisal and said, "It's ready. You just need to make the wish."

"Thank you, Delia," Faisal said. He set both of his hands on the Lamp, then let go quickly, as if it had burned him. He rubbed his hands together. "This has only been done once before, years ago."

"By the woman who made the Lamps," added Delia.

"Where is she now?" I asked, edging closer.

"She died," Atish said. "Apparently, the wish was too much for her, and it took all of her to make it."

Faisal reached up to the torches burning in their brass sconces on the wall, a wish on his lips. The flames leaped off the torches and landed in his hands. The room dimmed and suddenly felt heavier, and I looked over my shoulder. The place was filling with jinn. Their faces were dark in shadow, but their owl-eye marks glowed, blue and blazing. They were like a ring of power, encircling us and the Lamp. Every one of them was focused on Faisal.

"Faisal," I said, uneasy, "are you sure this is the only way?"

He blew on his fingers. "Yes." How did he know for sure? "Just give me a moment to clear my mind." Faisal closed his eyes, took in a deep breath, and let it out slowly. Then he brought his fingertips to his lips and said in a broad, commanding tone, "*Narush.*"

A chorus of jinn repeated, "*Narush,*" until the wish echoed and filled the chamber.

There was nothing but silence. Then a lick of flame leaped from the tips of Faisal's outstretched fingers. It dove into the Lamp's spout and disappeared. A second later, a golden flame sprouted from the Lamp, long as my hand. It flickered and danced, twisting in the silent air.

Faisal dropped his hands and exhaled, exhausted. Delia, who had been standing pensively behind him, sighed and crossed her arms.

"I don't want to ever watch you do something as risky as that again," she said to Faisal, whose face had spread into a smile, exposing a dimple in both of his cheeks.

"I will let you do it next time, my dear," he said. Then he clapped his hands and turned to face the jinn who had joined him in the wish. "Thank you all for helping. I couldn't have done that by myself." They bowed to him, and several departed.

Then Faisal turned back to the Lamp and said, "It's time, Zayele. Come here. No, not that close. Do you remember the invisibility wish? Good." He held out his hand to Delia. "Do you have the map?" She gave him a rolled-up sheet of paper, which he unrolled and held out for us all to see. "Do you see these markings? These are where we believe the wards to be positioned." He pointed to three red marks.

"You don't *know*?" I asked.

Faisal snorted and shook the map in front of my face. "Trust our spy network, Zayele. We have been working on this for longer than you've been able to walk. All the mathematical calculations point to this being the best layout for the wards. I say I *believe* they are there because I have *faith* in those who made this map. I would bet my life on their calculations, and I am willing to bet yours as well."

I snapped my mouth shut and took the map. "How will the Lamp get me there?" I asked.

"I can't believe I get to watch this," Shirin whispered to Atish. Despite everything, she looked more excited than afraid.

Faisal patted her shoulder. "Yes, Shirin, you may watch because your skills may be needed in the palace, unfortunately." He gestured for me to come to the Lamp. "Each ward is set inside a copper cylinder and hung beside the frame of a door or window. Once you destroy them, drop them into the flame of the Palace Lamp."

"How do I destroy the wards?" I asked.

He smiled again and lifted his brow at Delia. "Do you have it?"

"Yes." She went to a table against a wall, picked up a small box, and brought it to us. Then she opened it, revealing three glass vials stoppered with tiny corks. A clear liquid sloshed inside. "Open one and pour it on a ward. It will melt the ink. Once you've soaked them all, bring them to the Lamp and set them in the flame."

I took one of the vials and held it up to the light. "What is in this?"

"It's an acid," Delia said. She took the vial, placed it back in the box, and shut the lid. "Can you really do this?"

"I *believe* so," I said, eyeing Faisal. His mouth twitched, and he pulled me into an embrace.

"I am glad to have gotten a chance to meet Mariam's other daughter," he said into my ear. "Go, and watch for your sister."

I hadn't gotten used to the idea of having a sister yet, much less the idea that an entire race was depending on me to save it.

Atish came to me then, and held my elbow. "I will come as soon as I can. Be careful."

"All you have to do is touch the flame with your fingers and ask it to take you to the other Lamp," Faisal said, pulling me away from Atish. "When you arrive, you will be in the very heart of the palace. Make your *shahtabi* wish as soon as you arrive. With luck, no one will see you first."

I tucked the box under one arm and the rolled-up map under the other, and touched the flame. It tickled my fingertips, and then it *pulled* and I was sucked into the fire.

✦ 4I ✦

NAJWA

I RAN DOWN the corridor, jumping out of the way of anyone who happened to be there. No one saw me, but they could feel me brushing past, and some surprised shouts trailed behind me. I kept running until I came to a door I recognized. The room would be empty, because the man it belonged to was still in the Court of Honor.

I flung open the door, ran in, and shut it behind me.

The room gleamed. Light streamed in from a wall of windows and illuminated a series of bookshelves stuffed with books and scrolls. The tops of the bookshelves were heavy with large hunks of uncut rock, shattered geodes, and molded metals of various kinds, and spheres dangled from above. Six barrels lined the left wall, and in the center was the long, narrow table the selenite orb had sat upon.

This was the laboratory where I had seen Kamal playing his oud on that first day. The doorway to the garden with Janna's roses was at the back, in the wall of windows, but this time, it was closed.

The orb was missing from its cushion, but the rest of the table was covered in charts, and I raced to it, scanning the sheets of paper. The charts were spread open and weighted down by brass spheres. Half the charts were of the stars and planets, but the other half were the ones that caught my eye. They laid out, in clear detail, everything Kamal knew about the jinn, including the effects of moonstone powder.

This was the sort of chart the Eyes of Iblis Corps needed to see. I stood back so that I could see all of it at once. Then I pressed on my mark, sure that something here would alert the Corps to what the humans were planning to do.

I turned to the row of barrels and lifted the lids. Half of them were filled with an acrid black powder. The others held a luminescent white powder. I squeezed the drop of moonstone that hung from the silver pendant around my neck, and compared the sparkling powder and the stone. They had the same color, the same sheen.

Moonstone. He had jars and jars of powdered moonstone.

That was what the selenite sphere was for. It was hollowed out, leaving room for the powder. He was going to fill it with moonstone . . . and then what?

I looked at another chart that had a diagram of the sphere on it, titled "The Pomegranate." Scratched in thin ink was a description of how much black powder to mix with the moonstone for the "pomegranate" to explode.

I thought of how many soldiers the caliphate must have, and what it would be like if they each had an exploding sphere filled with moonstone powder. Our tunnel guards wouldn't stand a chance against them. Then, armed with enough powder to poison the entire Cavern, the caliph's army would force its way in.

I took image after image, until my body was weak from exhaustion. How was I going to tell the Corps what this meant? What if they couldn't read the faded scratching on the paper?

I thought, then grabbed a sheet of blank paper and one of the many quills. I dipped it in the bottle of ink and wrote, in my own alphabet, "The sphere is a type of weapon, and will be filled with moonstone powder. They will use it—"

The door flung open and slammed against the wall, but I was still invisible. Quickly, I pressed the owl-eye mark on my skin to send what I had written. I turned as three armored guards, with swords drawn, ran into the room.

Hashim followed, just two steps behind them. He scanned the room while I willed myself to be still. But it was the quill that betrayed me. It slipped off the table and fluttered to the floor.

"There," he said, pointing straight at me. "Surround her, and make sure she can't slip past you. In another minute, you will be able to see her again." While he said this, he unwound a braided rope and made his way over to where I stood, unable to move.

My skin was tingling, and I knew I was trapped. The *shahtabi* wish was fading, and soon they would capture me. I wasn't a match for three guards and a man who seemed to understand jinn better than I did.

I waited, unable to slip between the three guards, and watched a bit of moonstone dust float in a ray of light. By the time it slipped out of the sunbeam, the wish was gone, and the guards grabbed me by the wrists.

✦ 42 ✦

ZAYELE

I WAS A red cloud. My breath was pulled from my lungs and I doubled over, aching for air. But I *was* air. I was also a flame, soaring through the crystals, through the hundreds of layers of rock and dirt, flickering, flickering, and then I was there.

My body twisted back together, and I inhaled all the flame and air that I had been. I was whole now, but my fingers still burned. Confused, I looked down and saw they were in the flames coming out of the Lamp. I pulled them out, worried I hadn't gone anywhere at all.

But this wasn't the Cavern. I was alone, and this Lamp stood on a marble plinth inscribed in Arabic that twisted down into the marble floor. This was the twin. Faisal's Lamp had gotten me into the palace. I was whole. And people could see me.

I took in a long deep breath. *"Shahtabi."*

I had about two seconds before the wish would be tested, because a throng of guards came running into the hall from a corridor and turned down another. I had barely enough time to crouch down beside the Lamp. They stirred the air around me, and I had to resist the urge to reach out and trip them.

No one noticed the girl hunkered down by the plinth, so I opened the map to figure out where to go first. Three circles highlighted where the wards should be, and each was as far from the Lamp as the others.

One circle was near the front entrance to the palace. The corridor to my back would take me straight there, so I took in another deep breath and stood up. I tucked the map back under my arm and held the box with both hands. Then I strode down the blue-painted corridor, ready for the first ward.

A few minutes later, after several jumps to the side to avoid getting touched by the palace staff, I reached a wide, high-ceilinged entry ending in intricately carved wooden doors. The doors were guarded by six men dressed in the red-and-green colors of Zab. I stared, shocked to see men from my home, until I remembered that my father—my uncle—had sent men as part of my dowry. But now, knowing who my real parents were, I wasn't sure why he'd given up so many soldiers. Unless Hashim had something to do with it.

I pushed the thought aside and scanned the walls and doors for any sign of a copper cylinder. There, hanging on a hook beside one of the doors, was a small metallic cylinder. It was so close to the doorframe it would have been hidden if the door had been open. Skirting around the guards, I inched my way to the wall.

They weren't paying attention to the wall behind them. They were facing into the hall, as if they were trying to keep someone in. I pulled the cylindrical case off the hook.

This was one of the jinni wards. The cylinder was inscribed in calligraphy I could barely read, but I didn't bother. I flipped open the cap and pulled out a scrolled piece of paper. Something powerful must have been written on it, and I thought about not reading it. But I couldn't resist. I pulled it open and found the first and last letters of the Arabic alphabet written across the paper.

That was it? Just *alef* and *ya*? How could two insignificant letters prevent anyone, much less a jinni, from entering the palace?

I didn't have time to think about it. Carefully, I set the box on the floor and pulled out one of the vials of acid. Instead of pouring the acid over the scroll, and probably my hands, I slipped the paper into the vial and stopped it back up.

Then I closed the box, looked at the map, and took off past the guards. As I ran, I thought of how this palace would have been my home. I wouldn't have known about my parents, or my sister. I wouldn't have seen the Cavern, or hidden behind its waterfall. Or met Atish.

The second ward was outside the caliph's rooms. Or at least that was what the map said. I found a wide golden door in a hallway that was blindingly white, and tucked just above it was another ward. This time, I didn't bother to read it and just stuffed it into a vial of acid.

The last ward was inside the House of Wisdom, but the map didn't say where. I blew through the opened doors, skirted around a handful of men who were shouting at each other, and scanned the stacks and stacks of books. There must have been a book for every person in the caliphate!

There, in the very center of the room, on a pedestal and encased in a glass dome, was the last ward. It was larger than the other two, but I knew without any doubt that it was a jinni ward. There was a plaque beneath it declaring it so.

I suppressed a snort and looked over my shoulder. I didn't want the men to see the glass dome lifting in the air all by itself. They were still talking excitedly, shaking their heads at each other, so I took the chance and slipped the ward out from its protective case. After I tucked it into the acid vial, I tossed the cylinder onto the nearest rug, closed the box, and snuck past the men, grateful they were too busy to have noticed what I'd just taken.

Now I ran back to the Lamp. By the time I got there, I was breathing hard and my fingers were shaking. I slipped the sheets of paper out of the vials, carefully using the wrist of my gown to keep the acid from touching me, and dropped them into the flame.

The paper caught on fire and erupted in a ball of flame. I fell backward, landing hard on the ground, and climbed back up. While I waited for the flame to return to normal, the *shahtabi* wish fell away, leaving me exposed at the Lamp. Quickly, I dropped a stone Faisal had given me into the flame. The stone turned into smoke and slipped into the Lamp.

Then someone clapped a hand on my shoulder.

43

NAJWA

HASHIM WRAPPED THE rope around my wrists, then took my chin in his fingers.

"You've got the mark of Iblis," he said. His eyes were wide and wild, and in them I could see nothing but the end of me. His fingers pressed hard into my chin. "How did Sergewaz—your *uncle*—not know of this? When did this happen?"

"I thought you said I wasn't Zayele." I bit my tongue while I said it, and my mouth flooded with the taste of blood.

He sneered at me. "Of course you're Zayele. But they don't know that, now do they? All they care about is that you're a jinni. I wasn't sure how I was going to convince the prince—"

"But I'm not—"

"Oh, but your disappearing act settled it. Everyone knows you're a jinni now. And to keep you from making that wish again, I've brought this." He held up a ball of silk and stuffed it into my mouth before I could protest.

I screamed and tried to twist away, but he held me in place while he made sure I couldn't push the gag out. It hurt, and

I almost vomited into the cloth. He dropped his hand and shoved me into the guards. "Come," he growled to the guards, "we're taking her to my rooms."

They dragged me out of the laboratory and down the corridor, with one of the guards ahead of us clearing the way. I knew I should kick, or pull away, but it wouldn't have changed anything. I was powerless against them, and now I couldn't even make the simplest of wishes, so I fell limp in their arms. They had to carry me every step of the way.

After a single turn, Hashim threw open the door to a room, and I was carried inside and tossed onto the floor. I hit the ground, which was padded by layers of overlapping carpets, and stayed there. The wool pile dug into my cheek. I'd been discovered. It didn't matter that Hashim had his facts mixed up. He was right about the most important one.

I was a jinni. And I was trussed up like a sacrifice, lying in the middle of the vizier's rug.

Hashim said something to the men, and they left the room. Then he knelt beside my face. He was so close I could see the perspiration falling into his eyebrows. "Well, Zayele, it's time for you to pay for all the years you lived as a human."

My blood turned cold and slowed in my veins, as if it were afraid of offending the man before me, the man with all the power. Why did he still think I was Zayele? What was he going to do to me?

I tried to talk, but all the sounds I made came out as moans.

"Now that the entire palace knows a jinni is running free, they're expecting her to do something. Therefore, I leave you here. I must ensure they're not disappointed."

He stood up, hoisted me over his shoulder, and carried me to the back of the room. Something slid to the side, and I was tossed onto the floor inside a small, stone-walled room. I hit my head, so the last remaining light, from the main room, sparkled until the door slid shut and left me in utter darkness.

Behind the door, I heard Hashim's voice: "It won't be long now." I didn't know if he was talking to me or to himself. He sounded like he was rummaging through something, but then he stopped. "What are you doing here?" he asked someone.

"I'm looking for Zayele." It was Kamal! "Or whatever her name is."

"I haven't seen her," Hashim lied. "If you'll excuse me, I'll go search for her. Those invisibility spells don't last long, so I'm sure someone will see her soon."

A door closed, and then I heard the rummaging sound again. Hashim must have left to do whatever it was he had planned, which meant Kamal was looking for something in Hashim's room.

I scrambled to the door and kicked it as hard as I could. Silence. I kicked it again.

Lamplight poured in through a crack as Kamal slid open the door.

✦ 44 ✦

ZAYELE

A MAN WITH sour breath grabbed hold of me and turned me around.

"I caught you!" he growled. Then I was surrounded by a handful of guards, all wearing the colors of my tribe.

"Let go of me!" I shouted. "I'm Zayele! I'm from Zab too!"

"You're a jinni," one of the other men called back. "You're not one of us!"

How did they know?

Then, in a flash of light and a great curling of smoke, jinn poured out of the Lamp, brandishing swords and daggers. Atish, his friends Cyril and Dabar, Rashid, and ten other Shaitan leaped into the guards, giving them no chance to unsheathe their weapons. Atish pushed through and grabbed hold of my arm.

"Get back!" he shouted. He pushed me in the direction of the Lamp.

The Shaitan forced the guards against the wall, but the clashing of blades had drawn others to our location. The

Shaitan stood their ground against thirty or forty soldiers who jumped in, slashing at them when they made their strikes. The jinn turned invisible between attacks, and a few had time to send off flaming balls. There were some, though, who didn't bother with invisibility. Atish was amongst them, as smooth and lethal as a leopard.

He stood at the front. Cyril and Dabar held back the humans while Atish scanned the crowd, looking for his next target. Then, with a yell, he moved, stepping over the fallen soldiers.

Faisal and Shirin appeared just as a soldier managed to catch Cyril off guard. Shirin yelped when Cyril fell, and she started to run over to him, but Faisal held her back.

"We need to find Najwa," Faisal said.

"I need to help him," Shirin said, pointing at Cyril. He had pushed himself up off the floor, but blood was falling freely from his left arm.

"You'll get yourself killed," Faisal said. "Come." He pulled Shirin and me away from the fighting, and I turned just long enough to see Atish standing over Cyril, protecting him against the soldier. The fearlessness in his eyes terrified me.

We made ourselves invisible, slipped past the soldiers, and trotted down a corridor. Shirin grabbed my hand and squeezed.

"Where are you taking us?" Shirin asked Faisal.

"To the laboratory that Najwa discovered. She may be there," Faisal said.

We turned a corner and ran into a group of soldiers who were plowing their way toward the Lamp. Quickly, I leaped into them and wove between their swords and shields, careful not to touch anyone. I spun, ducked, and made it through, but they were followed by another group. This time, I was able to press myself against a potted tree.

When it was over, I had lost Faisal and Shirin. They must have stayed back at the corner. I waited, my heart pounding in my chest, but I never heard them. Finally, I crept out and slunk back to the corner, hoping to find them. When I had waited several minutes and they still hadn't called out for me, I decided I'd have to go for it myself. I didn't know where the laboratory was, but I had the map.

I was pressed against the wall, studying the map, when someone bumped into me. I gasped, then saw that it was a woman. She had been creeping along the wall too.

It took a second to recognize her. Rahela had changed. She had lost some of the all-knowing look she had carried. Now her eyes were as wide as a startled deer's.

"Najwa!" she shrieked, then reached up to my face, as if to make sure she was clutching the correct invisible jinni. "They're looking everywhere for you." She grabbed my wrist and pulled me along the corridor, away from the Lamp.

"Rahela, it's me," I said, rolling up the map. "Zayele." I undid the *shahtabi* wish.

She turned and looked, taking a step back. "Merciful Allah, Zayele! Is it really you? Why are you here? Why were you invisible?" I opened my mouth, but she held up a hand. "Never mind. Follow me."

She brought me to a door, pulled it open, and ushered me

inside. It was filled with shelves of crockery, and we had to push a gigantic clay pot aside in order to fit. She shut the door and turned on me, her face red as a poppy.

"Where have you been? I could slap you for what you did to me! To Najwa! Have you any idea what sort of trouble she's in now?"

"I'm sorry," I said, looking at my feet. "I'm sorry. I don't know what else to say but that. Just trust that I am trying as hard as I can to set everything right again."

She took my hands in hers, squeezing them. "Don't you dare leave me again, Zayele, or I will hunt you down."

"I'm sorry I left you. With a jinni."

She nudged the pot with her toe. "I was scared of her at first. But she's been trying to undo what you did, and it has nearly killed her. You have no idea what you did, Zayele," she said, shaking her head.

"Yes, I do," I whispered. I told her, as quickly as possible, where I had been and what I had discovered.

"Your mother isn't a jinni!" she exclaimed.

"Not Yadigar. My real mother, Mariam. The night Hashim said we were attacked by jinn—we weren't. *He* attacked. He killed my parents and *blamed it on a jinni.*" The scene reentered my mind, and I clutched my stomach. I had to push it away. I couldn't think of Mariam's blood pooling in the tent. Not now.

"No," she said flatly. "I can believe Najwa is your sister. I can even believe that you're half-jinni. But I cannot believe that Hashim lied about the attack."

"Rahela, you've got to believe me! Hashim knows I'm

half-jinni—he knew my real mother, Mariam. He wanted me here for a reason."

Her nostrils flared. This was the Rahela I knew. "We need to find her."

"You don't know where she is? What happened?"

"Hashim brought us to the Court of Honor and told everyone that Zayele had been murdered by a jinni, and that the jinni had replaced her. Najwa panicked and ran off, turning invisible along the way. The court surrounded me, and I had to push some old men aside to get away. I've been running around looking for her ever since."

I unrolled the map and pointed at a section nearby. "One of the jinn said Najwa might have gone to a laboratory. Have you looked there?"

"No."

I rolled up the map. "Let's go."

✦ 45 ✦

NAJWA

KAMAL KNELT DOWN before me. His turban was gone, and his hair fell over his eyes, leaving them in shadow. I couldn't see if he was angry or not, but he moved quickly to pull out the gag. "What is going on?" he asked. He pushed his hair off his face. "Give me a good reason why I should untie your wrists and let you go."

I swallowed back the saliva that had built up in my mouth. My jaw ached, as if I'd been trying to chew a rock. "Hashim was partly right," I said. I couldn't look him in the eye. "I'm not human. And I am a jinni. But I didn't kill Zayele, and I don't believe she is dead. If she was, I wouldn't still be here." He rocked back onto his heels, and I was afraid he'd leave me, still bound. "Please, I need to stop him! He is going to do something—I don't even know what, but it's not good. He is trying to make it look like I've done something horrible."

"Who are you?" he asked. His voice was low and cracked.

"My name is Najwa. I was only here because Zayele

caught me. She wished on me," I said, and suddenly the heat of oncoming tears crept up my cheeks. "She wished for me to take her place, because she didn't want to come to Baghdad."

"So this whole time, it was you and not Zayele?"

I nodded, and the tears began to fall. "I don't know where she is. Rahela has been so worried."

"Your friend *knew* you weren't Zayele? And she didn't *tell* us?"

"She couldn't have! It would have dishonored Zayele and the whole tribe. And so I had to pretend."

"Then why didn't Hashim let us know when he saw you? He has seen Zayele. He was the one who brought her here."

"Rahela says we could easily pass for each other. But I don't know. I only saw her for a moment. After she made her wish, she disappeared. I didn't kill her, Kamal."

He smoldered, like charcoal that had been cold but suddenly flashed back to life. "Why would Hashim claim such a thing? And why would he say you're a jinni if he didn't know what had happened?"

"I don't know," I said. "But please. Untie me. I promise I will not hurt you, or anyone."

He reached to his belt and unsheathed his dagger while I held my wrists out to let him slit the binding. As he put his dagger away, I rubbed my hands and then touched the necklace he'd given me. The moonstone was smooth and hard. "Thank you," I said.

His eyes were on the necklace. Was he regretting that he had made something for me? Or was he regretting all of it, every moment he'd wasted with me? After a long moment of silence, he took the stone gently from my fingers. "Perhaps you should take that off."

My heart was like a pomegranate, with each ruby seed spilling onto the floor. He regretted all of it. The necklace, the nights of music, and the words we had shared. Because I had lied, because I hadn't been Zayele, none of it mattered.

I reached behind my neck for the clasp, but my hands were shaking and I couldn't find it. "I can't get it undone," I said.

"Here." He reached up and wrapped his arms around my neck, then took the clasp from my fingers. His face was so close I could smell the soap he had washed with. "I don't want it to hurt you."

Then he looked at me, just inches away. I couldn't breathe, and it was like the moment we had shared the night before, beneath the stars. "It doesn't hurt," I whispered. "As long as I don't hold it for too long."

His fingers fell to the back of my neck, and my skin erupted in goose bumps. "In that case," he said, "keep it."

"But I'm—"

"I know. But you're still the same person I spoke with in the garden, aren't you? You didn't switch places with her this morning."

My heart beat a little faster. "It's still me," I said.

He smiled. It was like the sun rising after an endless night. "Then it doesn't matter what you are." He pulled me closer, and I was melting in his eyes. They were like jasper, green and brown, and they drew me in. He closed them, then placed his lips on mine. He was warm and tasted like cinnamon.

His kiss was like transporting to another world, and it

was just as frightening and exciting as my first trip to the palace had been. My entire body flushed, knowing that he didn't care I was a jinni. I didn't have to pretend I was a human, or a princess, anymore. He pulled away and a lopsided smile spread across his face.

"I forgot what you said your name is."

"Najwa," I breathed.

"Najwa," he said, then chuckled. "I never thought I'd learn the name of a woman *after* I kissed her."

"Since you have your hands on her," Hashim said behind him, "you should make a wish." We jumped to our feet, and Kamal whipped around. He held his arm out in front of me, pushing me behind him.

"Hashim! What is going on?"

Hashim frowned. "You should tell me, Prince Kamal. You know this woman is not human, and yet you're—"

"This isn't about her. What have you been planning, Hashim?"

"You mean, what have *we* been planning? You're as much a part of this as I am." Hashim's grin was oily. "If you wait a moment, you'll hear what we've been working on come to fruition."

"What did you *do?*" I shrieked, pushing my way past Kamal's arm.

"It's what you did, Zayele. You have been running around the palace, wreaking havoc. In a second or two—"

Boom!

The walls shook as an explosion rocked the palace. Plaster rained down in the room behind Hashim, where it hit a vase, which crashed to the floor amidst chunks of broken ceiling and glass.

"You've just blown apart the barracks."

"What?" Kamal ran at Hashim, but Hashim stopped him with a blow to his face.

"Your weapon works, Kamal," Hashim said. "You should be proud. You've done more damage in one blow than your brother ever dreamed of. Unfortunately, it was to your own people, but no one has to know it was your weapon."

"Let me go past!" Kamal yelled. He pushed at Hashim, who stood as still as a stone pillar.

"I cannot. I apologize, I have to keep you here for the moment. At least until my men—the men her 'father,' Sergewaz, gave me—have replaced the caliph's guards."

"She's not Zayele," Kamal said, gritting his teeth. "And you *will* let us pass."

"On the contrary," Hashim said, and with a flick of his wrist, he pulled a dagger from his robes and pressed it against Kamal's neck. "You're coming with me."

✦ 46 ✦

ZAYELE

RAHELA TOOK US down the corridor, holding my hand tight. After pausing behind a screen, we dashed across an empty courtyard, went through a rose garden, and stopped behind a closed door. We had run the entire way and were catching our breath when we saw Faisal and Shirin. Both had lost their *shahtabi,* and Shirin kept glancing over her shoulder.

"Who's this?" Faisal asked, eyeing Rahela.

"She's my cousin," I answered.

Faisal nodded and snapped a rosebud off the nearest bush. "This is where Najwa got her rose," he said to Shirin. He pointed at an archway cut into the palace's wall. "The laboratory must be in there."

Rahela looked surprised. "How did you know?"

"Najwa came here the first time she transported, and brought me back one of these blossoms."

"All right," I said, putting my hand on the door. I didn't have time for talk about flowers. "Let's go in."

I pressed on the raised designs that covered the door,

and it swung open. A jar of powder lay on its side by my feet. My eyes swept across the room and landed on three people. I froze, stricken. On the other side of a long wooden table were Hashim, Najwa, and a young man. Hashim stood behind the man, pressing a knife into his throat, while Najwa, tears dripping down her cheeks, was holding a spoonful of gray powder above a white sphere.

She held the spoon in the air, then dropped it, scattering powder all over the table. The man behind Najwa gasped, but Hashim pressed the knife harder against his neck.

"*Both* of you!" Hashim said incredulously. "Never in all my planning did I account for this. This is a boon." He gestured for me to come closer, using his free hand.

I didn't move.

"Come closer, or I kill the prince," Hashim said. "Which one are you, then? Zayele or the other mutt?"

I lifted my chin. "I'm not coming any closer until you release him," I said.

The others pressed me into the room. Hashim took one look at Faisal and nearly let go of the prince. His cheeks flushed above his beard, but his eyes darkened and narrowed. "You've returned. But it's too late. Just like it was for Mariam. Just like it was for your dear brother. It's always been too late."

Najwa wiped her face, staring openmouthed at Faisal. "How did you—"

"Yes, how did you get into the palace?" Hashim asked. "The girls I can understand, since they're only half-breeds, but *you*. You're a full jinni."

Faisal walked toward them, not stopping until the prince

winced in pain. "Zayele took down the wards. The Shaitan have come with us, Hashim. Let the boy go."

"Let him go like I let Mariam's father go? And receive nothing in return but death and loss?" Hashim spat out the words. "Over my dead body. The weapon this girl is filling— don't stop, dear—will end all of it. Yes, fill it to the brim. I don't care that your army is here. My army is more than strong enough. Thanks to this young prince here, we've found a way to protect ourselves. We now have the upper hand. And on top of all that, I've got a jinni of my very own," he said, pointing at Najwa's back. "And it looks like I might get her sister too."

Najwa almost dropped the spoon again, and looked at me with wonder. Clearly, she was putting the pieces of our puzzle together.

"Don't do it, Najwa," Kamal croaked. "I couldn't live with myself."

Najwa sniffed, but shook her head. "Faisal, help me" was all she said. Hashim sneered at her, taking his eyes off Faisal for the first time since he'd entered the laboratory.

Faisal leaped over the table and landed on top of Hashim. Kamal rolled out from between them, jumping up just in time before Hashim shoved Faisal to the side. Both of the older men jumped to their feet and faced off, dagger to dagger.

"You can't fight me fairly, Hashim." Faisal's dagger glowed red-hot.

"You're right, I can't," Hashim said, and he pulled another dagger from his belt and launched it at Najwa. Faisal turned and, in a split second, shouted out a wish. A wave of energy shook across the space in front of Najwa and Kamal, stopping the dagger in midair. It stayed there, stuck in a wavering, translucent wall that stretched the width of the laboratory, leaving Faisal and Hashim on the opposite side.

"Faisal!" Najwa screamed, pounding at the wall. But Faisal didn't have time to respond. Hashim had pounced on him, and he lurched backward, holding Hashim's dagger back with his own.

"Gah!" Faisal growled, pushing Hashim back. Hashim stumbled, then caught his footing. They danced, circling each other, while their blades flashed.

"I think my dagger is sharper," Hashim said. "It's funny. I was thinking about Mariam this morning." He twisted the blade till it reflected the sunlight into Faisal's eyes. Then he slashed, narrowly missing Faisal.

Faisal growled again, slicing at the air, but Hashim dipped down and moved to the side like a spider. Then Faisal plunged and cut into Hashim's robes. Hashim twisted and landed safely beside Faisal, his indigo robes spinning behind him.

"That's Mariam's blade," Faisal said. He sent a ball of fire straight at Hashim. It glanced off his shoulder and sent him careening into the shelves of jars. They exploded, raining white powder down over Hashim, who picked up one of the cracked jars and threw it at Faisal.

"No!" Najwa screamed. The jar flew through the air, trailing a cloud of white behind it, and hit Faisal squarely in the chest. The rest of the jar cracked apart and dropped to the floor. Faisal looked down at the bits of glass embedded in his chest. He stood frozen like a moonbeam, then fell onto his hands and knees, heaving and coughing. His hands slipped out from beneath him and he fell to the floor.

Everything was still and silent. I couldn't move and I couldn't breathe. Quickly, Hashim leaped over Faisal's body, broke through the energy wall, and grabbed Najwa. His grimace was wild, and he snarled at Kamal, who had been too slow to move. "One less magus," he said. He pinched Najwa's chin between his fingers and turned on Kamal. "If you follow us, I will kill her." He reached out with an opened hand. "The sphere, please, dear prince." Kamal hesitated, and handed the white sphere to Hashim. Then Hashim dragged Najwa toward the front door. She struggled, tears pouring down her face, and when he pulled her over Faisal's body, she shuddered, whispering something to Hashim that I couldn't hear.

Hashim paused at the door, with Najwa in one arm and the sphere in the other hand. "Kamal, explain to the others what will happen if any of you follow me." Then, with a kick, the door slammed shut.

Shirin ran to Faisal, but it was too late. "No, sir!" she sobbed. "You can't go. You can't."

47

NAJWA

I COULDN'T BREATHE without hiccupping, but it didn't matter. Faisal was gone, and the emptiness he left was greater than my entire soul. He had been my only father, my only teacher. He was the only person I had ever wanted to make proud. And Hashim had killed him.

I struggled, but Hashim's grip was too tight. "You can't get away, jinni." I was half dragged, half carried down the corridor, and I screamed the entire way, letting loose all the fear, all the pain, all the longing I'd been harboring since I'd come to Baghdad. The people we passed backed away, bowing at Hashim. Finally, he thrust me forward, into stone.

"At last something goes better than I'd planned. They've already relit the flame," he said. We were standing in front of the stone plinth that held up the Lamp. But unlike before, it was bursting with a long golden flame. Faisal must have lit it, and again, I choked on a sob.

There was a clashing of swords down one of the halls, and I looked up, hoping someone was fighting their way to me. But Hashim jerked my arm, knocking me into the plinth.

"I need you to send the sphere to the Cavern."

He was going to destroy the entire Cavern—the waterfall, the Lake of Fire, the houses of sparkling colors, and all the people. I thought of the children running along the wall, flying streamers in the air. I thought of my mother, at her loom. I thought of Faisal, and I pressed my lips together and shook my head in defiance.

"You will do this, because I will wish it. You cannot resist a human's wish."

That might have been true before, but I would *not* send the sphere down into the Cavern and cover everyone in exploding moonstone powder.

"I have been planning this moment for years," he went on. "Don't look so surprised. I knew your mother. I was there when she died, and your human father too."

I looked him in the eye then, not quite believing what I'd just heard. "My father was a jinni," I said.

"So you're the one who grew up in the Cavern, then," he said. "Let me begin our lifelong relationship of master and slave by saying that I killed your true parents. Your sister grew up in Zab, believing herself to be a daughter of Zab. I brought her here, just for this moment. I don't care how you switched places, but you both carry the same blood in your veins. And I've been meaning to catch a jinni with this particular blood for half my life."

"You're lying!" I said, and I snapped my teeth at him. He leaned back, still not letting go of me, and laughed.

"I swear on the Prophet that I am not. Now let's not waste time. This needs to happen before the Shaitan take care of my pitiful men." He smiled, like he was just going to ask me to behave nicely. "I wish for you to send this sphere to the Cavern."

I shook my head, but I could feel the wish pressing in on me. Like the jinni's in the memory, my lungs felt like they were twisting around barbs. I pulled against Hashim, but he wouldn't let go, and as the moments passed, the pain increased. My eyes stung, and my nostrils burned for air, but I would not open my mouth. I bit my lips closed, and screamed inside my mouth. I could not let the wish out. I would not let the wish out.

There is a point at which a person will break. I knew at which point the jinni from the Memory Crystal had reached it, and I held on, past the shredding of the lungs, past the sensation of fire flooding throughout my limbs.

But it was too great, and I reached my breaking point. I opened my mouth, gasping for air, and let the wish pour out. My hand grabbed the sphere from Hashim, all on its own, while tears, hotter than they were a moment ago, streamed off my cheeks. Then I croaked, "Granted."

I held the sphere over the flame, and let go.

✦ 48 ✦

ZAYELE

ATISH WAS THE one who brought us back to the moment. Shirin and I had been kneeling over Faisal, crying, while Kamal stood frowning beside Rahela, until Atish ran into the room from the front door.

"What happened?" he asked. When his gaze landed on Faisal, his eyes widened. He ran to Faisal, knelt down and stroked his forehead with his thumb, and then stood back up. "We cannot stay here. Have you found Najwa yet?"

"Who are you?" Kamal asked.

"A friend of Najwa's."

"You're Shaitan," Kamal said, gesturing at Atish's mark.

Atish nodded at Kamal and turned to me. "Have you found Najwa?"

"Hashim just took her down the corridor," I said, wiping my face and climbing up off the floor. "But we can't follow her or he will kill her."

"He will kill her no matter what," Atish said. "That's the sort of man he is. Najwa knows that."

There wasn't anything we could do. She was trapped behind Hashim's dagger, and she was there because of me. All of us were. If I didn't do something, Hashim would kill everyone in the Cavern. Everything beautiful about the place my mother was from would be destroyed.

I ran to Rahela then, took her hands, and brought them to my lips. "I'm sorry for everything," I said, choking on my words. Then I looked at Atish, at his deep, shadowed eyes.

"I wish we'd had more time," I said. His face darkened as he realized what I meant.

"No, Zayele!" he shouted. He ran toward me, pushing the table out of the way, but I was faster.

I closed my eyes. If I thought any more about Atish, I might not be able to do it.

"Umnisha-la narush," I shouted into the broken room.

They were the words Faisal had taught me to say once I saw Najwa again. They would free her from the Fire Wish and send me to my rightful place.

The wish unraveled faster than I expected. I blinked and dissolved, feeling the energy sucked out of me. When I opened my eyes again, I was behind Hashim's blade, pressed against his chest. The sphere was in the air, falling into the flame, and I hit it away. It flew sideways, smacked against the wall, and broke open onto the floor. A cloud of white powder puffed up into the air and fell all around us. We were as white as angels, and I almost laughed. We weren't anything like angels.

"No!" Hashim cried. "You demon!" Then the blade sliced against my throat. I tried to scream, but my words gurgled out, red and slick. I fell over, and as the light dimmed, I watched Hashim try to put the pieces of the sphere back together.

Everything was lost, and I was so tired. But it didn't matter. I had realized what I cared about most. And I had a home, even if I would never see it again. I thought of the Cavern and the way the gypsum shards sparkled from the ceiling, as real as stars but closer. I thought of Yashar, and how he would have loved to see that. I imagined I was there with him, but as I rowed him out onto the Lake of Fire, I was so tired. So very tired.

It was so very, very dark.

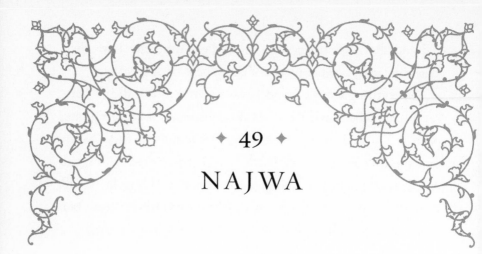

✦ 49 ✦

NAJWA

IN A FLASH of light and a twist of smoke, I was in the laboratory. Zayele had switched us back! With a flicker of hope, I grabbed Kamal's hand and pulled him with me.

"She's at the Lamp!" I yelled, gesturing at the others. We ran out the door and down the corridor, but when we reached them, my stomach lurched.

Zayele lay on the floor with her hair fanned out in a puddle of blood, covered in powder, and Hashim was on his knees, staring in disbelief at the cracked sphere.

"What have you done?" I cried to Hashim. He looked up at Kamal.

"I did it for us," he whispered. "They can't take over, Kamal. Don't let them take over."

Someone cried in anguish and rushed at Hashim. It was Atish, and his eyes were on fire. Before I could stop him from running into the moonstone powder, he pulled out his dagger and plunged it into Hashim's chest. Hashim gasped and opened his mouth to say something, but Atish shook his blade free and pushed the man onto his face.

"Don't *ever* speak again," he said. Hashim lay in the pool of Zayele's blood, and soon it was impossible to tell whose was whose.

It was over, but it didn't feel like a victory. Hashim was dead, the man who had murdered my parents and started a war, and all it had taken was the flick of a dagger. And a girl I hardly knew had died for me.

"Kamal," I said, broken and empty, "the moonstone powder."

He shook his head. "It's not moonstone. When Faisal and Hashim were fighting, I emptied the orb and put talcum in instead. It's not going to kill your friends." I fell onto him, unable to cry anymore, even in relief.

"Thank you."

Atish knelt beside Zayele, and although he wasn't going to die of the powder anymore, something was cracking apart inside him. His jawline was tight and fierce, and in that moment I knew why he had killed Hashim. It hadn't been for Faisal. It wasn't to protect any of us. It was for her. He cradled Zayele's head and wrapped her veil around her neck, but it kept bleeding. He pressed on it and stared at the blood that seeped through his fingers.

Her face was my face, but soft in sleep. Her hair was my hair, but wet with blood. Atish looked up to let me in and together we held her.

Rahela sobbed behind me. "She can't be dead." But

Zayele's body was as still as Hashim's. I closed my eyes. A wish couldn't bring someone back to life, but what if she wasn't dead yet? I looked over to Shirin, who sucked in her breath and then jumped over to my side. Together, we breathed in and out, pressing our hands onto her bloodied neck. I imagined her whole again. I remembered her voice, desperate and pleading, when I had first met her. Her neck had been smooth and whole. Her movements had been swift and sure.

Shirin squeezed my hand and said, *"Shushfa."*

The wish flowed slowly, like the first trickle of water across a dry and dusty stone. Then Atish put his hand over ours and the energy rushed forward, spreading our wishpower faster, deeper into Zayele.

It was like breaking open a dam. All our energy poured into Zayele, flooding her with *shushfa,* with health and strength. We gritted our teeth, shaking with exhaustion. I felt it shudder through my bones, and I thought they'd turn to powder.

Then it was done. The wish was complete.

For a long time, nothing happened. Then she trembled. It was such a slight tremor, I could have imagined it. Atish's eyes widened. Then it happened again. Shirin started crying freely, sobbing in relief.

I looked over to Kamal then, and saw him watching us in silence. His gaze drifted away, to Hashim.

Her body began to shake in great, wide waves, and her eyelids fluttered. She heaved a sigh and blinked. I shrieked and cried, squeezing her hands. She opened her eyes and melted into Atish's arms.

"It's all right, Zayele. It's over," he said. Then he grinned. "But don't do anything like that ever again."

She wiped at her neck and the blood slipped away, revealing a pink scar. Rahela wiped the remaining blood off her neck and hugged her fiercely.

"How is she alive?" Rahela asked.

"It was the healing wish. She must not have been dead yet."

"I don't know," Zayele said. Her voice was thick and scratchy. "It felt like I was dead. It hurt like you wouldn't believe."

"But it didn't kill you," I said.

Zayele wrapped her arms around herself and cried. "I was afraid," she croaked, "that I'd be too late. That I wouldn't be able to fix it. I'm so sorry about the Fire Wish, Najwa. I shouldn't have taken your life from you."

She had made a Fire Wish. Suddenly I understood why I could do certain wishes, but not any that would alter her wish. I understood why I'd been stuck in the palace.

She had risked her life to undo the wish, and she was still apologizing. I shushed her.

"It's over."

✦ 50 ✦

ZAYELE

WE TOOK FAISAL'S body home, wrapped in one of Najwa's veils. All of us, including Kamal and Rahela, held on to a part of him and placed our fingers in the Lamp's golden flame. As we whirled into the air, I noticed Najwa's eyes on me. They were dark with sadness, and then they were only bits of fire like the rest of us.

When we were whole again and standing in the Cavern, I helped set Faisal on the ground. Najwa explained to Kamal and Rahela what was going to happen, and then she knelt beside Faisal and cried over his body.

Kamal and Rahela looked around the Cavern, at the shards of gypsum and the waterfall pouring out of the wall. This time, I saw it for what it really was: my home. My real mother had come from all this, the blue canal, the lake with the dancing flames, and the homes that changed as their occupants wished. I could change them now, thanks to Faisal. He had saved my sister, and I was sure he had kept Hashim from killing me. I had hardly known him, but he had been a part of my life since I was born.

The two men who guarded the school left their posts and stood by Faisal's body. Delia, dressed all in red, came forward and bowed her head. The whole Cavern lit up. Not just the lamps, but each crystal that hung from the ceiling glowed a rich emerald green, lighting every building, every person, every wave on the lake. Delia had wished, and the Cavern turned into a living jewel.

Rahela gasped, and I took her hand. "Do you like it?" I asked.

"Yes, but it's sad light. Mourning light." She went to Najwa and helped her off Faisal's body so the men could carry him away. They nodded at Najwa as if she had been Faisal's daughter, and in a way, she was.

They carried him across a narrow bridge over the canal, to a golden dome. There, dozens of jinn gathered, waiting. They wore robes of emerald-and-black silk, and the women wore black scarves. They began singing a song that carried over the city and echoed off the crystal walls.

Najwa walked behind the guards—alongside Laira, her adoptive mother and Faisal's sister—and we kept behind them. Laira no longer wore the glowworm shawl, but something as airy and dark as a cobweb in the night. The remaining jinn followed us into the golden dome. Rahela and I held hands, and Atish and Kamal walked stiffly behind. Together, we went down a flight of steps into the dark, and the song drifted away.

The stairs carried us a hundred feet below the Cavern to a field of crushed volcanic rock. Gypsum, amethyst, and topaz monoliths sprouted from the gravel, creating a garden of jewels as far as we could see. Scattered lamps hung from the granite ceiling, casting jewel-toned shadows across the black rocks. Each monolith was engraved with letters of the jinni alphabet. Were the inscriptions names?

The guards took Faisal to a granite table ringed by rounded white stones. They laid him down, and a man with a long sapphire beard stepped forward. He pressed his palm onto a clear crystal protruding from the table and bowed his head. The crystal lit up, and a beam of light spread across the ceiling, projecting images of Faisal. They moved so quickly I could barely catch any of them, but I could see Faisal, younger, wearing a bathing suit and diving into the lake.

"What are they doing?" Kamal asked.

Atish whispered, "He's saving his memories of Faisal. We put our memories into the crystals, and then whenever you want to remember a loved one, you can come here and touch their stones."

Each monolith held memories? I looked at the field—the graveyard—and thought of the thousands of memories it contained, going as far back as the first jinni, Iblis. The shard of crystal Faisal had shown me before had been like these, but smaller. Maybe he had only preserved a few memories. Maybe Mariam didn't have a funeral like this one because she'd died so far from home. The thought made me feel lonely, and I pushed it away, forcing myself to think of Faisal instead.

When the man was done, he gestured for Najwa to come

to the table. She walked slowly and placed her hands on the crystal. Then we all saw what Faisal had meant to her. He was in a boat on the lake, teaching her how to sail between the flames. He was walking through the courtyard, telling her to stop splashing in the fountain. He was giving her trinkets from the human world, wooden dolls and woven baskets. But most of all, he was in his artifact room, cataloging everything that was brought in, fingering each object with love and admiration.

I wiped away my tears and watched the others do the same. Yashar would have loved all this, even the funeral. How would I explain the beauty of it to him if he had never seen a crystal? How could I help him see what a wonderful world existed down here?

He needed to see again.

A rush went through me. I could give him sight. I could wish it for him, and then I would bring him here. I would show him what jinn were really like.

Najwa came over to me. Her cheeks were dry now, but the loss was like an echo in the way she held her lips together. We looked past Faisal's body at the thousands of monoliths. Our ancestors were out there.

"Najwa," I said, "Faisal showed me a crystal like these. With a bit of our mother—Mariam—in it."

She looked startled. "Where is it?"

I told her quickly, and described what I had seen in it.

"Could there be more of her? A bigger one, here?" I asked.

The tears returned and she smiled, mirroring what I felt. And how I looked. I took her hands in mine and stared at her tiny owl-eye tattoo.

"We'll have to come back and look for her sometime," she said.

The other jinn deposited their memories, which took a long time. Each memory added a bit of color to the crystal, and in the end it was filled with an ocher smoke. Faisal's spirit, his memory, was now a glowing emerald shard. It took two men to lift the monolith. Then it was wished into place beside a pale yellow monolith that looked like it was filled with lemon juice.

✦ 51 ✦

NAJWA

SAVING MY MEMORIES of Faisal gave me a sense of peace. I wouldn't forget him, and no one else would either. People would talk of the man who had loved the humans, and if I wanted, I could show them what he was like.

After the funeral, we went out to the lake wall. Zayele had wanted to show Rahela the Cavern, so she and the others took off toward the canal. I stayed behind with Kamal and was leaning against the wall, watching the flames flicker on the water, when he got very close.

"I need to get back," he said. "I don't want anyone to think I was killed by a jinni. The war is still going on up there."

I nodded, but everything in me wanted to shout out in protest. I didn't want him to go back. Here, I could be with him. I could protect him, stay with him. But in Baghdad, he was a prince. He had duties. And one of them was to marry a princess.

I swallowed back the agony I felt. "What's going to happen?"

He smiled and wrapped his arm around me. "I'm bringing you with me."

"What will your father say?" The words were out of my mouth before I remembered that the caliph was unconscious. "I mean—"

"It doesn't matter. I'm not letting you go."

Our races were still at war, even if the battle had ended. Everyone knew I was a jinni. I shook my head. "They won't let us be together."

A flame erupted just on the other side of the wall, shooting into the air beside us, and Kamal reached out to grab it. It flowed over his hand before flitting off, blown away by the motion.

"Can I see the necklace?"

I felt at my throat and lifted it up to him. He took the bit of moonstone between his fingers and yanked it from where it hung below the silver window.

"What did you—"

"I'll give you sapphire when we get home. It won't be quite so toxic." Then he bent down and kissed me. Our lips were still pressed together when the thought came to me. I had an idea that would change everything between jinn and humans. It would frustrate half the Shaitan. But it would give us a chance, and I could not ignore it.

I reached into his hair, held him tight against me, and transferred us out of the Cavern.

It took just a moment. When the kiss was over, we were in a room I hadn't seen before. On a platform, draped in linens, lay a man asleep. His beard was trimmed into a point, resting on his collarbone. White smoke billowed out from a burner beside his bed, filling the room with frankincense.

"Father!" Kamal said. He let go of me, knelt beside the caliph, and looked up at me. "Are you—"

"Shh," I said. I couldn't go back to the Cavern and live like I had before. Half of me would always be here, in the land where feathered birds called down from tree branches and princes sang songs that haunted my dreams. I had to protect both places, and to do that, I needed to speak to a man who could change things. So I knelt over the caliph, and I *wished*.

ACKNOWLEDGMENTS

WITH HEARTFELT THANKS to Emma Kress, who is there on every page but is hiding behind a very strong *shahtabi* wish. Without you, this story wouldn't have had Zayele. I cannot express enough how grateful I am to have you with me on this journey. Faisal would have wanted you to pick up where he left off.

Much thanks goes to Scott Kaple, English teacher extraordinaire. You wrote things like "Touché!" in the margins of my essays, which spurred me on.

Gratitude, respect, and love go to my critique friends, both past and present: MJ Auch, Suzanne Bloom, Bruce Coville, Kirsten Kinney, Mark McDonough, Cindy Pon, Tudy Woolf, and Ellen Yeomans. Your warmth, support, and yes, even your show tunes have made all of this more fun.

Stephanie Gaither, Anna Dahlstein, and Hardik Panjawani were wonderful beta readers at a time when I needed them greatly. Thank you!

To the RockSugarBeets and The Fourteenery: thank you for holding me up against the solitude. Writing friends FTW!

Thanks to Verity Cast, my first-ever writing friend. I think we were writing fan fiction before there *was* "fan fiction."

Love and thanks to Diane Miller, Bee Messenger, Kendra

Harper, Mary Piron, and Hope Kuniholm. You told me it was okay to pursue my dream *and* be a mother. For this, and for helping raise my children, I cannot thank you enough.

Sincere gratitude goes to my editor, Diane Landolf, for truly understanding Najwa and Zayele's story. I could not have *wished* for a better editor.

Laura Rennert, you are the best agent in the world. Thank you for believing in me at the beginning and never giving up. ありがとう!

An entire lifetime of thanks goes to my parents, who understood my love of adventure and showed me the world. Mom, thank you for the musicals, the love of reading, and every single handmade Halloween costume. Dad, thank you for all the stories, especially those with shadows against the wall. You shared your love of magic and other worlds, and reminded me to hold on to a sense of wonder. I love you both.

Grandma Janis, thank you for telling me in second grade that I was *already* a writer. I wish I could have gotten this to you in time.

Hazel, I could not have written about sisters without having one, and I am thankful you are mine. (No, really. I am.)

Elizabeth and Henry, thank you for being good sports and for all the snowflakes you made out of my printer paper. I love watching you both fall in love with stories and words.

And last but not least, to my husband, Jim: thank you for the thousands of little things and the many big things. Without your trust and constant support, I wouldn't have had this story to share. I love you with all my heart.

ABOUT THE AUTHOR

AMBER LOUGH lives in Syracuse, New York, with her husband, their two kids, and their cat, Popcorn. She spent much of her childhood in Japan and Bahrain—an island nation off the coast of Saudi Arabia. Later, she returned to the Middle East as an Air Force intelligence officer and spent eight months in Baghdad, where the ancient sands still echo the voices lost to wind and time. For a pronunciation guide, character guide, and more, please visit amberlough.com.